IN THE
SHADOW
OF
HEROES

NICHOLAS BOWLING

Chicken House

2 PALMER STREET, FROME, SOMERSET BA11 1DS
WWW.CHICKENHOUSEBOOKS.COM

Text © Nicholas Bowling 2019
Illustration © Erica Williams 2019

First published in Great Britain in 2019
Chicken House
2 Palmer Street
Frome, Somerset BA11 1DS
United Kingdom
www.chickenhousebooks.com

Cover design and interior design by Steve Wells
Typeset by Dorchester Typesetting Group Ltd
Printed and bound in Great Britain by CPI Group (UK) Ltd, Croydon CR0 4YY

The paper used in this Chicken House book is made
from wood grown in sustainable forests.

1 3 5 7 9 10 8 6 4 2

British Library Cataloguing in Publication data available.

ISBN 978-1-911077-68-8
eISBN 978-1-911490-98-2

For PSF and MJP
magistris merentissimis

Also by Nicholas Bowling

Witchborn

PROLOGUS

The girl was like a visitor from the world below. Even if Silvanus had been able to stand, she still would have been a head taller than him; from where he lay, spread out on the couch and delirious with fever, she seemed inhumanly large, dark, insubstantial. Pluto himself come to take him away.

He motioned to his slave to bring him a little water, then dismissed him. With difficulty he propped himself up on one elbow and beckoned the girl into the room. She approached the couch in two giant strides, bringing with her a clean smell of dust and hot air from outside. Healthy visitors only reminded Silvanus of how sick he was. His room was damp and fetid. The plaster on the walls seemed to sweat as much as he did.

'You speak Latin?' he asked. The girl stared at him and didn't reply.

That was good. It meant she wouldn't be able to read what she was delivering.

'Greek?' he said.

She nodded slowly.

'You want to get out of this place, don't you?'

Her face remained expressionless, as though weighing up whether this might be some sort of trap. Then she nodded again.

'Well, then,' said Silvanus. 'I have a job for you.'

He hauled himself upright, his body sagging like a sack of grain. He waited for the throbbing in his temples to subside, and made his way to a strongbox in the corner of the room. Three times he stumbled and fell, three times the girl made no move to help him, but simply stood by the couch, watching with curiosity.

Silvanus opened the box and took out a scroll and a wax tablet. He put the scroll on the desk and handed the tablet to the girl.

'I've watched you,' he said. 'With the other slaves. You seem . . .' He groped for the word. 'Resilient.'

Still she said nothing.

'I want you to look after this tablet with the same vigour that you look after yourself. Do you understand? Its contents are very important. More important than I can tell you.'

She was starting to look bored now.

'*Listen.*' Silvanus tried to shake her by the arm, but found himself clutching on to her to stop himself from falling. He coughed, tasting blood in the back of his mouth. 'Listen to me. You must take this to a man in Rome. His name is written inside. Go to the harbour and get a boat to Italy. As quickly as possible. By any means possible. No one else is to read it.'

His slave trotted back into the room behind them both, holding a circle of iron in his hands.

'You'll have to wear this, I'm afraid. I can't afford to have the message going astray.'

Silvanus took the collar from the boy and fumbled with the clasp. He fitted it around the girl's neck. A wooden tag hung by a chain on to her chest, which read, in Latin:

I BELONG TO GAIUS DOMITIUS TULLUS, SENATOR. IF YOU FIND ME, RETURN ME TO MY MASTER AT ROME.

Silvanus could see that the collar was too tight around the girl's muscular neck, and her brow twitched with discomfort.

'Go,' he said. 'Don't rest. The man in Rome will look after you. I promise.'

He nodded to his slave, who led her out of the room, taking three steps for every one of hers. She never said a thing, and she never looked back.

Silvanus watched them go and wondered, through the fog of his sickness, if he was making a terrible mistake. Perhaps, he thought, it would be better if all he knew went with him to his grave.

He swayed a little on his feet. He rolled up the edge of his toga and looked at the two tiny puncture wounds on his thigh. The flesh around them had gone a sickening shade of yellow, threaded through with dark purple veins. No doctor in all of Athens had been able to do anything for him. Now he was resigned to prayer, and he very much doubted the gods wanted to listen to him.

Behind him, the scroll that he had taken from his strongbox was still lying on the writing desk. He picked it up and held it for a moment, enjoying its weight, tracing his finger around the bosses at the top and bottom.

Then he took the oil lamp from the tabletop, held it to the corner of the scroll, and set fire to it. He dropped it on to the tiles, and watched the tightly rolled papyrus burn and blacken and flutter like a crow's feathers. His eyes watered from the smoke. He may have been crying, though he hardly had the energy for it. Either way, it was done. Now it was all down to the girl.

Outside, he could hear the streets of Athens singing and clattering with life. Silvanus smiled. He'd hated the noise when he'd arrived, strange men hollering in strange accents. Now, on the brink of death, it sounded like music.

He crushed the remains on the scroll with his heel. Then he stumbled back to the couch, pulled the coverlet over his body, and waited for night.

I

Cadmus draped a cold flannel over the polished, pink dome of his master's head.

'Remember,' he said, 'Antonius Macer lost his case in court today. It wouldn't be wise to bring it up.'

His master nodded. 'Yes, yes, of course.'

'And Paulinus has just been elected *praetor*, so remember to congratulate him.'

'I will.'

'And Silvanus will eat three times as much as everyone else, so you'll have to be, ah, *tactical* in where you place the dishes.'

'Fine.'

'And remember not to open the Falernian wine

until the third course.'

'*Cadmus!*' His master whipped the damp cloth from his forehead and threw it with a slap against the wall. 'If this is your attempt at calming me down, you are doing miserably.'

'Forgive me, Master,' said Cadmus, looking at the damp patch and trying not to laugh. The flannel had hit the painting of Venus square on her rosy cheeks. 'Would you like me to fetch you something to drink?'

'What I would *like*,' his master said, massaging his temples, 'is for you to be like every other slave and speak only when you're spoken to.'

'Of course, Master.'

Poor old Gaius Domitius Tullus hosted one dinner party a year. Even that was too much for him, and when it came around he became nothing short of a nervous wreck. The prospect of raucous socializing and a drunken, interrupted night's sleep had been a storm cloud hanging over him all week.

'What need has a man of friends,' Cadmus remembered him declaring (many, *many* times), 'when he has his books?' Cadmus tended to agree with that. Although, as a slave, his opportunities for making friends were fairly limited anyway.

Tullus heaved himself from his couch and went out into the garden. Dusk had shrouded the city of Rome in purple. The crickets sang to each other in the silence, the air warm and heavy with the scents of cypress and lavender. The old man sighed to himself. Cadmus thought he looked particularly thin that night.

There was a knock at the door of the villa. Tullus whirled around in dismay.

'Cadmus? Who is that?'

'I'm afraid the gods haven't granted me the gift of foresight, Master.'

'Don't be *clever* with me, Cadmus. What are they doing here? Dinner won't be served for another hour!'

Tullus clutched at the folds of his toga and marched into the atrium, turned, marched back, then turned again and went for the door. The two slave girls sweeping the floor watched him in bewilderment.

'Don't just *stand* there,' Tullus hissed at no one in particular. 'Light some lamps!' He reached the bronze door handle and stopped. 'No, what am I thinking? Cadmus, you open it. Opening my own front door! Gods above!'

One of the slave girls brought an oil lamp, which only served to highlight the sweat beading on his master's head. Tullus stood back, a little to the side of the pool in the middle of the atrium, and composed himself. He looked rigid as a statue.

When Cadmus eventually opened the door, the man on the other side was not a dinner guest at all. Neither were the praetorian guards who flanked him on both sides. Nobody acknowledged Cadmus as they barged noisily into the villa, the two armed men carrying a bronze strongbox between them. Tullus's face, which had been so ruddy moments before, was now completely colourless.

'Greetings, Tullus,' said the man at the front. He was wearing a toga but he spoke his Latin with a strong Greek accent. A foreigner. One of Cadmus's countrymen.

His master looked like he was about to be sick. 'Oh, I . . . Yes. Good evening. I'm sorry the house is in such a state, if I had known you were coming I would have . . .' There was a flicker of recognition between the two of them, Cadmus noticed.

The Greek man laughed. 'Do not worry yourself, this is not a social call. Let's be honest, Gaius, you aren't exactly renowned for your hospitality, are you?' Tullus tried to laugh but it just sounded like he was hacking some phlegm from the back of his throat. 'No,' the man continued, 'I have actually come to bring you a gift.'

'A gift?'

'From Nero.'

The guards dropped the chest on the floor of the atrium and it echoed coldly. Cadmus looked at it, then at the guards, then at the Greek intruder. Something wasn't right.

'The emperor?' Tullus's face didn't know what to do with itself. 'What have I deserved from the, ah, Divine Caesar?'

'Nero wants to thank you.'

'What for?'

The man smiled. 'For all the fine work you are about to do for him.'

Tullus gaped like a speared fish. Then, for the first time, the Greek turned to look at Cadmus.

'Dismiss this one,' he said. 'We have much to discuss.'

Cadmus kicked a stone from the peristyle into the garden.

This one. He hated being spoken about like that. Living in Tullus's household it was easy to forget how most other people viewed him.

He went to the kitchen first, to tell the cooks they would need to delay serving the dinner for perhaps another hour. They took this news just as he expected them to, like a mouthful of sour fish sauce, and went back to the stoves sullenly and without reply. Worst of the lot was old Bufo, 'the toad', whose name really didn't do justice to either his squatness or his ugliness.

Tullus had inherited him years ago, before Cadmus had even been born, and treated him like an heirloom, some old piece of furniture to be treasured even though nobody wanted it in the house. While the others returned to work, Bufo dropped his ladle noisily into the bottom of the pan and stared at Cadmus out of the sagging folds of his face. He shook his head and tutted. Another black mark against his name, Cadmus knew.

He'd grown used to it all, though. The educated didn't talk to him because he was a slave, and the other slaves didn't talk to him because he was educated – and certainly far too educated for a boy of fourteen – so he'd carved a lonely little niche for himself. There was also the matter of his appearance. He was too pale to look like he was Greek or Roman, even though he was born in Athens; so pale, in fact, he felt luminous when he wandered the house by night. And then there were his eyes. His right eye was perfectly normal, but his left was a strange yellowish colour that seemed to belong more to an animal than a human being. Most people never noticed, but when they did they had a tendency to sidestep him in the street. He was a prodigy, certainly, but not the good kind.

Quite right, Tullus, he thought to himself. *Who needs friends?*

He went back to his tiny bedroom, hearing the low talk of his master and the new guests as he passed the study. Their murmurs were tantalizing.

He tried to ignore them, and pulled his blanket over his bare legs. It was tatty and thin and not particularly comfortable, but it was just about the only thing he could call his own – everything else in the room belonged to his master, just like Cadmus himself did. He spent a few moments writing up a letter that Tullus had dictated to him earlier in the day, then scraped down his wax tablet, cleaned and arranged his writing implements. He attempted to read some scrolls of his own.

But it was no good. Occasionally he would catch a word of the discussion from across the atrium, and try to hear the rest. Tullus was agitated about something, but Cadmus couldn't work out what.

He couldn't help himself. He threw down the scroll on to his bed, crept from his room and tiptoed through the darkness to where the curtain had been pulled across Tullus's study. He stood with his back against the cool, smooth plaster, and listened.

'It goes without saying,' Tullus said, tiredness plain in his voice, 'that this is a great honour. And it is not my place to refuse the will of the emperor.'

'The will of the gods, wouldn't you say?'

'Yes, yes, I'm not questioning Nero's divinity. Not

at all.' Cadmus heard his master slurping nervously from a wine cup.

'Then shouldn't a god be in possession of godly things?'

'Yes, of course, it's just . . .'

'Just what?'

'I'm just not sure how *useful* I can be.'

'Well, you can certainly be more useful than the last man who was in charge of the project.'

'Why do you say that?'

'He is dead, Tullus. That's why we've come to you.'

Cadmus's heart was hammering so loudly in his ribcage he was sure the visitors would hear it. Whatever the 'project' was, his master almost certainly wasn't up to the task. The man couldn't cope with planning the menu for his dinner party – being made to work according to the whims of the emperor would probably kill him.

There was silence in the study for a moment.

'Dead?'

'Sadly.'

'Who was he?'

'You knew him, I think. Quintus Aemilius Silvanus.'

'Silvanus? He was meant to be coming here tonight! I didn't even know he was out of the city!' It sounded, just for a moment, like Tullus was more annoyed at having to change his seating plan than shocked at the man's death. But Cadmus knew that his master would take it heavily. Silvanus was a scholar, like Tullus – younger than him, but still one of his few really close friends. He'd been due to read from his *Argonautica* after dinner, an epic poem he had been working on for years. Cadmus had been rather looking forward to it.

Tullus sighed. 'Gods above. How did it happen?'

'A fever, I think. Something he caught on his way to the excavation.'

Excavation? What did he mean by that?

'And the emperor is certain he would like me to replace him?' said Tullus.

'Sadly Silvanus's research was destroyed in the hours before he died. Burnt by Silvanus himself. Or by one of his slaves, perhaps. At any rate, we need to start from scratch, and you come highly recommended. By Silvanus himself, I believe.'

There was a long and strained pause.

'I cannot,' said Tullus, very quietly. 'It is not proper. The gods—'

'Nero is your god. You need to ask yourself whose displeasure you would rather risk: Jupiter's, or Nero's.'

'Don't force me to make that choice, Epaphroditus. Look at me. I'm an old man. I have no more hair to lose. Does he really think a frame like this is up to the task? Look what happened to Silvanus – and he was younger than me!'

'He thinks you are the *only* person who is up to the task. With greater age comes greater wisdom. You are a scholar without equal, especially in this area of research. Or so Silvanus said.'

'But I haven't given this sort of thing any thought for decades. Silvanus was the real expert.' Tullus paused. 'I respectfully ask, if I may, that Nero lets me live out my few remaining years in peace.'

Cadmus was surprised at the firmness in his master's voice. He never would have thought the old man had the kind of backbone to turn down the emperor – he saw that backbone daily, and it was bent and arthritic from too much time in his library.

The Greek man laughed unpleasantly through his nose.

'I was assured you would be stubborn. Hence the gift.'

'What is it?'

'An incentive. Not yours to keep. The gift is simply to lay your eyes upon it.'

There was the sound of the praetorians shuffling around in their armour, then two heavy *clunks* as the clasps of the strongbox were opened. A voice inside Cadmus's head screamed at him to look. No, he couldn't risk it. Tullus wouldn't punish him if he were caught, but this visitor had a cruel look about him. And if Nero himself found out that a slave had been eavesdropping on official imperial business . . . Well, he'd be lucky to get away with crucifixion.

But then he was edging silently to the doorway anyway, against all of his better judgement, pressing himself as close to the wall as possible and holding his breath. He squinted through the narrow gap in the curtain. The three newcomers had their backs to him, Tullus sitting opposite, the box resting on the table between them.

One of the guards lifted the lid and the hinges groaned. Tullus's brow wrinkled, but for a fleeting moment his eyes were as bright and clear as those of a man half his age.

'Silvanus's slaves found it a week after he died,' said the Greek man. 'An abandoned shrine to the south-east of the city. Silvanus had been right all along. It's a shame he didn't live to see the fruits of his labour.'

Tullus stood up and slammed the lid of the box shut. The room seemed to darken.

'Is this a joke?' he said.

'Not at all. It is the thing itself.'

'But . . . it can't be.'

Suddenly, Cadmus felt a shiver between his shoulder blades that told him he was being watched. He whirled around. It was Bufo, standing behind him with his arms folded and a grin like a split wineskin. He beckoned Cadmus into the middle of the atrium. Cadmus lost the thread of the conversation in the study.

'Now,' whispered Bufo, licking his swollen lips, 'what do you reckon they'd do to you if I went in there and told them you were spying?'

'I wasn't spying.'

'Might find yourself out of the master's good books then, mightn't you? At long last.'

'Give it up, Bufo, I just wanted to—'

'You just wanted to know everyone else's business, as per usual!'

'Shouldn't you be in the kitchen? No, wait: it's probably a good thing you aren't giving everything your unique flavouring.'

The older slave took Cadmus's hand in his greasy, calloused fingers. 'I'll make you a deal, boy. How about: I'll only tell them what you were doing if you give me a reason to. Understand?'

He tightened his grip, and Cadmus grimaced. He wanted to cry out.

Bufo laughed. 'Hush, hush! You'll give yourself away. Not a very good spy, are you? Can you see anything with that horrible eye of yours anyway?'

In Tullus's study, somebody closed the box. The visitors were getting ready to leave. Cadmus had missed the most important part of their talk.

By the time the curtain twitched and the group emerged, Cadmus and Bufo had retreated into the shadows. The old slave's fingers were still pressed around Cadmus's wrist so hard he could feel his pulse straining against them.

From the corner of the atrium, he could see the Greek man's face was slack and grim.

'You will apologize to Caesar, won't you?' said Tullus. An air of desperation had crept into his voice.

No reply. The visitor's toga whisked over the atrium's mosaic floor.

'I'm sure there are many more capable men in Rome. I'm thinking of the emperor, first and fore-most, not myself. I wouldn't want to let him down, you see?'

They reached the front door.

'You have made your answer clear enough. I shall give it to Nero tonight. And you shall receive his answer tomorrow.'

Tullus's slender throat bulged like a heron trying to swallow an apple. Without another word, the Greek man and the guards left, taking the chest with them. The door slammed behind them with such force Cadmus felt it in the soles of his sandals.

He watched his master rest against a pillar for a moment, his eyes closed but fluttering slightly underneath their lids. Then, with a short, hot sigh, he wandered back to the dining room.

'How about that?' whispered Bufo. 'Praetorian guards! Must have been important. Imperial business, maybe. And there you were, listening in with your greedy little ears. Maybe I should just go straight and tell the emperor?'

Cadmus yanked his arm free of Bufo's grasp. 'You go for it, Bufo,' he said. Then he sniffed. 'But perhaps sober up first, if you want him to take you seriously.'

The old slave slapped him around the ear. 'Remember what I said, you little runt. You give me a reason to, I'll tell the master *everything*.'

'You give me a reason, and I'll tell him why his wine cellar is practically empty.'

Bufo grunted, then swayed on the spot for a moment, either because he was drunk or because he didn't know how to respond. He spat at Cadmus's feet.

'No one wants you here,' he said. 'Not even the master. He's only keeping you out of pity. But he'll see sense. I'll *make* him see sense.'

He slunk back to the kitchen, leaving Cadmus's head and heart pounding in the silence.

II

When Cadmus went to wake his master the next morning, it was obvious that neither of them had slept. The air in Tullus's bedroom was sour with the smell of garlic and old wine, and Cadmus's eyes were watering as soon as he set foot through the door. Tullus himself was staring at the ceiling, still fully clothed.

'It's dawn, Master. The Senate will be sitting soon.'

Tullus grunted.

The party had been an unequivocal disaster. Gaius Domitius Tullus was terrible at small talk even at the best of times, but he had obviously been shaken by the unexpected visit, and Silvanus's absence had cast a long shadow over the dinner table. Antonius Macer was already upset about his court case too. Conversation was quiet; laughter was rare, and felt too loud when it happened. Cadmus had spent the evening watching his master picking morosely at a plate of fried snails, and nursing several cups of very strong Falernian.

The other guests had wondered aloud about the empty couch, joked about the surprising excess of food on the table without Silvanus there to claim his portion. Tullus had remained silent, face buried in his goblet, shooting occasional furtive glances at Cadmus.

Needless to say, most of the guests had left early.

Cadmus withdrew from Tullus's bedroom and went to fetch his tablets and his satchel. He waited at the front door while Clitus, a Syrian slave who'd said precisely nothing to him in the two years they had shared a house, helped his master into fresh clothes and brought him water and a little fruit. When he finally emerged he didn't look much better than he had the previous night, and smelt much worse. Cadmus decided not to comment. He drew back the bar from the door, and they stepped out into the morning.

Tullus's house was on the Caelian Hill, a once grand villa that was starting to sag and crumble in recent years. He claimed he'd run out of money. He knew their more aristocratic neighbours were embarrassed by him, but he didn't seem to care. Cadmus was rather fond of its dilapidation.

Below them, the sprawl of Rome was concealed in a blanket of mist. Clusters of cypress and umbrella pine raised their heads above the haze, along with the roofs of temples and municipal buildings; but the Forum and Subura were sunk in gloom, and the city's thousand different flavours of pleasure and suffering were hidden from the heavens. From here it looked almost peaceful.

And suddenly Cadmus was homesick again. Homesick for a place he'd couldn't even remember. That heaviness, deep in his bones, knowing that he wasn't where he belonged, and maybe never would be.

He waited patiently at Tullus's side while his master surveyed the city.

'Sometimes I wonder what kind of Rome will be left to my grandchildren, Cadmus,' he said over his shoulder.

Cadmus wanted to point out that it was generally necessary to have children before one could have grandchildren, and it was necessary to find a wife before one could have children, but he bit his tongue.

'You seem preoccupied, Master,' he said. 'May I ask what's weighing on your mind?'

'You may not.'

'Very well.' He paused. 'Only, if it is something to do with last night's visitors, I may be able to help. A problem shared is a problem halved, and all that.'

Tullus turned and looked at him with tired, watery eyes, and managed a smile. 'Shared? I don't think I need to *share* anything about the meeting with you, do I?'

'Master?'

'Don't pretend you weren't listening in on every word, boy. I know you too well.'

This would be difficult to play, Cadmus realized. Of course, he *had* been eavesdropping. Just not eavesdropping attentively enough.

'I overheard a few words as I was coming and going,' he muttered. 'Nothing more.'

'And the box?'

'What box?' The lie didn't sound at all convincing. He'd been awake all night thinking about what might have been inside.

'For all your learning, Cadmus, you're a terrible liar.' Tullus sighed like a winter gale. 'Come on, we shouldn't talk about it out here. Besides, I need time to, ah, digest what happened last night. And I don't mean the fried snails.'

With that he set off down the hill. Cadmus followed, frustrated, his satchel thumping against his hip.

Cadmus's relationship with his master was a strange one, to be sure. For much of the time, Tullus was more like his father than his owner. His master had found him outside Athens when he was a baby, exposed on the roadside like so many unwanted children. He had taken pity on the tiny Cadmus, screaming among the folds of an old blanket, and brought him back to Rome to be raised in his household. When he was of an age, Tullus had instructed him in languages, literature, rhetoric, philosophy, mathematics; and since then barely a day had gone by when Tullus hadn't relied upon him to take notes, or write letters, or seek out some obscure text to help him with his own philosophical and historical works. Cadmus tried to be grateful, especially when he saw how slaves in other households were treated — but as generous and affectionate as Gaius Domitius Tullus was, it didn't make up for not having any real family.

He thought he saw them sometimes, in his dreams. His parents, their house, the city of Athens. But that was nonsense — he hadn't been a year old when they had abandoned him.

Although the sun hadn't yet risen, the Caelian was busy. Clients hurried up the hill to greet their wealthy patrons, slaves hurried down on errands for their masters. Some of Tullus's neighbours were also up, drawn by the call of the Senate House, making their slow way into the city and talking in low and serious voices.

'Is there anything I can do while the Senate is in session, Master?' asked Cadmus.

'We're not going to the Senate,' said Tullus.

Cadmus frowned. 'We're not? But they're debating taxation in the provinces. You *love* talking about taxation.'

That got another laugh out of Tullus, and it made Cadmus glad.

'As tempting as that sounds, I have more pressing business. Regarding last night. Regarding that box you claim to know nothing about.'

'And you wouldn't care to tell me what that business is?'

'No,' he said distantly. And then, drifting back to Cadmus: 'But I need to check something. Something I thought I had laid to rest a very long time ago . . .'

Cadmus wanted to press the matter, but could see his master's mood was fragile.

'Very well,' he said. 'Then where are we going?'

'The same place we always go for answers, my friend. The library.'

The Palatine Hill rose out of the mist in front of them, smaller, steeper, and groaning under the weight of marble built upon it. The hill itself could hardly be seen for the mass of columns and porticoes and vaulted roofs clinging to its sides. This was where Nero had his residence – just as all previous emperors had – overlooking Rome's million crawling inhabitants. Cadmus and his master walked around to the west side of the hill, where the Circus Maximus stretched into the distance. In the shadow of Nero's vast palace they climbed the steps to the Temple of Apollo, and the library connected to it.

In front of the temple doors, Tullus stopped to catch his breath. Cadmus offered his arm to steady him, but then suddenly withdrew it, and his master nearly tumbled to the floor.

'That's a cruel joke to play on an old man . . .'

Cadmus held a finger in the air. 'Hush.'

'Are you trying to silence your own master? This is brave new level of insolence, Cadmus!'

'No, *listen*.' He turned on the spot. They were alone. 'Can you hear that?'

'Hear what?'

'Footsteps.'

Tullus sighed. 'I can only hear my ancient blood creaking around my body.'

Cadmus listened again. The footsteps had gone, replaced with the echoes of their breath.

'I am sorry, Master. I think I'm just tired. I must be imagining things.'

Tullus looked at him suspiciously from the corner of one eye, before the pair of them set off down the high marble portico leading from the temple's entrance to the library. His master was muttering something, but Cadmus was straining to listen beyond it. He glanced once, twice, over each shoulder. He was *sure* he could hear three sets of feet.

They weren't the first in the library, something which always seemed to annoy Tullus, but the only other reader was asleep at his table, using a scroll as a pillow.

'You have to *read* it, Afrinus,' said Tullus, nudging his chair as he passed. 'You can't just absorb the information through your forehead.'

The other man opened his eyes suddenly, yawned, and sniffed. 'Gods above, Tullus, how much garlic have you eaten?'

He sneezed, spraying the scroll in phlegm and setting the whole room booming. The librarian appeared from behind the shelves and stared at the three of them, his face a tombstone. Tullus made an apologetic noise and left Afrinus to his nap.

The Palatine Library was enormous. It contained two floors of texts, Greek on one side, Latin on the other, set into alcoves with statues and portraits of famous authors displayed at intervals between them. It had a cold smell of marble and sandalwood, of silence and thought. Cadmus loved it.

Tullus gave him a list of scrolls to find from the Greek section, whose titles Cadmus scribbled into his wax tablet. Hesiod, Pindar, Palaephatus, Diodorus Siculus, Apollonius Rhodius. He tried to look for a connection between the authors, to work out what Tullus was investigating. But nothing came to him.

He looked high and low for the scrolls he needed, but every single one was missing. That wasn't right. You weren't supposed to take the texts out of the library. And the authors weren't obscure, so there was no reason why there wouldn't be a copy on the open shelves.

Then the echoing steps again. Slow, heavy, deliberate. Each one rang out like the footfall of a giant – it couldn't have been Tullus or the librarian, and the man called Afrinus had gone back to sleep at his table.

Cadmus turned from the alcove and looked back towards the library's main reading room. A huge figure stalked past the oblivious Afrinus, at least a head taller than the most athletic Romans Cadmus had ever seen. He was in full armour, its colours vibrant and gleaming as fresh paint. It looked as though a statue had been given all the suppleness of a living human.

Cadmus blinked and shook his head and emerged from among the shelves. He could still hear the mighty steps, but couldn't see the figure any more. His heart began to surge uncomfortably. Either the vision was real, or he was losing his mind. Neither option was appealing.

Then there was the sound of a brief scuffle, a smothered groan. He ran across the floor of the library to the shelves on the other side, the gloomy librarian appearing again like a phantom to show his disapproval.

He couldn't find Tullus. Still those relentless, thundering footsteps, but the library was such an unforgiving echo chamber that he couldn't pinpoint where they were coming from, or where they were going. Cadmus ran from one alcove to the next, in and out of the private reading rooms that adjoined the main library. His master was gone. And all the while the sound of the intruder was fading, fading.

He came back to the middle of the hall in time to see a massive silhouette disappear out of the door.

'Hey! Stop!' he shouted.

Afrinus's nose twitched, and he rolled his head on to the opposite side.

Cadmus ran for the exit, his satchel flying behind him, one of his cheap sandals starting to loosen around his ankle. The ghostly librarian materialized for a third time, but Cadmus sprinted past him and out into the open air.

The portico was deserted. A few Romans were making their way up the hill to the adjoining temple of Apollo, but the statuesque figure was nowhere to be seen. Three times Cadmus ran down the steps of the Palatine and back up, three times he saw nothing of his master. On the fourth time, his left sandal came apart completely, and he went rolling over the hard marble corners and landed in a heap at the bottom of the hill.

The sun rose. Priests and worshippers stepped over and around him.

'Where's your master, boy?' one asked, nudging him with his foot.

Cadmus sat up and took a moment to check his limbs, amazed that he hadn't broken anything.

'Well?' said the priest, his veiled head looming above him and blocking the sunrise.

'I don't know,' he said. 'He's gone.'

'Then you'd better find him before he gives you a whipping!'

III

Cadmus hobbled about the Forum in a daze, lost in the ebb and flow of bodies. The sun was up and the square was heaving. The smoke and spice of incense wafted from the temples and mingled with the sweat of the crowds, and every stifled breath stung the nostrils. He couldn't hear himself think over the din of voices: heralds, merchants, beggars, priests, out-of-work lawyers and two-penny prophets, all competing for the attention of the citizenry, who were themselves shouting to be heard. Cadmus had come here hoping to find someone who would listen to him about what had happened to Tullus. Fat chance of that. No one was listening to anyone.

He suddenly remembered: the Megalesia was still in full swing. It was the sixth of seven festival days in honour of the Great Mother, and Rome boiled like an unwatched pot. It was the worst time, the worst place to lose someone.

Finding himself without a master was not a pleasant sensation. What was he, without Tullus? A person halved. He hated himself a little for thinking that. But it was true. For the first time he could remember, he was without purpose. No one to tell him what to do or where to go. He felt rudderless, a skiff caught in a gale.

He took a deep breath to steady himself.

Tullus had always taught him to be a good Stoic: to accept one's fate, to endure the trials of life with a steady mind. It looked so easy when it was written down, but it was difficult to put in practice when the wheel of fortune cast you downwards.

Outside the steps of the Curia he managed to extricate himself from the swirling currents of the plebs. He scanned the crowd, thinking he might see another marble figure striding head and shoulders above the rest, but almost everyone was short and dark-haired. Above him a messenger was proclaiming news from the east. Something about a rebellion in Judaea. On any other day he would have listened, but right now the man's loud, nasal voice only added to his discomfort.

He turned to look at the Senate House. Technically Tullus was a member of the Senate, though he only occasionally took his seat these days. The men in there would know him, might care about his disappearance. But Cadmus could hardly go barging into that sacred space while the Senate was in session, telling tall tales about giants. What if Nero himself had the floor? He could wait until dusk, when the debate would finish, try and find a sympathetic ear then. But that would be too late. Tullus had no family, no particularly close friends, apart from Silvanus and his wife.

The thought struck him like a bolt from above.

Drusilla. She'd know what to do. She was better connected, commanded more respect, and exerted far more influence than her husband – out of necessity, since Silvanus himself had spent all his time pottering about in libraries rather than climbing the ladders of political or military office. He'd go to their house on the Esquiline, speak with her. With any luck he might also find out a bit more about what Tullus had got himself involved in, since he was supposed to be replacing Silvanus.

He clutched his satchel to his hip and set off to the rear of the Forum. Past the rows of market stalls, past the basilica, past the temples of Janus and Vesta and Venus, the crowds began to thin and Cadmus followed the Via Sacra to the Esquiline Hill.

Silvanus and Drusilla's house was situated in a wealthy residential district perhaps not quite as respectable as Tullus's, but certainly more fashionable. No aged grandeur here – every villa sparkled like it had been freshly carved from a single block of marble. You could practically smell the money in the air.

So it struck Cadmus as very odd when he arrived at the house and found the front door wide open, with no one standing guard. Anyone from the street could have slipped in and taken what they wanted.

He stuck his head into the gloom and called out.

'Hello?'

No reply. He clasped his hands in front of him and tried to look as innocent as possible, not wanting to be taken for a thief. The hallway was dark, but he could see it wasn't well kept. There was dirt on the floor, a broken vase, an up-ended wine jug next to the *impluvium*. This was another surprise. Silvanus was a slob, but his wife ran a tight ship when it came to their household.

'My lady?' he called again.

There was a cry from a room at the back of the villa. Cadmus ran through the empty atrium, across the garden, and threw back the curtain to Silvanus's private library.

Cadmus felt his heart lurch before he could take in the whole scene. He couldn't say which was the more wretched picture, the library or its owner. Drusilla, dressed in the long black gown of mourning, eyes sunken and hair grimed with dust, was on her knees in her husband's study. She was weeping uncontrollably. Around her looked like the aftermath of an earthquake. The desk and chairs were overturned, the surrounding shelves empty and broken in places. Silvanus's strongbox had been forced, the few scrolls that remained strewn all over the floor, unravelled and torn. The place had been thoroughly ransacked.

Cadmus went straight to Drusilla, who was being comforted half-heartedly by one of her own slaves. Two more were picking through the debris.

'My lady,' he said, awkwardly proffering a hand. The other slave glared at him. 'Can you stand?'

She looked up at him, eyes streaming, as though she'd never seen him before in her life.

'Cadmus?'

'What happened? Are you hurt?'

She didn't answer either question. 'Thank the gods you're here! Is your master with you? Where is Tullus?'

Cadmus shook his head. 'My master's gone.'

'Gone?'

'Taken.'

Drusilla sank even lower to the ground, her face a mask of despair. 'Taken? By whom?'

'I don't know,' said Cadmus, looking around the library. 'But I would bet a million sesterces that whoever did this knows something about it.'

An hour later, Drusilla was a different woman. Back to her usual impressive, imperious self. Her hair was still matted and dishevelled, and there was something ghostly about her mourning clothes, but her face was composed. She reclined a little stiffly on a couch in the *triclinium*, taking tiny sips from a cup of something herbal and aromatic. Whatever it was, it seemed to have put some of the old steel back in her.

'That library was all I had left of him,' she said. 'His books. I could read his words and feel like he was speaking to me. But now they've torn that from me too. For the gods' sake, sit down, boy, you're making me anxious.'

Cadmus stared at her a moment. No one apart from Tullus had ever offered him a seat. In some circumstances, such an invitation was the equivalent of giving a slave his freedom.

He suddenly came to, and found himself pierced by her sharp, grey eyes. 'Yes, Mistress,' he said, and went to perch on the couch opposite.

'Oh, no,' she said, wagging a finger. 'Don't "Mistress" me. Just because you've lost Tullus doesn't mean you're one of my slaves now. I have enough trouble with the ones I've already got.'

As if to make her point, she clicked her fingers and another slave came in. She raised her cup at him.

'This is vile,' she said. 'Put some honey in it.'

The slave nodded and silently took it from her. Cadmus sat bolt upright and watched him go.

He admired Drusilla, but that didn't make her any less intimidating. When Tullus had first brought Cadmus to Silvanus's house, she had laughed openly at the way he corrected his master, at his gentle mockery and his wry asides. Then she had suggested Tullus beat him for his insolence, and to that day Cadmus had never worked out whether she'd been joking or not. That was how she'd been ever since, and it set him on edge – never sure whether his words would get him laughter or lashes.

'When did it happen?' he asked tentatively.

'Early this morning,' she said.

'Do you have any ideas about who might have done it?'

She looked at him like he had said something idiotic. 'Of course I know who did it. It was Nero's men.'

'How do you know?'

'Because I was the one who let them in. They came to claim my husband's research. All of it. They haven't even returned Silvanus's body to me yet, and they think it is acceptable to barge into our home and take everything that was dearest to him.'

Tears rose in her eyes and disappeared as quickly as they had come.

'Why was he sent to Athens?' Cadmus asked carefully.

'Why?' She laughed, and the sound was like two flints striking. 'Because our emperor is a madman, that's why. A madman and a fool. He sent my husband chasing after children's stories, and now my husband is dead. I hope the Furies take his eyes. I hope they flay him and drag him to the lowest pit of hell.'

Cadmus thought he saw a reflection of that hell in her eyes. She could have been one of the Furies herself, girt in black, her hair unbound.

'What do you mean by children's stories?' he asked.

The slave returned with her sweetened drink. She fell silent, and waited until he had left before continuing.

'About a month ago, we were paid a visit by Epaphroditus. Nero's personal secretary. An ex-slave, I believe. Greek filth.' She paused. 'No offence.'

'None taken.' Cadmus's skin crawled, but he put on a smile.

'He arrived unannounced at our door, saying that Silvanus had been chosen by the emperor for an important task.' *Just like last night*, Cadmus thought. 'Nero, it seems, has grown tired of gold and wine and women. He is after gifts of a very different kind. Godly gifts. Gifts worthy of his divinity. His mother's bedtime stories must have made quite the impression on him, because he has become obsessed with the heroes of old, and has decided he is their natural successor. A god on earth. And he wants what they had.'

'What do you mean?'

'You know the stories. Heracles's club; Orpheus's lyre; Jason's Golden Fleece.' She laughed again. 'I cannot believe it myself, when I say it out loud. But Nero, spoilt child that he is, has decreed that he shall have them. The Golden Fleece is his current obsession – he thinks it will grant him everlasting kingship, or some such rubbish.'

'And he thought your husband would know where to start looking. Silvanus must have been well versed in the myth if he was writing his own *Argonautica*.'

She nodded. 'Exactly. But the emperor was completely misguided. Silvanus was interested in myths, yes, their origins, their authors, their inconsistencies. He found it all an interesting puzzle, but I'm sure he never thought any of them were true.'

'Well,' said Cadmus, 'it's difficult to say. Truth and fact are two very different things.'

Drusilla stared at him.

'Um,' he said, and looked at his broken sandal.

'You are too clever by half, Cadmus. Perhaps I should take you into my household. Have your philosophizing beaten out of you.'

'I assure you, my lady, I receive all the beatings I need at the hands of Tullus's other slaves.'

She smiled, and for a fleeting moment Cadmus thought he could see sympathy in her cold eyes.

'Whatever you think about Nero's grand plan,' she continued, 'it makes no difference. My husband is dead. That *is* a fact.'

There was a pause, filled with the sound of the fountain trickling in her garden.

'Nero's men paid us a visit last night too,' Cadmus said.

Drusilla arched an eyebrow.

'I should have said earlier. I didn't hear everything, but I think they want Tullus to take over where Silvanus left off.'

'That makes sense,' she said. 'My husband always saw Tullus as his mentor. You know they worked together on the *Argonautica* in the beginning? That was years back, though. Your master seemed to lose interest suddenly. Silvanus never understood why.'

'I didn't know that,' said Cadmus. That was odd. Tullus was definitely not a poet, and had never mentioned anything about it to Cadmus.

'Half of the texts they've stolen from this library

probably belonged to your master at some point. Nero went to my husband first because he was younger, but neither of them should be getting involved in work like this.' She took another sip of the cordial. 'Some people are made for travelling and war and adventure. Others are made for sitting in libraries. Look at you, boy. Skin like milk, skinny as a reed pipe. You wouldn't survive a trip to Baiae, let alone an expedition to Greece. Tullus is the same. Silvanus was the same. It is a waste. A terrible, pointless waste.'

'Hopefully neither Tullus nor I will have to go anywhere,' said Cadmus. Drusilla raised an eyebrow. 'My master turned down the offer.'

'Come on, Cadmus, it wasn't an offer. It was an order. Nero doesn't *offer* anything.'

He considered this. She was right, of course – there was no way the emperor would accept Tullus's refusal, however polite.

'I suppose so,' he said.

'How did he leave things?'

'The secretary, Epaphroditus, said he would deliver Nero's reply today.'

'Well, there you have it.'

Cadmus blinked. 'Have what?'

'That's Nero's reply,' said Drusilla. 'He's kidnapped Tullus.'

IV

The climb back to Tullus's house felt like scaling Mount Etna. Cadmus's knees were still raw and bruised from his fall outside the library, his left sandal was still broken, and his afternoon in the formidable presence of Drusilla had left him physically and mentally drained.

And he was alone. His heart sank along with the sun.

Again he thought of himself on a boat, on the open sea, tossed by cold black waves. No living thing for miles around. He may have been his own master temporarily, but that wasn't the same thing as being free. He had no money, no food, no clothes, apart from those that Tullus provided for him. If he didn't find the old man, he'd be sold on to a different house-hold, and there was little chance he would find someone as generous or as appreciative as Tullus.

He kept thinking of Drusilla's half-joke. *Perhaps I should take you into my household. Have your philosophizing beaten out of you.*

That was a very real possibility if he was sent else-where. His current situation was as good as it could get for a Greek slave in Rome. Not just that – Tullus was his best hope, maybe his only hope, of being freed. His only hope of returning home.

Cadmus stopped to secure his sandal. The strap had snapped, and he had to keep retying the leather. No matter how tight the knot was it always came undone again after about twenty paces.

Of course, it wasn't as if there was a home waiting for him in Athens. He couldn't even conjure a picture of what his home had been like. All he knew was what he had read in books, and he had to rely on that to feed his imagination.

By the time he reached Tullus's house, the sun was beginning to set. Cadmus basked in the amber light for a moment before knocking. The bronze studs of the front door were hot to the touch. A lizard scuttled nervously from the doorstep, then zigzagged up a crack in the plaster to the roof.

Someone opened the slot at eye level. It was Bufo.

'Let me in,' said Cadmus. 'Something's happened to the master.'

The watery eyes narrowed. 'What do you mean something's happened? Weren't you looking after him?'

'It's not my job to look after him, and even if it were—'

'Not your *job*?'

'Bufo, I know you have difficulty with long words, but try to concentrate.'

Bufo produced a stream of swearing so obscure that Cadmus was almost tempted to make notes in his tablet.

'Are you finished?' he said, when the torrent of abuse had dried up. 'Listen. Tullus has gone missing. Disappeared. We have to go looking for him. But you have to let me in first.'

'Missing?' Bufo laughed. 'More like he gave you the slip because he'd finally got tired of listening to you talk rubbish all day.'

'I'm not making this up. This is serious.'

'And what makes you think he's disappeared? Does he have to let you know every time he wants to go somewhere on his own? He's probably gone off for a walk. Or he's gone out drinking. And when he's out, you know who runs the show.'

'Just because you're the oldest, Bufo . . .'

'I've served Tullus for twenty years, boy. Don't think there's any contest for who's the most senior slave in this place.'

'Most senior slave? That's not much to be proud of. You may as well claim to be the world's tallest dwarf.'

Bufo swore again. 'Make all the jokes you like, but you'll be making them from that side of the door. I'm in charge of the household while the master's away, and I say you're not coming in tonight.'

'But—'

'And if you complain about me when he gets back, maybe I'll tell him about what I found you doing last night.' The greasy skin around his eyes crinkled.

'That's what I'm trying to *tell* you, Bufo, he's not *coming back.* This affects all of us.'

The slave closed the slot violently. Cadmus heard him laughing from the other side.

He stepped back from the door and surveyed the house. In theory he might be able to climb to the roof and drop into the garden, but if anyone were to see him he'd have a hard time explaining himself. Especially without Tullus here to vouch for him.

From the top of the Caelian, Rome looked like the embers of a dying fire. The terracotta roofs shone intensely red. Somewhere below, drunken men were shouting at each other; the faint strains of music from pipes and a lyre drifted from a house further down the road.

Cadmus rested his back against the outer wall, still warm from the afternoon's sun, and slumped down to the ground. A braver slave would perhaps have gone looking for his master. Walked right up to the imperial palace and asked if he was inside. But Cadmus knew he wasn't brave. He *thought* things rather than *did* them. So here he was, thinking.

He thought about what Drusilla had said. He thought about Nero and his ridiculous mythic project. He thought about where Tullus might be, whether he'd ever see him again. Was it more or less reassuring to imagine that the masked giant had been working for the emperor? What if Tullus's kidnapper *wasn't* anything to do with Nero? Then where had Tullus gone?

Two hours passed and his stomach began curdling with hunger. He knocked on the door a few more times. On one occasion Clitus peered out, then the new slave girl — but they both lived in fear of Bufo and wouldn't let him in.

Cadmus went back to his spot in the dirt, closed his eyes, and fell asleep sitting bolt upright.

When he woke up it was the middle of the night. The air was cold and damp, and his tunic clung to him.

He'd been dreaming about the giant, dreaming that he was the one who'd been kidnapped, smothered by a great marble hand.

When he opened his eyes, a real hand emerged from the darkness and shook him.

'Hey,' someone said.

Cadmus squinted. Two meaty calves were planted in the dust in front of him. Above them, silhouetted against the starlight, was a tall, broad-backed figure. The sort of figure forged by years of hard labour. Soldier, it looked like, although there was also the glint of an iron collar around the neck, which suggested they belonged to somebody.

'Hey, wake up.'

The voice didn't match the body, though. It was deep, but unmistakably belonged to a girl.

'Wake *up*.'

The girl shook him so hard he felt his arm almost pop from its socket.

'Ow!' he cried. 'All right, I'm up! Niobe wept, what's the matter with you?'

'Whose house is this?'

She spoke Greek, but her accent was unlike anything Cadmus had heard before. Not Thracian, not Near-Eastern. A little like Gaulish, but more clipped, and without so much saliva involved.

He shivered, and not from the cold. Maybe she was

working for Nero too. She was nearly the same size as the figure from the library.

'It's my master's house,' he said, trying to stall her. He had little hope of fending off the intruder any other way. *Words, words, words*, he scolded himself. *That's all you have, Cadmus.*

'Don't waste my time, friend,' the girl sighed. 'I've had enough trouble getting here.'

'If you tell me your business, I'll try and help you.' His voice didn't sound half as steady as he wanted it to.

'I have a message. For Gaius Domitius Tullus.' She said the name like she had been rehearsing it for days. 'From Athens.'

Cadmus got to his feet, suddenly flushed with warmth. Even when he was standing upright, she towered over him.

'Athens?'

'Yes.'

'You were there?'

'Yes.'

'Who sent you?'

'The man.'

'Which man?'

'Silveranus.'

'Silvanus?'

'Yes.'

A long pause.

'And?' Cadmus prompted.

'And he gave me a wax tablet. To bring to your master.'

'A tablet?'

'Yes.'

'Not a scroll?'

'No.'

The girl was obviously not in the mood for talking. In the darkness her face was a vague, expressionless circle. The silence was broken by the sound of dogs barking down in the city.

'Can I look at the tablet?' he asked eventually.

'Are you Gaius Domitius Tullus?'

'No, I'm Cadmus—'

'Then, no. It's only for him.'

'Tullus isn't here. He's disappeared.'

The girl's huge shoulders sagged. 'Are you joking? Do you know what I went through to get here? You don't get any special treatment for carrying an important message. Just chained up in the ship and beaten like all the other slaves, thanks to this.' She pointed at the collar.

Cadmus looked at the tag. These things were usually reserved for runaways. Slaves with a history of disobedience.

'That's funny,' he said, reading the words etched

into the wood. 'I don't *remember* you belonging to Gaius Domitius Tullus.'

'He really isn't here?'

'I'm sorry to disappoint you.'

'What's happened to him?'

'Someone's taken him away,' said Cadmus. 'But that tablet might help him. Or help *us* to help him.'

'I don't understand how it can be so important. The message is very short.'

'You looked inside?'

'Might have done.'

'I thought you said it was for his eyes only?'

The girl shrugged. 'It doesn't matter. I can't read anyway.'

Cadmus didn't know what to make of her. After his initial trepidation, he felt strangely calmed when she spoke. Her words were slow and rhythmic, rising and falling, tinged with that odd, lyrical accent. It was like listening to waves breaking on a shore.

'Can we go inside?' she said. 'I need a rest.'

There was something frank and direct about the way she spoke too. Most slaves didn't just ask for things outright.

'You and me both,' said Cadmus. 'But we're locked out. I had, um, a *disagreement* with one of the household.'

'Wife?'

'No.'

'Son or daughter?'

'No, my master isn't married. It's just him living here.'

'So then who have you been arguing with?'

'One of the other slaves. Thinks he owns the place.'

'Another slave? You need to stand up for yourself, friend. Come on.'

'Come on what . . . ?'

The girl walked to the entrance of the villa, Cadmus trailing behind her. She ran her fingers over the bronze handle, and pushed at it gently. She hummed. Then she took two, three, four paces backwards, dropped her shoulder and threw all of her weight at the door.

The whole house seemed to vibrate like a struck drum. The door swung inwards, shuddering on its hinges, as though it had never been locked in the first place. The draw bar on the other side clattered to the floor. A piece of oak, thick as Cadmus's forearm, split neatly into two. He looked at her and gaped.

'Wait, you can't—'

She didn't even turn around. She pushed again at the swinging door and strolled calmly into the atrium.

The house still seemed to be ringing when he followed her inside. The rest of the slaves had their lodgings at the back of the garden – another reason for them to hate Cadmus, since Tullus had offered him a *cubiculum* at the front, near his study – but it was highly likely that the echo of the intrusion had reached their ears.

He listened carefully for shouts or footsteps. Nothing yet. He closed the door behind him and tried his best to secure it with the broken stub of the bar.

The girl looked around, hands on hips. 'Hmmm. Very nice. What about your master?'

'What about him?' Cadmus wrung his hands. What was he going to do about her? Why couldn't she just hand over the tablet and leave?

'Is he nice?'

'Why do you ask?'

'The old man said your master would look after me. In return for delivering the message. I'm wondering if I'm going to be happy here.'

Cadmus was lost for words. And that never happened.

'You seem nice,' she continued. 'And a lot of the time that's because of the master. Slaves are nicer if they're treated right. And the other way round. Although that doesn't follow in my case. Ow!' She stubbed her toe in the darkness.

'Wait a moment,' Cadmus said. 'Let me get a lamp.'

A small flame was flickering in the shrine to the household gods, its feeble light barely reaching the floor. Cadmus used it to light the wick of an oil lamp, and brought it over to where she was standing. She rubbed her foot vigorously, and then stood up. That was when he saw her properly for the first time.

'Gods above,' he muttered.

'Yes. You don't know how lucky you are being so small. They'll never put you to work in the mines, not with those arms.' She pinched his bicep.

The girl's skin was a fibrous mess of scars. They criss-crossed in pale, white ridges down from her shoulders to her hands, and arced across one side of her face.

'Did this . . .' Cadmus swallowed drily. 'Did this all happen on the journey here?'

'What? Oh. No. I've just not been very lucky with masters, last few years. You always get the worst jobs when you're my size. Even if you're a girl.' She paused. 'Especially if you're a girl, sometimes.'

'Your masters gave you all these?'

'Yes. Apart from this one,' she said, pointing to a puckered line along her collarbone. 'Got that at home. Got into a fight with a wild boar. You should see what *he* looks like now.'

The girl chuckled, and then looked strangely distant. Cadmus knew what she was feeling. He'd understood from the moment that she mentioned 'home'. There was a moment when he thought he might like to sit with her the whole night, to find out who she was, to tell his story and to hear hers. But then he saw the wax tablet in her hand and remembered there was more pressing business.

'You need to give me that tablet.' He directed a finger at her, and she slapped his hand away.

'Ow!' The sharp sting turned to a deep throbbing. Cadmus tried to soothe the pain by putting his hand under his armpit. 'What was that for?'

'Don't point at me.'

He looked at her. She was deadly serious.

'And ask more nicely,' she added.

'Sorry,' he said, frowning. What a peculiar creature she was. '*May I please* have the tablet?'

'You're sure your master isn't coming back?'

'Not any time soon. But whatever's in that message could be very helpful to him.' *And to me*, he thought. If it was vital information, if might give him a reason to go with Tullus on whatever expedition Nero had planned.

'I told you, it's only a couple of lines. I don't know why the man thought it was so urgent. Maybe I'm wrong.'

She paused, but made no move to hand over the message.

'So . . .' said Cadmus. 'Can I see it?'

'I suppose. But seeing as your master isn't here, you have to make good on the promise the man made.'

'What do you mean?'

'I want to a place to stay. And things to eat.'

Cadmus looked over her huge frame in the flicker of the lamplight and wondered just how much she *would* eat.

What was he supposed to do? He almost missed having Tullus make all his decisions for him. Bufo couldn't claim to be in charge, but then again neither could Cadmus. He couldn't just allow another slave into the household. He couldn't throw her out on the street again either – quite literally, since there was no way he would be able to manhandle her out of the house, and he suspected she wouldn't go without a fight.

Then he imagined what Bufo himself would say or do when he saw her, and he felt a tingle of rebellious excitement. He'd pay good money to see Bufo try and wrestle the girl across the threshold.

'Fine. As long as you don't mind sleeping on the floor.'

'I've never slept anywhere else.'

As she handed over the tablet Cadmus heard the sound of something being knocked over in the kitchen. He froze, both of their hands on the wooden frame.

'Quick, through here!'

He ran into his bedroom, expecting the girl to follow. She did eventually, but not quite as urgently as he'd hoped. He watched her duck under his door frame, her face a picture of broad bemusement, and then pulled the curtain across behind her. He was poised to blow out the oil lamp, but they heard nothing else. No footsteps, no voices. The house sank into silence again.

Cadmus handed the lamp to the girl and sat on the edge of his bed with the tablet. He untied the string holding the frame together, opened it on his lap, and read the message.

From Quintus Aemilius Silvanus
To Gaius Domitius Tullus, Senator

Greetings, friend,

I hope all is well at Rome. Thank you for your invitation to dinner, I would be delighted to attend. Make sure you clean the tables!

That was all it said. He turned it over in his hands. There was no postscript. Nothing written on the back.

The girl had been right. She'd risked her life crossing land and sea just to arrange a dinner party.

V

As tired as he was, Cadmus hardly slept for the second night in a row. The girl snored like a bear and seemed to speak more when she was asleep than when she was awake. Sometimes in Greek, sometimes in her own language. He stared at the ceiling and tried to piece together everything that had happened. Images rose and fell before his blind eyes: the giant's vividly coloured face and clothes; the ruin of Silvanus's library; the distraught Drusilla; the mystery of Epaphroditus's box. In the dark their strangeness only became more vivid. When he wasn't thinking of these, he was looking at the wax tablet again, tracing the inscribed letters with his fingers. There *had* to be more to it than just Silvanus's reply to

Tullus's invitation. Some other meaning lurked behind its simplicity. And why the request about cleaning the tables? Some kind of in-joke?

He'd snatched a couple of hours of uneasy sleep when he was woken by the patter of feet outside the room. The other slaves were up. Dawn, maybe later. They were talking in low voices near the front door, and had obviously discovered the evidence of the break-in.

Below him, the girl rolled over heavily and muttered something in her native tongue, the words seeming to resonate through the floor and into his mattress. He watched the vague outline of her back rising and falling as she breathed. Now that the dust of the previous evening had settled, he knew in his tired bones that letting her stay had been a bad idea. He knew nothing about her. What had he been thinking?

She suddenly sat upright and yelled something into the darkness, more foreign sounds that Cadmus didn't understand. They poured from her lips, terrified and terrifying.

'What? What is it?' hissed Cadmus.

She didn't even realize he was there. Her hands thrashed and groped in front of her face. Cadmus scrambled from his bed and on to the floor, cupping a hand over her mouth. He tried to grab both her wrists, then just one of them, but even using all his strength and all his bodyweight she swatted him back against the bed frame. Eventually he pinched her neck hard, and that seemed to wake her up. Her mouth closed and her shoulders slumped.

She turned slowly where she sat. 'What are you doing?'

'What am *I* doing? Your screaming's going to bring the whole house in here!'

'Screaming?' She looked into her lap. 'Hmmm. Sorry. Bad dream.'

The curtain behind them twitched. Cadmus could see two pairs of bare feet shuffling in the gap at the bottom. He got up off the floor and threw it open, to find both of the slave girls loitering guiltily outside. Charis looked over his shoulder and raised her eyebrows.

'Don't start with your gossiping,' he said, relieved that he hadn't been caught by someone else. 'This is none of your business. Go and find something useful to do.'

'You sound like Bufo.' She tutted, barely able to conceal her delight. 'He's not going to be happy when he finds out you broke the door down just so you could bring your girlfriend in.'

'She's not my—'

'Don't worry, we won't tell him, unless you give us a reason to.'

'Are you blackmailing me? *You're* the one who sounds like Bufo now.'

At that, the girl got to her feet. Cadmus watched Charis's and the other slave's eyes widen as they fully appreciated her size.

'Maybe I will tell him, after all,' Charis said. 'She looks like she'd put up a bit of fight. The old toad won't know what to do with himself.' She looked the girl up and down and shook her head as if in wonder. 'I'll tell you what, Cadmus, you've got strange taste in women.'

'I told you, she's not my—'

But before he could finish protesting, Charis and her friend had scampered away laughing. When he turned around, the girl was less amused.

'Sorry about that,' he said.

'Embarrassed by me, are you?'

Cadmus blinked. 'No. Not at all. If anything I'm rather proud of you.'

'Oh, right. Proud of me. Proud to show me off.'

The girl's displeasure was all the more unsettling for the fact that she hadn't moved her face, or raised her voice, since she started speaking.

'That's not what I mean.'

'Don't lie to me. I know when I'm being made fun of. I've been up for auction twice. You don't know what it's like.'

'No, but . . .'

'You don't know how it feels to be the youngest slave in the line-up, but also the tallest. To have hundreds of men gasping and pointing and laughing at you.'

'I'm sorry,' he said, and he meant it. He was ashamed.

The girl *humphed*, and fiddled with the metal collar around her neck. She'd broken off the tag, he saw, but the collar itself was locked shut.

'How shall I introduce you in future?' Cadmus asked. 'Do you have a name?'

'I have a few,' she said quietly. 'They gave me nicknames after they captured me.'

'Such as?'

'Everyone in the camp just called me Ursa.'

The bear. Cadmus imagined the slave dealer who'd given her the moniker, thought of his grinning face. He didn't find it funny.

'Well, that won't do,' he said. 'What's your real name?'

She sighed. 'I can tell you, but you won't be able to pronounce it. No one can.'

'Try me.'

She opened her mouth, and out fell a jumble of syllables. They sounded like the noises she'd been making in her sleep.

'Tog . . . what?'

'I told you,' she said. Then she spoke very slowly. Her tongue seemed to be working incredibly hard as she enunciated the name again: 'Tog-o-dum-na.'

'Togidubina.'

'Close enough.'

'Maybe I'll just call you Tog.'

She shrugged. 'Fine. That's more effort than most people go to. And your name is . . . ?'

'Cadmus.'

'Is that your real name?'

'I suppose it is now. I can't remember what I was called when I was born.'

'Oh. I'm sorry.'

'Don't be. There are plenty more like me, plenty more like you. Can't be sorry for everyone. There's not enough sorrow to go around.'

They shook hands, Cadmus's slim fingers disappearing completely within hers.

'Right,' he said decisively. 'Seeing as Charis is now probably spreading the secret through the house, there's not much point in hiding in here any more. Let's get something to eat, then I want to ask you more about this tablet, and about what happened in Athens. I want to know everything.'

They stepped out into the atrium, which was now deserted, Cadmus taking the tablet with him. From there he led Tog into the garden. The sun was beginning to coax the dew from the grasses; flowers in terracotta pots were opening themselves to the day, their petals warm like flesh. Thrushes hopped from branches to bathe in the fountain. The edges of everything seemed softened.

He'd nearly reached the kitchen before he realized that she'd stopped following him. She was standing next to the fountain, her eyes closed, breathing deeply. In the sunlight he saw how pale Tog's hair was – like silver and gold thread, in a ponytail that reached her shoulder blades. He rarely saw anything like it in Rome.

He was still staring when she finally turned and blinked at him. She smiled briefly and came over to where he stood in the shade of the peristyle.

'I can't remember the last time I could just stand and listen to the birds,' she said.

Inside the kitchen, it soon became clear why Bufo hadn't heard them breaking into the house the night before. He was slumped in the corner, cradling an amphora of wine, sleeping off a hangover. It was well known that he liked to drink on the job, but the absence of Tullus had obviously encouraged him to really push the boat out.

Cadmus put a finger to his lips, laid the tablet down next to the stove, and began to gather fruit and bread from the shelves.

'Oh, hello!' said Tog in a voice that wasn't even close to a whisper.

Bufo gurgled like a baby, then went back to whatever wine-drenched dream he was having. Cadmus turned around. Tog had her finger in the bars of a tiny cage resting on a work surface, in which a dozen or so small furry bodies were wriggling.

'What are they doing here?' she asked, still too loud, her face a mask of concern. 'Poor things.'

'Dormice,' Cadmus whispered, in an attempt to encourage her to lower her volume. 'For dinner.'

'For *dinner*?'

Bufo stirred again.

Cadmus pointed at the door. 'Go!' he mouthed, a bag of provisions in one hand, the tablet in another.

'You mean, you *eat* them?' She wasn't even trying to keep her voice down any more.

'Can we discuss this some other time?' he hissed, and made to leave.

Tog didn't move. She looked so sad all of a sudden. 'The poor things.'

'They're just mice.'

'What do you mean, *just* mice?' she said loudly.

Bufo's eyes opened. For a moment he seemed unsure of where he was. He frowned and slurped at the saliva pooling around his lips. He looked at Cadmus, then at Tog, then at Cadmus again. Then at the food he'd pilfered. The toad's face and neck swelled.

'What do you think you're *doing*?' he slurred. 'Who's she? And who let you in?'

He spoke to them in Latin, and Tog frowned in incomprehension.

'Calm down, Bufo,' said Cadmus. He could hear a quiver in his voice. Perhaps this wouldn't be as entertaining as he'd hoped. The old slave was unpredictable when he was drunk. Tog, meanwhile, seemed unconcerned by the whole situation, and was still trying to find a way to open the cage.

'I'll have you whipped!' he said. 'When the master comes back, he'll beat you black and blue! Thieves!'

'He's not coming back,' said Cadmus, feeling like the soles of his feet had melted and stuck him to the spot. 'I told you that. But she might be able to help us find out what's happened to him.'

Bufo laughed and got unsteadily to his feet. Cadmus watched his cheeks and forehead turn the colour of raw meat. 'Well, if you're so sure Tullus has gone, I suppose I'll have to discipline you myself . . .'

He seized a rolling pin from the bench next to the stove, and lurched forward. At exactly the same time, Tog opened the cage.

The dormice scattered in all directions in twos and threes. Tog smiled, her face transformed again. Bufo tried to stop himself mid-lunge, but he already had too much drunken momentum. His legs buckled and he fell to his hands and knees, swiping wildly at the grey smudges as they raced away to freedom. He was far too slow. In the space of two heartbeats, all of the mice had disappeared.

Tog clapped and muttered a word of triumph in her own language. She turned to follow Cadmus out of the door, but hadn't noticed Bufo groping for the rolling pin again and picking himself off the floor. He was growling like an animal.

'You *useless* . . .'

'Look out!' Cadmus yelled, but it was too late. The old toad staggered into her and brought his club down heavily, clumsily, on the back of her neck. Cadmus's feet still didn't want to move.

Tog didn't go down, though. Instead, she turned, as though someone had tapped her on the shoulder. Bufo tried to swing the rolling pin again, but she caught his hand in hers, and squeezed. He dropped the weapon.

'Go back to sleep,' she said in that calm, deep, undulating voice.

Bufo winced, his face now almost the same shade as the wine he was pickled in. Cadmus remembered, with some satisfaction, when he'd been in the same position as Bufo, his hand crushed, after the old slave had caught him eavesdropping.

'Who are you, monster?' Bufo snarled, creased in pain.

'What's he saying?' Tog asked.

'He wants to know who you are.'

'Then tell him. I am Togodumna, daughter of Caradog, granddaughter of Cunobeline, King of the Catuvellauni. And I am asking him nicely to go back to sleep.'

Cadmus saw her knuckles flex, and Bufo made a wet-sounding cry. Then she released him and he tottered backwards, holding one hand in the other.

'You'll *pay* for this! Both of you!'

She left him whimpering, pushed past Cadmus, who was still standing frozen on the threshold, and returned to the atrium. When Cadmus finally tore himself away from the scene, he found Charis, Clitus, the other slave girl and two of the other cooks peering into the kitchen. He couldn't decide whether their expressions were of admiration, or disapproval, or fear, or some mixture of the three. He didn't waste time trying to explain. He turned, smiled weakly, and followed Tog – although, as she'd just revealed, she was so much more than just Tog – back into the house.

When he reached the atrium, the front door was wide open, and she was standing in the white sunlight with her hands on her hips.

He stepped through after her.

'It's probably not wise for us to stay here,' he said. He chewed on his lower lip. Masterless, now homeless.

'Agreed,' she said. 'You've got the food, though, haven't you?'

'A little, yes.'

'We should look for your master.'

'Yes.'

An awkward pause. One of Tullus's wealthy neighbours bobbed past them in a litter, carried by two slaves. She leant out of the window and ogled them. Halfway down the hill, she was still craning her neck.

'Why didn't you tell me?' Cadmus said at last. 'About who you were?'

'You didn't think to ask,' Tog said.

VI

The pair of them sat on a pontoon on the banks of the Tiber, legs dangling, the yellow waters lapping at their feet. Tog was eating her third fig from the satchel, juice dripping from her chin. Cadmus chewed morosely on a piece of stale bread, his broken sandal on the floor next to him. A little further down the bank he could see the waste from the Cloaca Maxima sluicing into the stream, and when the wind was in a certain direction all he could smell was raw sewage. In the exact same spot he could see men fishing with nets. He grimaced.

'What are you doing?' Tog said, with her mouth full. The stench apparently didn't bother her.

He didn't reply. Her large head came looming into

the corner of his vision.

'Hey. What are you doing?'

'I'm *thinking*.'

'Oh. I thought you were just bored.' She went back to eating, and there were another few moments of silence. 'What are you thinking about?'

'What we should do. If Tullus doesn't come back, then both of us are homeless. And I'm worried about this message from Silvanus. He was trying to tell Tullus something, I'm sure of it. Like you said, he wouldn't have gone to the trouble of sending you all this way if the message was really that simple.'

'Then we go looking for him.'

'But he could be anywhere!'

'Then we just look *really* hard.'

'I don't think even that would help. If he's been recruited by Nero, then he's either in the imperial palace – ' Cadmus flapped his arm behind him at the Palatine Hill – 'or he's already left for Athens.'

'If that's where you're headed, you're on your own. I'm not going back there.'

Cadmus shuffled on the pontoon to face her. 'What exactly *were* you doing there?'

Tog inspected her half-eaten fig, and then put the remainder on the edge of the pontoon. She'd done the same with the others. Three morsels of fruit in a neat row.

'Well,' she said, wiping her hands on her tunic, 'I was working in the mines, to begin with. I'm good at digging. I suppose that's why they picked me. Important people. A few us were taken away to the other side of the city, to dig for something else. I didn't really understand what. From listening to Silveranus—'

'Silvanus.'

'Him. From what he was saying it sounded like some treasure. Something made of gold?'

'The Golden Fleece,' Cadmus murmured.

'Yes, that's it. That's what they called it. *Fleece*. Strange word.' She seemed lost in thought for a moment. 'Anyway, we didn't find anything while I was there. Then suddenly your man fell ill. He called me back to Athens with him. That was when he told me I had to deliver the message. He didn't look so good. I wonder how he is.'

Cadmus cleared his throat.

'He's dead,' he said. 'The fever took him. That's why Tullus was asked to replace him.'

'Oh,' she said. 'Shame.' She took a radish out of their bag of provisions and bit it cleanly in half.

Cadmus scowled into the currents of the Tiber. The matter of the tablet still didn't make sense. He might not have expected Silvanus to mention the expedition if it was a secret project, but why agree to a dinner party when he was racked with fever?

'What even is this treasure?' asked Tog. 'Something you wear?'

'It's from one of our myths. A Greek story, not Roman. A man called Jason, a hero, went on a quest to claim the fleece of a sacred golden ram. His uncle had taken his kingdom from him, and gave Jason the task of finding the fleece to win it back – but he knew the task was impossible, and hoped it would get Jason out of the way. But Jason agreed. He built a ship called the *Argo*, and he collected together a group of famous heroes to be his crew, the Argonauts. Then he sailed to Colchis, in the far east, and had to complete three trials to win the fleece back from the king there, called Aeëtes.'

Tog yawned.

'He had to plough a field with some fire-breathing bulls; then he had to defeat a field of warriors who had grown out of the ground; and then he had to find a way past a giant serpent who was guarding the Golden Fleece itself. He was only able to complete the task with the help of the king's daughter, Medea, who was a sorceress. She gave him the potions that allowed him to get the fleece – the flames of the bulls didn't touch him, and he was able to put the serpent to sleep.'

'What's a sorceress?'

'Like a priestess. Or a witch. Do you know what I mean by a witch?'

She nodded. 'Sounds like she is the hero of the story. Sounds like Jason didn't really do anything, apart from sail a ship around.'

Cadmus thought for a moment. 'I suppose you *could* look at it that way. But there's more to the story. They fell in love, and she came back to Greece with him. Jason got, um, *embarrassed* because his wife wasn't quite normal.'

'I know what that feels like.'

'He went off with another woman, and abandoned Medea in a country where she wasn't welcome.'

'Bet she didn't stand for that.'

'Absolutely not. To get her revenge, she killed their children.'

'Oh. Fair.' She yawned again. 'And the treasure. The fleece. What happened to it?'

'No one really knows. There are lots of different accounts.'

'And now your emperor wants it?'

'*The* emperor,' he corrected. 'Not *my* emperor. But, yes, he's trying to find where it's got to. The fleece has always been a symbol of kingship. Of divine power. They said it had healing properties. That it protected its wearer. Even made him invulnerable.'

'Hm. Sounds good.'

Cadmus gave a low, humourless laugh. 'It does, doesn't it? But then all bedtime stories do.'

'You don't believe it?'

'Of course not,' Cadmus said. 'Myths are fascinating things, and they can tell us a lot about ourselves, but we mustn't believe any of these things actually *happened*.'

He shook his head. Ridiculous, that people should be dying for the sake of something that never existed. People like Silvanus. Perhaps people like Tullus too.

He looked at the heel of bread in his hand, so hard it was inedible, and threw it into the water.

'Hey! Don't do that.' Tog got on to her knees and stretched out into the yellow-brown ripples to fetch it back. 'That's perfectly good food.' She placed the waterlogged crust next to the other bits of fruit. She'd also balanced the other half of the radish on the edge of the boards as well.

Cadmus rubbed his brow, his brain already too overwhelmed to make sense of this extra bit of strangeness. She seemed to be leaving offerings for some tiny god or goddess. 'What are you *doing*?' he said.

'I'm preparing a little feast.'

'You've already eaten half of our supplies, Tog. These were meant to last longer than today.'

'It's not for me.'

Cadmus closed his eyes and shook his head. 'You've lost me.'

'It's for him.'

When he opened them again, she was holding the tiny body of a dormouse in one of her hands. It explored the edges of her huge palm, nose twitching, and then ran up to the crook of her elbow.

'Where did that come from?'

'From the kitchen.'

'I know that, but how is it here?'

'*He* is here because *he* took a ride in the sleeve of my tunic.'

'I thought you said you wanted to set them free!'

'I did. But this one jumped on to me and hasn't left me since. It's his choice. I'm not forcing him. Here you are, friend . . .'

She plucked the mouse from her arm with thumb and forefinger and set him down next to the meal she'd arranged on the edge of the pontoon. The creature ran from one piece to the next, with steps so fast and small it looked like he was on tiny wheels.

'How do you know it's a *he*?'

Tog shrugged. 'Just a feeling.'

The dormouse settled on a piece of fig and began nibbling.

'Great,' said Cadmus. 'Another mouth to feed.'

Tog didn't bother replying to that. She just watched her new companion tucking in and smiled, smiled like she had in the garden. She so rarely made any expression, it was like the sun clearing storm clouds.

While she was preoccupied, Cadmus reached into his satchel and took out the wax tablet. When he opened it again he groaned.

'Oh, no . . .'

Tog looked up. 'What?'

'The wax. It's melted. I must have left it too close to the stove in the kitchens. Damn it!' The yellow sheet was twice as thick at the bottom as at the top, the text was warped and sagging and in some areas had been swallowed up completely.

'Why is that a problem? It was only a couple of lines. You can remember them, can't you?'

'Of course I can remember them, it's just—' Then he saw something. In the top left-hand corner of the wax tablet's wooden frame. A pale, stained corner of papyrus, exposed where the wax had melted and thinned.

'Just what?'

'I don't believe it.' Cadmus laughed. 'Of course. I'm so *stupid*.'

'Well. I didn't want to say so.'

'It's the oldest trick there is!' He looked up at Tog, beaming. '*Make sure you clean the tables!* He's hidden his real message *under* the wax. He wanted Tullus to clean off the top layer.'

He began to pick at the smooth, hard surface, but it just came off in tiny chunks and got stuck under his fingernails. He tried using the edge of the pontoon, the edge of his sandal, but nothing would take the wax off cleanly, and he was afraid of damaging the papyrus underneath.

'We need to get it melted again,' he said. 'We need heat. A fire of some kind.'

'Here, use this.'

From a fold in her grubby tunic, where it was cinched around the waist, she produced a razor; a broad, flat piece of iron with a wolf's head as a handle. He recognized it immediately.

'By Heracles, Tog, what else have you stolen from my house?'

'What? Is your master going to miss it?'

'No, but—'

'I liked the wolf. Reminds me of home.'

That word again.

'Right,' said Cadmus.

'Don't worry, I'll give it back when we find him. I just thought it would be useful. And looks like I was right, doesn't it?'

He eyed her warily, suddenly aware again of how little he knew about her. How little he could trust her. You didn't just *steal* things that you liked the look of from your master. That sort of thing could get you killed. He looked at the scars on her arms and caught himself wondering how much they were her own fault.

No, he had to reprimand himself. *None of it is her fault.*

Tog proffered the blade and he took it from her carefully. She went back to fussing over the mouse, and he began to slowly scrape the wax from the tablet. It peeled off in thin, pale curls, until the entirety of Silvanus's secret message was revealed. He removed the square of papyrus from the frame and unfolded it. The letters were cramped and half-formed, written by a hasty or a failing hand.

'Well?' said Tog, lifting the mouse and the fig he was gorging on back into her palm. 'What does it say?'

He showed it to her.

'You'll have to say it out loud. Can't read, remember?'

'Oh, yes. Sorry.' Cadmus scanned the whole thing. It was in shorthand, a sort of code that Silvanus and Tullus had taught their slaves, for transcribing notes at speed. To any other readers it would have been completely indecipherable. 'It says: *Greetings from Athens, old friend. I wish I had more space to write, more time to explain. I am not long for this world – that'll teach me for sticking my nose into matters of the gods. I won't say you didn't warn me.*'

Cadmus looked up.

'Strange,' he said. 'Drusilla said they had worked together in the past, but Tullus never mentioned it to me.'

Tog shrugged. He went back to reading the letter.

'I know you wished to leave all of this behind you, but I thought this was something you needed to know. I have found it, Tullus. Medea's grave. In an abandoned shrine near Athens. I'm amazed we never discovered the site earlier, it seems too obvious! It wasn't mentioned in any of your notes, but I have found someone who is an even better guide than you. She is a prophetess. I can hear you laughing now – a prophetess indeed – but this young woman is different. She claims descent from Medea herself.

'We have hit a snag, though. The slaves have been digging for days, but the fleece is nowhere to be found. Nor the trials mentioned in the historia Brutorum. *I returned to the prophetess to ask for more information, and I am sorry to say I lost my temper with her. I should have known not to be so forceful – and now here I am, confined to my bed, staring Death in the face.*

'But I am choosing to see this as a blessing. A sign from the gods. While work has stopped, I am asking you to pick up where I have left off. This is your chance to find the Golden Fleece before the emperor does – a blessing, like I say. I have destroyed my notes here, so they do not fall into the wrong hands, but much of the research you gave me is

- 79 -

still in Rome. It is hidden in the Aemilii family tomb, watched over by the gorgon. I need not remind you what a disaster it would be if Nero were to claim the fleece first.

'*I am sorry I will not be there to take these final steps with you — but then, it is only fitting that you should be the one to enjoy the fruits of our labours. A word of caution, though: if you choose to visit the prophetess, take great care. She is more dangerous than she seems.*' Cadmus paused again, before continuing. '*Reward this slave, she has suffered a great deal. Love to my wife. See you in the world below.*'

He looked up at Tog, whose face was strangely blank. 'A reward?' she said. 'That's good. Wonder what it'll be.'

Cadmus scanned the letter again. He couldn't help feeling slightly betrayed. Why hadn't Tullus said anything? Here were two of Rome's most renowned scholars, convinced that the Golden Fleece was not only real, but within their grasp. Why was it so important that Nero not get his hands upon it? Surely they didn't subscribe to the same superstitions as Nero?

There was only way to find out, and that was to read the research that Silvanus had taken such pains to hide.

'Tog,' he said, starting to fasten his broken sandal, 'it looks like you and I have a date with the dead.'

VII

It was the final day of the Megalesia, and the Via Appia was almost at a standstill. Somewhere along the road a cart had broken down and in the blazing midday sun nobody was in the mood to be patient. A fight had already broken out at the bottleneck. Slaves and journeymen shoved and shouted, while patricians leant from their brightly painted litters and demanded to be let through first. To make matters worse, the entire community of beggars from the Porta Capena had now descended upon the gridlocked road to ply their trade, bringing with them their various exotic smells and afflictions.

Tog went ahead and forced a way through the compacted bodies, Cadmus following in her wake, grateful for the human shield. Once they were through the Porta Capena and beyond the city walls, the air seemed to immediately freshen, and even though the road was almost as busy, people were noticeably more subdued. Out here, travellers kept different company.

The route was lined with the tombs of the great patrician families, whose long-dead ancestors watched the living come and go from the city. Rich or poor, citizen or slave, everyone leaving or arriving at Rome did so under their stern, marble gaze. The imposing facades of the tombs demanded silence. Their doors yawned open. They seemed to invite passers-by out of the summer heat and into the cool, blue shade of death.

'This was the road I came in on,' said Tog. 'From the coast.' Her mouse was perched on her shoulder. Only the gods knew how she'd got it to stay there.

'The Via Appia,' Cadmus said. 'Longest in Italy, I think. Definitely the most important.' They wandered slowly along the road, looking up at the names on the tombs. Cadmus already had a crick in his neck.

'I thought these were *houses*,' said Tog. 'They're so big!'

'Oh, yes. Just because you're dead doesn't mean you don't have to keep up with the neighbours,' he laughed.

'You bury your dead right here? Next to the road? Where everyone can see them?'

'The rich families do, yes. After they've been cremated. Poorer people have to make do with being chucked in the river.'

'I'd rather that. Not very peaceful here, is it?'

'I think that's the point. Keeps the dead fresh in everyone's mind. And gives them a bit of company, you know? Look.' He pointed to a more modest tomb a little further up the road. 'Some people still have dinner with them.'

In the small paved area in front of the monument was a table set with bread and oil and a jug of wine. There were flowers scattered among the meal too.

'Oh, I wonder if—'

'Don't even think about it, Tog. You can't feed your mouse with offerings to the dead. The gods below will not take it kindly.'

'That wasn't what I was thinking . . .' she said, but trailed off. 'He's had too much to eat anyway. I think he's a bit sick.'

Cadmus looked at the dormouse and laughed. She was right, somehow he *did* look a little green around the whiskers, and was moving very sluggishly around her broad shoulders.

She stared at the food and looked up at the bust of the tomb's owner. Then she moved on, as though lost in thought. The mouse crept under the golden-silver tumble of her hair.

'I think it's odd,' she said quietly. 'At home we buried them under the ground.'

'That's the third time you've mentioned home. Where exactly are you from?'

'Britannia.' She pronounced it slowly and deliberately. 'That's what you call it anyway. I don't like the way it sounds in your language.'

Britannia. Just the name sounded like fantasy. Like myth. She may as well have said she was from Mount Olympus, or the Elysian Fields. A rain-soaked island of monsters, cut off from the rest of the world by a cold and frothing sea, where the inhabitants painted their naked bodies in blue woad and never cut their hair. Whose priests sacrificed their fellow men and wielded strange and unnatural magic.

Or so he'd been told. Tog didn't quite fit the description.

'I see,' he said, swallowing hard. 'And those things you told Bufo in the house . . . were they all true?'

'Yes. My grandfather was our king. So was my father, but by the time he had the throne things were . . . changing. He led the fight against the Romans when they invaded, but he was captured. My mother and sister too. I don't know what happened to them. I assume they're dead.'

'I'm sorry,' said Cadmus.

'I thought we agreed not feel sorry for each other?' she said. 'Anyway, I hardly knew him. I just know the stories my aunt told me – she looked after me and my cousin when the others had gone. Then, three winters back, there were rumours of another uprising against the Romans. A queen from the east passed through our village, looking for people to join her. My aunt forbade me to go, but I saw it as my duty, after what had happened to my father. So I joined the queen.'

'Boudicca,' said Cadmus.

'You know her?'

'She made quite an impression on us, here at Rome. Obliterated the settlements. Brought the province to its knees.'

'No thanks to me . . .' She hung her head in shame. 'I got captured before I'd even seen my first battle.'

'And then what? How did you end up in Athens?'

'They took me back to Rome and put me up for public auction, like I said. Some businessman bought me and shipped me to Greece. I only worked in his house for a few days before he realized I wasn't going to behave. That was when he sent me to work in the mines.'

Cadmus had heard about the conditions in the silver mines of Greece. Slaves rarely made it out alive. It only added to his impression of Tog as a being not quite of this world.

'Your Greek is very good,' he said, because he couldn't think of anything else. Tog shrugged.

'Had to learn quickly. All the other slaves were Greek. And nothing gets you whipped faster than not understanding your master's instructions. You probably know that.'

He didn't, actually, and again felt faintly ashamed. He'd never been whipped in his life. Tog had endured things that were beyond the realms of his imagination.

They continued along the verge of the Via Appia, searching the inscriptions for Silvanus's family tomb. They passed the Metelli and the Sergii, their bones laid to rest in edifices larger than Tullus's villa.

'Do you miss it?' asked Cadmus.

'Of course.' She paused to let her mouse nibble at her finger. 'You know what I miss most? The weather. The rain, the wind. You don't have proper skies here. Your skies are dead. I miss the greens and the blues. You Romans—'

Cadmus cleared his throat noisily. 'Careful, Tog. I'm not a Roman any more than you are.'

'Fine. *These* Romans are always going on about their land. How much they love their countryside. But, to me, this whole country is just dirt. It's hot and it's yellow and it's dusty. Like nothing wants to grow. My home . . . Everything wants to grow. The whole world is leaves and grass and streams. And trees. Mighty trees, not like these little things.' She pointed at a poplar growing between the marble monuments. 'You should come with me, when I go back there.'

'*When* you go back?'

'Yes. When. It'll happen. One day.'

Cadmus knew that feeling. 'We just need to be patient,' he said. 'It'll happen. Tullus is a good man.'

'What does that have to do with anything?'

'I mean I think he'll free us. In the future.'

'I don't need his permission. I just need enough money and provisions for the journey.'

'I don't think it would be wise to just run away. Not with the collar on.'

'I knew you'd say that. You think too much.'

Cadmus went quiet and chewed his lip. She was right. Always worrying and thinking instead of doing. Suddenly he was full of regrets for not acting faster in the last two days.

'Let's just keep looking,' he mumbled. 'Whatever's in this tomb might be our route back to Tullus.'

They continued along the Via Appia in the broken shade of poplars and pines. The air was so hot it hummed with a sound all of its own. Still the men and women streamed towards Rome, beating heart of the world.

'Aha!' Cadmus pointed to the opposite side. 'Look.

Tombs of the Aemilii Lepidi. And the Aemilii Scauri.'

'What does that mean?'

'They're branches of the same family. The Aemilii Silvani aren't as important as them, but I bet they'll have built their tomb nearby.'

They were some way from the road, and its traffic seemed a distant murmur, when he finally saw it. A small house about the size of Cadmus's *cubiculum*, perhaps slightly bigger, fronted by two pillars and the graven heads of three men in togas. The inscription beneath them was badly worn, but Cadmus could make out, 'DIS MANIBUS' and, 'AEMILII' and, 'SILVANI'.

'You're not superstitious, are you?' Cadmus asked.

'Superstitious?'

'Afraid of ghosts. Spirits.'

Tog shook her head and stepped inside. She had to duck under the lintel.

The interior of the tomb was cold and dusty, but not unpleasant. There was no smell of death; just a smell of nothing at all. The marble of the exterior was only for show, it turned out – the walls themselves were made of brick, and there were alcoves built into them where urns had been placed and the busts of those whose ashes were inside. Underneath them were oil lamps and dishes for offerings. They were empty.

'Oh, dear,' whispered Cadmus, shivering. 'Looks like Silvanus hasn't been taking much care of his forefathers.'

'What exactly are we looking for?'

'I don't know. Silvanus just called it his work. Maybe a scroll or something.'

'Didn't it say someone was guarding it?'

'The gorgon. I'm not sure what he meant by that. It's a monster, from a Greek myth. I don't think he meant the real thing.'

He waited a few moments for his eyes to adjust to the darkness, then started exploring the abandoned shrines. Tog let the mouse run down her arm and on to one of the ledges, where it circled the dishes warily.

'What was that?' she said suddenly, straightening up and banging her head on the ceiling.

'What?'

'I think there's someone outside.' Tog shook the dust and plaster out of her hair, and went to the door, where the sun was painfully bright. She looked around. A bee buzzed lazily into the tomb and quickly left, as though aware it had taken a wrong turn.

'Well?' called Cadmus.

'Nothing,' she said, coming inside and making sure she ducked this time.

'I thought you said you weren't afraid,' said

Cadmus. She gave him an unimpressed look.

'So this monster . . .' she said.

'I think I've found it.'

In the back corner of the tomb was the head and shoulders of a heavy-browed, serious man – to be honest, they *all* looked serious – who wasn't wearing a toga but a military uniform. He must have been a distant ancestor because, as far as Cadmus knew, the Silvani were a family of scholars and lawyers. On the front of his breastplate Cadmus could just make out the carving of the gorgon's face, teeth bared, snakes writhing wildly around her head.

'Right. So where is this scroll?'

'I don't know.'

Cadmus looked around and behind the bust, even in the urn itself, but found only dust and ash.

'Looks cleaner, this one. Doesn't it?' said Tog. 'Look at the others. Covered in cobwebs.'

At the same time as she said this, her mouse came scuttling along the ledge, and disappeared into a crack at the base of the marble that seemed barely wide enough to fit a finger in. It was so small Cadmus hadn't even seen it.

'Hey!' cried Tog. 'Where are you going?'

She pushed Cadmus out of the way, and grasped each side of the bust.

'I'm not sure . . .' said Cadmus feebly, but before he

could reason with her, the muscles in her back and shoulders were taut and she was heaving the huge carving to one side so the grizzled face of old Marcus Aemilius Silvanus Probus was facing the wall.

And there it was. Beneath his image, maybe half a dozen bricks had been removed to create a sunken recess, and in it Cadmus could see a parcel of leather, about the size of his writing tablets. Tog's pet was perched on top of it, his tail curled around one of the strings holding it together.

'Well,' said Tog. 'Looks like you wouldn't have achieved very much without us.' She held out a finger and the dormouse ran up the length of her arm.

Cadmus reached in and drew the package carefully out of its hiding place. The leather was a little damp and faded at the corners, but it was otherwise in good condition. It looked well used. It was also heavier than he had expected. After watching Tog lift the marble bust without so much as breaking a sweat, he felt utterly feeble having to cradle it in both hands.

'This must be what Silvanus was talking about,' he said.

He walked back towards the light of day, blew the dust from the top and unwound the strings. Inside were hundreds of pieces of loose papyrus, yellowed and curling. Each page was crammed with text, written horizontally, vertically, diagonally, in long lines and in small clusters, to the margins and beyond. There were short passages in Greek and in Latin, and symbols that Cadmus didn't recognize as any language. The handwriting looked slightly crazed, but most of it without doubt belonged to his master. There were maps and diagrams too, sketches of pottery and statues and ruined buildings.

'What is it?' Tog asked.

'Tullus's notes. Everything he knew about the Argonaut myth. And it's not all about Jason and Medea – he's followed Heracles, Orpheus, Theseus . . .' He squinted. 'Hold on, I need a better look.'

He stepped out of the tomb and suddenly his eyes throbbed with a blinding whiteness, not from the sunlight, but from an explosion of pain on the back of his head.

Tog's shout came too late. He remembered the taste and smell of soil, and then nothing.

VIII

When Cadmus came round, he couldn't see anything. Then, out of the nothing-ness, a Roman face, a man's, ancient and furrowed. It stared down at him, as though in judge-ment. For a moment he thought he was still in the tomb. Then the face spoke.

'Cadmus! Are you all right?'

It was Tullus. Cadmus stood up, an instinct from when he was back in the villa and roused from sleep by some emergency.

'Master,' he burbled. 'What is it?'

He collapsed and Tullus caught him in his bony arms.

'Thank the gods you're awake!' The old man

gently, awkwardly, lowered him to the ground in a half-embrace. 'I thought you were dead when they brought you in.'

'I think I might be.' He rubbed his head. 'Where are we?'

'The Domus Transitoria,' said Tullus. Cadmus squinted. It took a huge amount of effort to understand what his master was saying.

'Eh?'

'The emperor's palace.'

Cadmus closed his eyes for a moment and breathed deeply. When he opened them again the throbbing started afresh, only this time in his eyes instead of his head. All around him the room was decorated with frescoes of mythological scenes, heroes and monsters in vivid reds and yellows and blues, lit by three braziers. He could see Heracles rushing at the jaws of the Nemean Lion, Perseus hiding behind his mirrored shield, Theseus descending into the darkness of the Labyrinth with the radiant Ariadne at his side. On the wall behind him was Jason, snatching the Golden Fleece from under the nose of the giant serpent. There was something odd about the appearance of these heroes, though. They looked overweight and ugly. For a while Cadmus thought his vision was still fuzzy from the blow to the head, but when he looked closer he started laughing.

'They've all got Nero's face,' he said, his laughter creating an exciting new type of pain in his ribs.

'Repulsive, isn't it?' said Tullus.

His master helped Cadmus back on to the couch where he had been resting. There were three of them, arranged in a horseshoe shape, for dining. The scent of perfume and overripe fruit clung to everything. There were no windows, and the light from the braziers was yellow and dirty.

'What time is it?' Cadmus asked.

'I don't know,' said Tullus. 'They don't let me out of this room. About the sixth hour, I think.'

'And what are we doing here?'

Tullus rubbed at his bald head. '*You* are here because I asked for you to be here. I didn't think Nero's men would be quite so ruthless about bringing you in, but more fool me.'

'Why do you need me here?'

'Because . . .' He stopped and looked at his old, shaking hands. 'Because I need to tell you something. Before it's too late.'

'Too late?'

'Nero is sending me to Greece,' he said. 'I am old, Cadmus. I fear it is a journey I will not return from. Obviously I shall accept my fate as any good Stoic should – but before I go there is something important I must discuss with you.'

'The Golden Fleece?'

Tullus looked shocked. 'What do you mean? What do you know about the fleece?'

'I know Nero is looking for it. I know he recruited Silvanus. And I know Silvanus thought he was close to finding it.'

Cadmus told him everything that had happened since his master's disappearance, about Tog, about Silvanus's letter, about the notes he'd found in the tomb.

'We found them, Master,' he said. 'We found Silvanus's notes. Only . . .'

He looked around the room. The notes weren't there. Neither was his satchel, containing Silvanus's hidden message. And, most worryingly, neither was Tog.

'I don't know where they've gone.'

'Don't worry, my boy,' Tullus said. 'I would give all of my estate to never have to look at those notes ever again.'

In the firelight the old man's eyes were bright and keen and quivering. He was looking at the couch in front of him, but he was seeing something else. There was loss in those eyes, and grief. Cadmus wondered what his master was thinking.

'You never told me this was your area of expertise,' he said. 'It doesn't seem . . . you.'

Tullus's eyes weren't focused. He was still miles and years away. 'That's because it isn't me. It is the work of a very different Gaius Domitius Tullus. But, yes, long before you were ever a member of the household, I was an avid mythographer. The story of the Golden Fleece interested me more than most, though, because it was where so many other myths crossed paths. The *Argo* was crewed by some of the greatest heroes – Heracles, Orpheus, Meleager, Atalanta. Theseus, in some versions . . . And then there was the fleece itself, as an artefact. I was seduced by it, like so many others. The emblem of eternal kingship.' He paused. 'The idea of Nero claiming it as his own chills the marrow of my bones. It would be catastrophic.'

Cadmus gave a nervous laugh. Tullus never spoke in such grave and mystic terms.

'Even if it exists,' Cadmus said briskly, 'I think you and Silvanus are slightly overstating things. It would be a shame, but hardly a disaster. Heaven knows, ever since he came to power Nero's been stealing holy relics from all over the world to refill the treasury.'

But Tullus wasn't smiling – not even his curious smile of self-mockery. The furrows in his face were so deep he looked like an actor in a tragic mask.

'The Golden Fleece is not just a pretty shawl, Cadmus. Nor is it simply holy. It holds power. An old power, the kind that left the world many generations ago.' He pointed at the frescoes of the mythological scenes. 'It belongs there and then, not here and now. It certainly doesn't belong in the hands of a lunatic like Nero. There are oracles, in the Sibylline books, that talk of the fleece lending its bearer unnaturally long life. Eternal dominion. It makes gods of men.'

Again Cadmus had that creeping sense of having been tricked. He thought he knew Tullus – he was the least superstitious man he'd ever met.

'You really believe all this?' he asked.

'I do.'

'But—'

'You think me a fool, I know. You're young and clever and you think you understand everything about the world. You think these are children's stories, that you've left them behind, but mark my words, Cadmus: they are more important than you know.'

He looked as though he was about to say something else, but his mouth made a thin, sealed line.

The two of them sat in silence for a moment, while the braziers crackled and hissed around them. The room was stiflingly hot. The heroes painted on the walls lurked behind a haze of smoke, their colours dulled, grim shadows of the divinities they were meant to represent.

'Let's just say all of this is true,' said Cadmus. 'The

myths, the oracles, everything. You've still got to find it, haven't you? Couldn't you conveniently, you know, *fail* to find it?'

'It's a little late for that, I'm afraid,' he said. 'Nero already has the Golden Fleece. At least, he has *a* Golden Fleece.'

'What do you mean by that?'

Tullus stared at him. Cadmus could make out every wrinkle, every blemish, every thin hair, thrown into sharp relief by the light of the coals.

'It was in the box they brought to the house the other night. It certainly looked convincing. It was a thing of divine beauty, that's for sure. But . . .'

His master looked pained.

'But what?' Cadmus said.

There were footsteps outside the door of the *triclinium*. A tuneless humming.

'Damn him,' Tullus muttered. 'No more of this. We will talk after he's gone.'

'Ah, wonderful! You are awake.'

A voice slithered into Cadmus's ears from across the room. He turned to see the same slender Greek man who had come to Tullus's house two nights ago. He had the pink, oily complexion of a man who drank too much and slept too little. In one hand he held the thick sheaf of papyrus that Cadmus and Tog had discovered in the tomb.

'Forgive me,' he said, with a slight bow of his head. 'I should have introduced myself the other night, but I didn't realize you were *the* Cadmus. Such a strange-looking boy. Not what I expected at all.' Cadmus blinked and looked at the floor. '"Little Socrates", wasn't that what you used to call him, Tullus? Your master holds you in very high regard, you know. He was quite assertive in his demands to have you here.'

'I am grateful for it,' was all Cadmus said.

'I wonder if we might speak in Greek?' the man said. 'It's always a bit of a treat for me, these days. I am Epaphroditus. Secretary to the Divine Caesar.'

'I see,' said Cadmus; and before he could stop it the rest tumbled out. 'I imagine gods have a lot of paper-work.'

Epaphroditus laughed, and his yellow teeth glittered with too much saliva.

'You don't disappoint, do you, boy?' he said. 'What a quick tongue you have.' Then his eyes narrowed and Cadmus knew he had misspoken. 'I used to be a slave, just like you. Did you know that?'

Cadmus nodded. Tullus was furiously massaging his brow.

'You know how I got to where I am now? Because I understood how to play the game. I understood that you do anything your master tells you to, anything at all, or you are punished. And I understood that cleverness and insolence get you killed.'

The smile never faltered, nor did his stare. His eyes were black, all pupil; a lizard's eyes.

'Now, then. Shall we get down to business?'

The secretary slipped in between the couches and laid the satchel on the central table. Then he fanned out the pages of Silvanus's notes. Tullus craned his neck to see.

'Your slave found this in Silvanus's family tomb,' said Epaphroditus. 'He has entitled it his *Argonautica*, though it is far more wide-ranging than the title suggests. It contains notes, sketches, diagrams. Everything he ever learnt about the myth of Jason and the lives of the other Argonauts. Frustratingly, Silvanus burnt his own copy just before he died. We searched his personal library, but it contained nothing we don't already have in the imperial archives. Thankfully, clever little Cadmus knew exactly where to look. Well done, my boy.' He brushed a clammy hand over Cadmus's hairline.

'If you have the notes,' said Tullus, 'then surely you don't need either of us? By Jupiter, my eyes are so bad I can barely read what's on those pages.'

'There is only one page we are particularly interested in.' He plucked a folded piece of papyrus from the bottom of the pile and opened it. 'A map.'

Cadmus looked at the hastily sketched picture, and

immediately recognized the outline of the city walls, the web of the roads, the surrounding topography.

'It's Athens,' he said.

'Very good, Little Socrates,' said Epaphroditus. Cadmus clenched his fists until it felt like he was drawing blood with his nails. 'It points to the location of a prophetess. A Sibyl. A woman who, we believe, gave Silvanus the final directions to the Golden Fleece. It seems – although, as I say, you will be better placed to decipher these things – that she claims to be descended from Medea herself.'

That was what Silvanus had said in his letter. It seemed preposterous. He turned to look at Tullus for reassurance, but the old man had his eyes closed, and his head quivered like it was caught in a draught.

'If you already have the fleece,' his master said, 'then what, exactly, am I supposed to be looking for?'

'The Divine Caesar is interested in far more than just the Golden Fleece. You of all people, Tullus, should know the treasures that the other heroes carried with them. And there is the *Argo* itself, the first ship, blessed by Hera and Athena – they say that its very timbers were able to speak prophecies. If this Sibyl knew of Medea's final resting place, who is to say she cannot help us find the other Argonauts?'

Cadmus was watching the secretary closely. The corners of his mouth twitched continually, as though he was trying very hard not to laugh. Did he believe any of this?

'You still don't need me!' said Tullus. 'Are you not able to read a simple map?'

Epaphroditus's smile faltered. 'The map is not the problem, old friend. Many of the accompanying notes are written in the shorthand that only you and he understood. And you know how misleading the words of oracles can be. An expert such as yourself will be invaluable in interpreting the Sibyl's utterances.'

Tullus hung his head, exhausted.

'Now,' the secretary continued. 'Nero is acutely aware of how much time has been wasted by the death of your friend, and he is keen for you to take these notes and accompany the expedition leaving for Greece tomorrow.'

The old man suddenly opened his eyes and coughed like he was choking on an olive stone.

'Tomorrow?'

'At first light. Cadmus, I presume you will be accompanying your master?'

Cadmus's heart fluttered like a caged sparrow. *Athens.* He was finally going to see his home.

'If that is what my master wishes,' he said.

'No,' croaked Tullus.

'No, Master?'

'You must stay here. I will not put you in danger.'

'But—'

'*No*, Cadmus. Do as you're told. There will be time for explanations. Not now.'

Cadmus's blood boiled with frustration. Epaphroditus was watching their exchange with open amusement.

'It seems a little odd, Tullus, to demand the boy's presence and then not to take him with you. But then, he is your slave. Do with him as you see fit.' He turned to Cadmus. 'Perhaps you can persuade him over dinner, my boy? A few sweet words in his ear?'

'Dinner?' said Tullus.

'Yes! Of course, I never told you. My deepest apologies. Nero has invited you both to dine with him tonight, in thanks for your work.'

Cadmus and his master looked at each other, their faces slack with horror.

'Tonight?'

'Right now, in fact.' He flashed his yellow smile again. 'Follow me, please. I hope you both have a good appetite!'

Epaphroditus stayed long enough to savour their discomfort, and then turned and left the room, his laughter echoing like bells rung out of tune.

IX

The Domus Transitoria was less a palace than a network of several palaces, designed by Nero to link all the imperial residences together. Epaphroditus led them left and right and left again, past so many rooms and through so many corridors Cadmus was certain he wouldn't be able to find his way back again. Eventually he could smell the cool, slightly damp air of the evening, and they emerged into a grand garden surrounded by a portico. All of the countryside was here, tamed and shaped and slotted neatly among the marble columns – little rolling hills, clear springs and pools, clusters of cypress that looked blue in the light of the fading day. After so many hours of sweating in the dark dining room, the garden was bliss.

They made their way around the portico to a corner where there was an outdoor dining area, its couches and canopy wreathed in vines and lit softly with hundreds of lamps. None of the food had been brought out yet, but rich coverlets were spread over the tabletops and festooned with fruit, flowers and expensive glass and silverware. The emperor wasn't there either, but most of the guests were already reclining while slaves served them generous helpings of wine.

Tullus surveyed the scene with barely concealed disgust as they approached.

'Ah,' said Epaphroditus, looking over the guests already assembled. 'It looks as though we're a little early, but do make yourself comfortable.'

They weren't early, Cadmus knew. Nero was late. But Nero was master of time as much as he was master of everything else in the world.

Cadmus accompanied his master as he circulated the open-air *triclinium*, reminding him of the names and ranks of a handful of guests. There were a handful of ex-magistrates, but most of the group were an eccentric mix of hangers-on: Nero's comrades in indulgence, a gaggle of wet-lipped, overweight and over-perfumed young men who laughed too loudly and never said a word they really meant.

It was Cadmus's job to remain inconspicuous, but he felt more introverted than usual among the dinner guests. It wasn't just the obnoxious, braying company. He was preoccupied. He was still angry with Tullus for not letting him go to Athens. And he kept thinking about Tog. He should have asked Epaphroditus what had happened to her, but now he'd missed his chance.

Tullus was refusing the offer of a drink for the third or fourth time when the emperor finally joined them. He sauntered across the grass like a dancer mid-routine, wrapped in a crimson, double-length toga, embracing the other guests and giggling in a disjointed, tuneless way.

Cadmus had never seen the emperor this close before. He was plainly wearing thick make-up to disguise his terrible complexion, and his hair and sideburns glistened with perfume or oil or sweat or a combination of all three. He looked much older than his twenty-five years. His eyes were glazed and wild.

A bizarre train followed him. At his heels were several young slave boys and slave girls, dressed to look like the god Bacchus with their faces painted gold and ivy wound into their hair. They danced and spun, showering Nero and the guests with fresh petals.

Behind them was another group, as stern and silent as the young Bacchuses were spirited. They looked the same as the giant who had come for Tullus in the library. Thirteen figures, dressed from head to toe in colourful, enamelled bronze, their faces concealed by smooth and exquisitely proportioned masks. As they came into the light, Cadmus saw they matched the paintings in the room he had just left. They were all dressed to look like the heroes.

Lastly, hobbling to keep up, was the most decrepit old man Cadmus had ever seen. Or was it a woman? The features were so ancient, the figure so stooped, it was impossible to tell. Under a white hood, Cadmus could see a whisper of a beard, although this didn't necessarily settle the matter. The sleeves and the lap of the robe were the colour of rust. Blood. The figure's clothes were stiff with it.

'Who are all these people?' Cadmus asked his master quietly. 'They look like they've come from the theatre.'

'That's Nero's soothsayer, Polydamas. He's an augur, a haruspex, a priest, and I don't know what else.'

'And the giants?'

'Some new personal guard Nero has created for himself,' said Tullus. 'Seems the praetorians aren't dramatic enough for him. He's recruited from the gladiator schools, I believe. They were the ones who took me from the library.'

Nero took his couch, with Epaphroditus reclining next to him. The old man bent double at his ear, while the bronze, statuesque guards took their positions on either side. Finally two more Bacchus-slaves entered from the other end of the *triclinium* carrying a box that Cadmus recognized. They placed it on the floor below Nero's elbow, undid the clasps and opened the lid.

'Gods above . . .' Cadmus muttered. 'It's real.'

The Golden Fleece shimmered like a fish catching the light. At one end, the ram's great, golden head hung slack and empty. The two slaves lifted it carefully from the chest and draped it over Nero's shoulders. Nero spread his hands as though to frame his splendour. The dinner guests gasped and burst into applause.

'Do you like my new outfit?' Nero made his strange giggling noise again. 'Isn't it beautiful?'

The faces on the couches nodded in agreement. They looked just as painted-on as the masks of Nero's guards.

'Beautiful . . .' Nero muttered again. His eyes darted in his head, as though following a fly circling over the tables. Behind him the old man in the robe rocked backwards and forwards, watching the sky, and then leant forward again to mutter in the emperor's ear.

'*Yes, I know,*' Nero snapped. He turned back to his

guests. 'You are all most welcome. But one of you is more welcome than the rest.' He suddenly looked directly at Cadmus and his master. 'Our friend Gaius Domitius Tullus will be travelling to Greece tomorrow in the service of his emperor. We drink to his health and his fortune. And we pray that he isn't as feeble as the fool who went before him.'

The emperor erupted into laughter, and the rest of the guests followed suit.

'I thank you for your prayers,' said Tullus. Cadmus could see he was quivering with rage, or fear, or both. 'I hope I can be of, ah, some service to you.'

'No, no, no – no need to worry. You won't fail me. Polydamas has seen it. He has just come from the sacrifice, and the omens were favourable. The gods have given their blessing to my every endeavour. Just as the Golden Fleece belongs to Caesar, so shall all the treasures of the heroes. I shall have Heracles's club, that I might wield it myself, and crush the enemies of Rome!' He stood up and made a sweeping gesture, as though armed with an imaginary weapon, and knocked Epaphroditus's goblet from his hand. The diners laughed again. 'I shall have Orpheus's lyre, that I might charm Rome's allies with my songs. I shall clad myself in Achilles's invincible armour, so I might lead my people into battle and inspire them to greatness. Shan't I, Tullus?'

He suddenly looked at Tullus with such a glare, Cadmus felt compelled to leap in front of his master and shield him from the blow. Tullus's whole body stiffened.

'I, ah, pray I will not disappoint you, Caesar,' he stuttered. 'And I pray that my old bones won't let *me* down. Aha.'

Nero stared at him for a moment, his expression unreadable. Then he smiled. 'You needn't worry about that, my old friend. It is your mind that we need, not your body. I have my *heroidai* for the hard work,' he said, gesturing to the guards either side of him.

His abrupt switch to Greek caught Cadmus by surprise. *Heroidai.* The Sons of the Heroes.

'I wonder, my friends; would you like to see my new toy?'

There was a brief, confused pause.

'*I want to show you my new toy.*'

Suddenly the guests were talking and nodding, begging him to show them what he was talking about.

Nero silenced them with a gesture, and then beckoned to one of the armoured men. The bronze figure came towards his couch in a couple of strides.

'I like my *heroidai* very much,' he said, caressing the mask with one of his fat, pink fingers. 'But today I think I found my favourite. Not one of the *sons* of the heroes, but a *daughter* of the heroes.'

The gait, the stature – Cadmus recognized them now. He tried to get Tullus's attention, but his master seemed lost in thought.

'Take off your mask, my dear,' said Nero. 'Show them how well-made you are.'

Mask and helmet came off as one, and a mass of golden-silver hair tumbled over the shoulders and breastplate. It was Tog.

'Isn't she beautiful?' The emperor stared at her with something like awe. His eyes shone in the lamplight and for a moment he looked like an infant about to burst into tears. The diners dutifully applauded.

'Atalanta, reborn! Or Penthesilea? Either way, quite, quite worthy of my little band of heroes. What's that?'

Nobody had spoken, but Nero looked around the couches as though he had been interrupted.

'You think it inappropriate that a woman be brought to symposium of civilized men? My friends, if only you knew. There is no one else in this palace I would trust more with my life.' He turned to Tog. 'Perhaps, my dear, you would like to give us a demonstration?'

The emperor clicked his fingers and demanded the tables be removed. Slaves appeared from the darkness of the colonnade and cleared the space in front of his couch, quickly, effortlessly, with the merest patter of feet on the mosaic floor. Tog herself looked utterly bewildered as Nero led her by the hand, as though she were a young bride, into the centre of the *triclinium*.

'Come, then,' he declared. 'Who would like to provide us with a little pre-dinner entertainment?'

The diners' laughter was muted, as though they were unsure if he was joking or not. Cadmus could see that he was quite serious.

'No one?' Nero's voice again took on the tone of a child who had been denied a treat by his mother. 'I'm surrounded by cowards! To hell with all of you! She's just a *girl*!'

The guests exchanged glances and elbowed each other in nervous encouragement. Finally, a man emerged from the shadows at Nero's back. He had been standing there all along, and Cadmus hadn't even realized. It was Tigellinus, the head of the praetorian guard. As soon as the man's trenched and broken face came into the lamplight, Cadmus could see that his reputation for cruelty was well deserved. He looked like he'd never smiled in his life. He wasn't much taller than Tog, but was thicker set, and the muscles in his arms stood out like banded iron.

'Ah, Tigellinus!' Nero clapped with delight. 'Of course. Good to see there are still some proper Roman men left in the city – not just these lazy, womanly creatures!' He licked his lips. 'Now, perhaps you would like to arm yourself? We should try and make this a fair fight.'

Every muscle in Cadmus's body was tensed. His teeth ached from clenching his jaw so much. Nero was setting the pair of them up for gladiatorial combat.

There was another ripple of nervous excitement as Tigellinus wandered along the line of the *heroidai*, and eventually chose the huge club of the guard dressed as Heracles. He hefted it in one hand. Tog, meanwhile, picked at something she had found in her ear.

'Very good, very good,' said Nero, as the tribune returned to the centre of the dining area. 'Two worthy adversaries! Now, salute your patron.'

Tigellinus made a small bow in the direction of the emperor, but scarcely took his eyes off Tog. Cadmus could see the man's knuckles going white around the handle of the club, the sinews in his forearm thick and taut under its weight.

'Are we ready?' cried Nero, as though appealing to the audience at a satyr play. The dinner guests cheered. He turned to Tog. 'Fight as though my life depends on it, yes? And be wary – ' he added this in a stage whisper – 'Tigellinus doesn't play very fair.'

Then he withdrew to his couch.

'*Begin!*' he shouted, in tones so shrill the whole room jumped.

Tigellinus immediately assumed the stance of a boxer, knees bent and shoulders hunched. Tog still hadn't moved. She regarded her opponent with curiosity. The atmosphere turned bitter and mocking, although Cadmus couldn't work out which of the two were the target of the laughter. Tigellinus seemed infuriated by what he took to be Tog's insolence, took his club in both hands, and swung it with brutal force into her midriff.

Cadmus winced and closed his eyes. When he opened them again, Tog was still upright, swaying slightly like a tree in a storm. Still she didn't move. The guests began to murmur. Nero came forward again, frowning.

'Come now, girl. Show a little spirit. Let's give our guests something to cheer about, shall we?'

Again he stirred the drunken enthusiasm of the onlookers, and before he was even back in his seat Tigellinus had brought the club down between Tog's neck and shoulder, with a blow heavy enough to crack marble.

Once more, Tog staggered backwards but made no move to defend herself or return the blow. The emperor stared at her, his tongue protruding a little as though it were too big for his mouth. He stepped forward and brought his face very close to hers.

'Listen to me, you wretch. I don't think you're

trying very hard. It's almost as if you don't like having fun.' He cocked his head like a chicken. 'I don't *like* people who don't like having fun. Do you understand?'

The other guests fell quiet.

'Now. Shall we try one more time?' he said.

Tigellinus clasped his club in two hands again, and gave a broken grin. This time, just before Nero screamed, Tog looked round and caught Cadmus's eye. He nodded fractionally, his body so rigid with worry that he couldn't manage anything more expressive.

'*Begin!*'

Down came the club, but this time Tog's arm flew up and caught the man's wrist in mid-air. Her biceps bulged. Opposite her, Tigellinus's eyes suddenly widened under his heavy brow, and Cadmus saw a flash of teeth behind his lips. He strained against her, and a vein on his forehead began to pulse and shine with sweat.

Nero cackled, and the dinner guests roared their approval. Even Tullus managed to peer out from behind his fingers. Slowly, inexorably, Tog brought the club down to the level of her waist, Tigellinus hissing like an irate asp. Even through the din of the onlookers, Cadmus thought he heard the crack of bones, though he didn't know whose. The weapon dropped heavily to the floor.

Tigellinus managed to free one of his broken hands from Tog's grasp and began to fumble frantically under his leather breastplate. He withdrew his hand. There was a flash of steel. Cadmus looked on, silent and sick, while Nero jumped and clapped like a lunatic.

An agonized groan undercut the cheering, and for a moment Cadmus thought that the dagger had found its target; but then the groan was echoed by the other guests, as Tigellinus slumped to the floor, clutching his abdomen.

The *triclinium* fell silent, apart from Tigellinus's whimpering. Tullus had clapped a hand over his mouth. Still Tog peered down at her floored opponent, frowning, as though he were something she didn't fully understand. She was barely out of breath.

Nero came forward, smiling broadly.

'You see!' he said. 'Atalanta reborn. A true daughter of the heroes!'

One man made a strangled laugh. Another clapped twice, and then stopped when he realized he was alone. Two slaves made their way among the couches and dragged the moaning Tigellinus into the inner rooms of the palace. He left a thick smear of red over the white tiles of the mosaic.

'Now,' Nero announced into the silence. 'Shall we eat?'

X

By the time the food started to arrive, everyone seemed to have forgotten that the head of the praetorian guard was bleeding out his life somewhere in another room. Perhaps, thought Cadmus, there was nothing unusual about this sort of occurrence at one of the emperor's dinner parties. But the whole episode had left him quite shaken, and even a dinner as lavish as Nero's didn't serve as much of a distraction.

Lavish, in fact, hardly did it justice. Each dish was a masterpiece of gastronomic design. There was a peacock, with its glittering tail feathers still attached to its crisped rump; a giant turbot on a bed of sea urchins, arranged to look as though it were leaping from its serving platter; a circular dish of different sweetmeats, big as a cartwheel, each selected to represent a different sign of the zodiac; a huge sow, the centrepiece of the whole dinner, with roasted fowl carved and shaped to look like piglets suckling at each of her teats. Not only that, but when the carver came to open up the pig, a dozen thrushes flew, alive and twittering, from inside its belly.

Amid all of these grotesque delights, Cadmus watched Tog standing awkwardly behind the top couch. Nero was feeding her scraps from his plate like she was a dog. She chewed what she was given with a kind of furious boredom, and then spat it on to the floor as soon as the emperor's back was turned. She looked like she'd forgotten about the evening's entertainment too. Her face was glowing and scarless in the reflected light of the Golden Fleece.

Cadmus leant in to his master, who was struggling to swallow a flamingo's tongue without retching, and whispered: 'What are we going to do about her? We can't just leave her with Nero.'

'Why not?' said Tullus, grimacing as the next plate was added to the table. 'She looks like she can take care of herself.'

'Well, for starters, she technically belongs to you. Silvanus gave you ownership.'

'What difference does that make? I thought my

mind and my body belonged to me, but that didn't stop Nero claiming them as his own.'

'But she helped us. Silvanus promised her that we'd look after her.'

'I'm sorry, Cadmus, but we have more pressing concerns than the life of a Gaulish slave—'

'British.'

'What?'

'She's from Britannia.'

'Same thing,' said Tullus, waving a hand dismissively.

'So you're not going to do anything?' Cadmus tried hard to keep his voice down. He knew this wasn't how a slave should speak to his master, even when his master was as innocuous as Tullus; but his anger from earlier was still simmering gently somewhere around his navel. 'You're happy to abandon both of us?'

Tullus looked at him sternly. 'You are unkind, Cadmus,' he hissed. 'None of this is going as I would have wished. But Fate and Fortune have their own plans. All we can do now is pray to the gods for deliverance.' He paused and looked at the plate in front of him. 'And for some food that's actually edible.'

Cadmus straightened up, the frustration of the situation contending with the frustration of knowing Tullus was right. Fortune raised you up one day and cast you down the next. All one could do, his master always told him, was endure. He tried to regain his sense of calm, his sense of balance, as a good Stoic should. But it was difficult when the room was whirling like it was.

The slaves still pranced about the diners, endlessly filling and refilling their wine cups. Some people had already passed out. As expected, the emperor looked more worse for wear than just about anyone. The Golden Fleece kept sliding off his back when he turned or rolled on his couch. Each time it did, Tog stepped forward and draped it back over him.

'Well, here's something positive,' said Cadmus. 'It looks like Nero's forgotten all about you.'

Just as the words left his mouth, he saw Polydamas staring at him, his eyes like curdled milk. Without looking away, the ancient priest said something into Nero's ear, and the emperor sat upright.

'Yes, yes, yes, yes, of *course*,' he burbled, lips wet with wine. 'Tullus! It is time for your performance!'

There was a chorus of laughter and belching from the diners who were still conscious.

Tullus tensed. 'My performance . . . ?'

'Yes, we must have our second round of entertainment. Something more cultured, perhaps? My secretary says that your slave found something *special* in Silvanus's tomb. Come out here, old man. Come, come, come. Tell me what that dog Silvanus was hiding from the Divine – ' he hiccoughed – 'Caesar.'

They both made their way out into the centre of the *triclinium*. Some of the guests began booing and hissing – they'd obviously been expecting the bar to be raised after the excitement of Tog's fight. Cadmus limped a little, his sandal strap loosening with every step. Nero had raised himself unsteadily from his couch and was trying to quell the noise. The fleece had fallen off his shoulders again, and behind him Tog was holding it in her fist like an old dishrag.

'We have made several, ah, useful discoveries,' said Tullus. No one heard a word of it. Cadmus felt like he'd been thrown into the middle of the amphitheatre. The guests roared and roared. A wine cup sailed across the room in front of Tullus's nose, and there was a cheer when it hit a diner on the other side.

'Speak up, Tullus!' cried Epaphroditus, sharing Nero's couch and obviously enjoying the old man's discomfort.

'In particular, ah, a map . . .'

'Louder!'

The emperor was laughing now too. Tullus shot a terrified glance at Cadmus.

'We think,' he said, his voice straining, 'that Athens may hold an interesting clue. There is a woman, a prophetess of some sort, who Silvanus thought might know the location of the heroes' graves. And possibly of the, ah, *Argo*.'

Suddenly the guests fell silent.

'The, ah, boat,' Tullus finished weakly.

Cadmus looked around. From where he was standing, the couches, the tables, the columns wreathed with vines, everything seemed to take on a strange, disorientating slant. At first he thought it was something to do with Tullus's mention of the *Argo*, but when he looked ahead he realized the party had frozen for a very different reason. The priest was upright. He was pointing a bloodstained finger at Cadmus.

The sound from the old creature's mouth sounded like wind over a desert. A collective shiver went through the mute dinner guests.

Polydamas lowered his finger and indicated Cadmus's foot.

Nero yelped like he was waking up from a bad dream. He began to tremble. His purple face now had the colour and consistency of unbaked dough. Cadmus looked down to see that he was missing half of his footwear.

'He is here!' said the emperor, a fat hand over his mouth. 'The boy! He is only wearing one sandal!'

A freezing sweat surged from Cadmus's skin. He knew what Nero was referring to. His lungs felt as cold and heavy as marble. In the silence he managed: 'I have two sandals, Caesar. Only, one of them is broken.'

'How *dare* you, Tullus?' said Nero, as though Cadmus had never spoken. 'You would bring this monster into my home?'

Tullus's lips quivered. 'Please . . .' was all he managed, and that wasn't more than a whisper.

'The boy will be the end of me!' Nero looked around frantically around him, and then screamed like a child: 'Kill him! *Kill him!*'

The *heroidai* – all but one – marched forward in their coloured armour, spears, swords, clubs raised. Cadmus looked at Tullus's face and then at Nero's, the one ashen and the other murderous, and knew there was no point in appealing to either of them.

Accept your fate, said that stern, philosophical voice at the back of his head. *Accept your suffering with equanimity.*

And then another voice, the voice of a fourteen-year-old boy with pale skin and one shoe replied firmly: *Run like hell.*

He bolted to one side as the first sword stroke landed, sending chips of mosaic flying into the air. He leapt up on to the couches, over the heaps of flesh drunkenly snatching at him, and disappeared into the darkness of the garden.

Outside the sweaty fog of the dinner party, the night air was a cold thrill. Cadmus felt suddenly very awake, his eyes watering, his one bare foot pounding the damp earth in time with his heart. The garden was enormous, cluttered with the dim shapes of trees and statues and fountains. There were plenty of places to hide, but no way to escape.

Behind him he could hear the rest of the diners baying for blood. Amid the cacophony he could distinguish Nero's scream and Epaphroditus's clipped instructions. What was he doing? A good Stoic wasn't meant to run from death; neither was a slave.

Cadmus was halfway to the other side of the garden when the ground suddenly disappeared beneath him, and his leg, followed by the rest of him, plunged into one of the garden's artificial lakes. His world went cold and silent for a moment, and then he struggled to the surface, thrashing and choking and feeling like his tunic was pulling him to his death. Tullus had taught him a great many things; swimming was not one of them.

He squirmed and flailed until his feet touched the slimy bottom. When he waded to the bank on the far side, he found one of the *heroidai* waiting for him. The giant picked him up with one hand and threw him on to the grass.

Cadmus curled up, too terrified to cry. He waited for the feeling of freezing steel in his belly.

'Get *up!*' said the giant.

He opened his eyes. He stopped shivering.

'Cadmus, it's *me!*' Tog lifted her mask. 'Come on, we can get up on the roof!'

He got to his feet, and now there really were tears in his eyes, but tears of relief rather than fear. He shook the water out of his ears and ran with Tog to the corner of the portico. Behind them the other *heroidai* drifted through the dark garden, like phantoms in their coloured armour.

Tog got down on one knee and interlaced her fingers to give him a boost. 'You go first, then pull me up.'

Cadmus thought of Tullus, said a quick prayer, and stepped into Tog's waiting palms. She lifted him up and he gripped on to one of the roof tiles. It came loose in his hand, and he tumbled back down on top of her. He heard her swearing in her native language.

Second time around, the displaced tile had created a convenient hole in the roof that he could hang on to. He hauled himself on to his stomach, and then, still lying flat, dangled an arm for Tog to use. She didn't need it. With the *heroidai* a few paces behind, she ran, kicked off one of the columns and caught the edge of the roof with both hands. She swung herself up as a spear shattered the tiles next to her head.

'Where are we going?' said Cadmus. His lips and fingers were still numb from falling in the lake.

'I don't know,' said Tog. 'Just run. Think later.'

They hobbled unsteadily over the ridge of the roof, tiles loosening with every other step, showering terracotta on the pursuers below. At the top Cadmus paused briefly, overcome by the sight that greeted him: the whole palace, and beyond it, Rome, its streets and corners sketched out in firelight.

Something was strange about Tog's breathing. It was loud and irregular and ragged. It was a moment before Cadmus realized she wasn't panting. She was laughing.

'Hey, Cadmus, wait,' she said. She took off the mask and helmet and tossed them back into the garden. There was a satisfying *clang* as it struck one of the other guards. 'Look what I got.'

She put her fingers down inside the enamelled breastplate, and pulled out a corner of what she was wearing underneath. Her neck and face reflected a golden light.

The fleece. She'd stolen it.

Before Cadmus could reply, another pair of missiles rained down on them. Something snagged on the shoulder of his tunic and he cried out in pain. Both of them lost their footing, slid down the other side of the roof, and fell off the edge. Cadmus hit the ground and began rolling, out of control, over the rocks and the roots on the steepest side of the Palatine Hill.

XI

Tog pulled him out from under the legs of a mule, idling in the street at the foot of the hill. Annoyed at the disturbance, it flicked its ears and kicked him in the stomach as he was standing up. The festival-goers pointed and laughed.

'Are you all right?' said Tog, grasping him by his shoulders.

'Guh . . .' said Cadmus.

'Good enough for me.'

The mule continued to dance irritably on the cobbles.

'Hush,' Tog said, turning and patting it on its flank. She rummaged in a leather bag that was hanging from its back, found a flask of water and took a swig. She offered some to Cadmus, and while he drank she removed the leather pack in its entirety.

'Oi!' came a shout from mule's owner. 'What are you— That's mine!'

Tog snatched the bag and ran, Cadmus gasping in her wake. His shoulder stung, and from elbow to wrist his skin felt hot and sticky. They pushed through the crowds of revellers, through priests, musicians, dwarves, troupes of actors plying their trade on street corners, through alleyways that stank of meat and stale wine and fresh urine, until they collapsed outside the back of a two-storey shop where a couple of dogs were fighting over something that looked and sounded a lot like miscellaneous entrails.

'We're . . . in . . . the Subura,' said Cadmus, in between pained lungfuls of air. 'Bad . . . place to be.'

'It's fine. We're not staying,' said Tog.

'That's . . . damn right,' said Cadmus. He took a few more ragged breaths and prodded at the wound in his arm. It gaped like a fish. 'We can't even . . . stay in Rome now. Nero's going to find us and kill us. Very slowly. Very painfully.'

'That's all right,' said Tog. 'I didn't want to stay in Rome anyway. I'll just head for home. It's a bit earlier than expected, but no time like the present.'

'And what about *me*?'

She shrugged. 'You can go home too.'

'I can't just go back to Tullus's house, they'll find me!'

'Not that home, your *real* home. Wherever you came from.'

For a moment, a vista opened up before Cadmus's eyes. He imagined himself walking the streets of Athens at liberty, with his own house, his own library, his own little garden. Maybe a plot of land with some vines outside the city walls. And then, as usual, the dream was muddied with rational thoughts. How would he find any money? How would he convince anyone he wasn't a slave? How would he even survive the journey? His skin was so pale he couldn't leave the house at midday without getting sunburnt.

Next to him, Tog had started removing the bronze plate armour and piling it on the floor.

'What was all that about your shoe?' she said.

Cadmus came back from his reverie. 'What?'

'Your shoe. Why was the emperor so worried you only had one shoe?'

He looked at his bare, bruised foot. 'It's an omen.'

'Omen?'

'Something that predicts the future. In the myth of Jason, his uncle, King Pelias, was told to beware of a traveller wearing only one sandal. It was said that such a man would unseat him from the throne. When Jason turned up at his palace, one of his sandals was missing.

That's why Pelias sent him away to get the fleece – he thought the mission would kill him.'

'But what does that have to do with you?'

'My thoughts exactly. Nero must think the omen is still relevant. I imagine that soothsayer has been pouring poison in his ear. And his brain is addled enough as it is.'

Tog removed the intricately decorated breastplate. As the clasps came undone, she peeled the Golden Fleece away from her body. She threw it to Cadmus, who caught it in both hands. The fibres of the fleece were like nothing he had ever felt before. They were cool and supple and flowed like water over his fingers. Looking at its otherworldly sheen, he thought he could start believing all the things that Tullus had said.

'Maybe this *omen*,' Tog said, pronouncing the word slowly, 'is true. I mean, look. You are his enemy. You took his fleece.'

'*Me?* I wasn't the one who stole it!'

'No, but you're the reason I did.'

Cadmus looked at her in mute disbelief.

'The letter,' she said, casually tying her hair back. On the nape of her neck Cadmus saw the mouse, somehow safe and sound and untroubled by their escape from the palace.

'What about the letter?'

'The secret letter said Nero shouldn't have the

fleece, didn't it?'

'Yes.'

'That it would be a disaster?'

'Yes . . .'

'So I took it.'

'Right.'

'And you were the one who showed me the letter. So it is *sort of* your doing.'

Cadmus blinked.

'What?' said Tog. 'That was what you wanted, wasn't it?'

'Well . . . I suppose so.'

A strange, joyless laughter exploded from the building behind them.

'Someone's coming,' said Tog. 'Throw it here.'

Cadmus tossed her the fleece. It was stained red where his bloodied fingers had touched it. Tog quickly stuffed it into the leather bag she'd taken from the mule, just as a red-faced woman appeared on the doorstep.

'What are you two doing here?' she said in Greek.

'Come on,' said Cadmus, getting up. 'We should go.'

'*Hey!* You!' The woman wasn't giving up. 'Yes, *you*, with the collar! Where's your master? If he's one of our customers then you should be waiting round the front, not skulking back here.'

'No, he's not here,' said Cadmus.

'Then where is he? Who do you belong to?'

'No one,' said Tog, before Cadmus could reply, and strode off into the night.

The Subura was a cramped and dirty labyrinth. It was only April, but the air felt unbearably hot, and it was heavy with incense and sweat and cheap perfume. Cadmus took them in the direction he thought was north, trying to move as quickly as possible without seeming suspicious.

They fought their way up the Vicus Longus, against the tide heading towards the Forum and the Circus. Cadmus's shoulder throbbed, and his one bare foot was getting bruised and swollen.

The Quirinal Hill rose gently out of the mess of the Subura, and they came to the imposing brick and marble of the city walls. All of Rome's gates had been thrown open for the festivities of the Megalesia, and the watchmen had better things to worry about than two young slaves heading *out* of the city. Cadmus and Tog passed under the nearest of the arches and suddenly Rome, with all its dark corners and dangerous alleyways, was behind them. From the top of the hill they looked out on the plain of the Campus Martius and saw the silver seam of the Tiber meandering through it.

'What do you think we should do?' said Tog.

'You said run now, think later.'

'It is later,' she said. She wasn't even out of breath.

So Cadmus thought. The situation seemed hopeless. They would be outlaws, barred from Rome, without even a roof over their heads. And no one would care if two slaves died of exposure.

'We should cross the river. Get as far from the city as possible. Head west to the coast and find somewhere to hide out. Maybe Ostia.'

'What's that?'

'Next town along. Rome's main port.'

'Maybe I could get a boat to Britannia from there.'

Cadmus looked at her scarred, hopeful face. He didn't have the heart to disappoint her.

'Maybe,' he said.

They walked quickly down the hillside and crossed the Campus Martius to the river. Over a footbridge they left the road entirely and disappeared into the fields, soft and furrowed from the rain and the plough. On the edge of a copse of ash trees, Cadmus turned and looked back at Rome. The city was bright with lamps and torches, but it didn't look festive any more. From where they stood, it looked like Nero had set fire to his own city in a fit of rage.

XII

They lost themselves in the darkness of the woods. Once Rome was out of sight they stumbled into a hollow in the earth, surrounded by a nest of thick roots, and decided to rest. For a while they didn't speak. Underneath their panting, the trees and the earth continued to rustle with the sounds of animals going about their secret nocturnal lives.

'Do you have wolves here?' said Tog.

'Um . . . I don't know. Maybe?'

'What about bears?'

'I don't know that either.'

'How can you know so little about your own land?' she said, getting to her feet. 'I'm going to make a fire. If I don't come back, the wolves got me.'

Cadmus opened his mouth but she was already gone, tramping through the undergrowth. He said prayers to Jupiter and to Diana while she went about finding flint and firewood, and then watched in amazement as she conjured flames, like magic, out of nothingness. The sudden warmth on his cold face was a miracle. She went foraging for berries and mushrooms too, and brought them back a rabbit, which she promptly gutted in front of him.

'I don't understand,' said Cadmus, his stomach turning as she emptied the intestines on to the forest floor. 'You seem to have a rather ambivalent attitude to fauna.'

'A what attitude to what?'

'I mean – you want to take care of them, but you also seem quite happy to kill them.'

'I'm not *happy* to kill them,' she said, frowning in the firelight. 'Out here, I have to kill them, if I'm hungry. And I accept that *they* might have to kill *me*, if they're hungry. It's about mutual respect. I've seen the way Greeks and Romans treat their animals. They could learn a few things about respect.'

She spitted the body of the rabbit and balanced it on two pairs of sticks over the fire. Soon the skin was charred and sizzling. She tore off a haunch and handed it to Cadmus with thumb and forefinger.

He lifted the rabbit to his mouth and winced as the wound in his arm opened again. Tog saw and immediately stood up.

'Oh, your arm,' she said. 'Wait.' She disappeared into the trees again.

When she returned she was holding something delicate in between her fingers. It looked like several fine silk threads, glittering in the firelight; though how she had found them in middle of the forest he had no idea.

'Turn that way.' She pointed. He did as he was told, showing her his shoulder. She laid what she was carrying over the gash where the spear had caught him. It felt cold, and tickled where it met the flesh.

'What is it?' he asked.

'Spiders' webs,' she said. 'They'll stop the bleeding. And when they—'

She made a motion with her fingers.

'Shrink?'

'Yes. They'll get smaller and close the wound. Don't touch it.'

He looked down at the network of tiny fibres, then up at her, and said: 'Thank you.'

She just nodded, and tore into her own portion of rabbit, fat spurting from around her teeth.

'Who taught you how to do all of this?' he asked after a moment.

She swallowed her mouthful. 'My aunt. Everyone in my tribe learns how to make the most of the land around them. You Romans—'

'*Stop* saying that, Tog. I'm not a Roman.'

'Sorry. *Those* Romans just want to stay in their big houses all the time. Getting other people to feed them, to clean them. Why would you want that? You don't feel proud. There's no . . . what's the word?'

'Dignity?'

'That's it. There's no *dignity* in shutting yourself off from the world.'

'Most Romans would say there's no dignity in hunting for your dinner. In a society without baths. They think you're all barbarians. Monsters.'

'We think the same about them. Can't both be right.'

'No, but you could both be wrong.'

She snorted.

'The Romans think they're so civilized, but they know nothing about the world. At home, in Britannia, you get taught how to take care of yourself. You learn about plants and animals, which ones will help you and which ones will harm you. I was taken hunting when I was eight years old. I could ride a horse before I could walk. That's what my aunt said.'

Cadmus felt that creeping shame returning, about how sheltered his life had been. He was glad he had

Tog with him – he wouldn't last a day on his own under the open sky. What good were all the books he'd read, all the teachings of the Stoics, when it came to keeping himself alive?

Tog manoeuvred a bone out of her mouth and spat it into the fire. 'You haven't told me anything about your family.'

'You didn't think to ask,' Cadmus said, deliberately repeating her words from the day before.

She looked at him over the flames and made a noise that was halfway between a sniff and a laugh. 'Well, I'm asking now.'

Cadmus sifted through the tatty fragments of his memory and found them blank.

'I'm sorry to disappoint, but I don't have any family,' he said. 'Apart from Tullus.'

'But before him?'

'There wasn't anyone before him. He found me, when I was a baby.'

'*Found* you?'

'Abandoned. On a road outside Athens. It happens more than you think. One too many mouths to feed. I don't blame them, really.'

'You should,' said Tog gruffly.

'Why? Look at the size of me. My skin. My eye.'

'I've seen your eye. It means you're lucky.'

'Ha! That's a laugh. I don't think my parents ever

saw it that way. They must have taken one look at me and seen I'd never grow up to work their fields, or join the army, or to defend their property in their old age. It's fair enough.' He poked at the fire with a stick. 'Tullus found me and took me back to Rome. He gave me another slave as my nurse. And I grew up into the fine physical specimen you see today.'

'But you are not a Roman,' said Tog, more a statement than a question.

'No,' Cadmus said without hesitation. 'It's hard to explain. It's just a feeling. I know it might not look like it, but I feel just as out of place in Rome as you do. There's something in my bones that knows I don't belong here.'

'And you don't remember anything about your parents? What they looked like? What they were called?'

'Nothing.'

Tog picked her mouse up off the ground and cradled it in front of the embers. She whispered something to it and then sat up straight, deep in thought, taking slow and measured breaths. Framed by the absolute darkness of the woods, her face seemed to glow like a hot, heart-shaped coal. And that was when Cadmus thought, clearly, for the first time: *she is beautiful.*

'That's probably a good thing,' Tog said at last.

'What do you mean?' said Cadmus, suddenly embarrassed, as though she had read his thoughts.

'I can picture my mother and father perfectly. They come back to me every night.' She paused. 'And every morning.'

Cadmus realized what she meant. 'Is that what you were dreaming about the other day? In Tullus's house?'

She nodded. 'It makes me want to not go to sleep.'

They were both silent, lost in their own and each other's thoughts.

'Well, tonight,' said Cadmus, 'I'll stay up to watch over the camp. If you start having nightmares, I'll wake you up.'

'That's kind, but I think I should be the one who stays awake. You're more tired than me. I can see it. You sleep first, and I'll take first watch. Then I'll wake you and you can take over. Deal?'

He looked at her for a moment.

'Very well,' he said. 'But don't be the hero and stay awake all night. You need rest too, even if you think you don't.'

Cadmus curled up facing the fire, but it was down to embers now, and the dark and the cold was starting to seep around him like spilt ink. He tossed and turned and shivered until Tog finally interjected:

'Use your blanket.'

Cadmus opened his eyes. She hadn't moved from

her spot opposite.

'What?'

'If you're cold, get under your blanket.'

'I don't have a blanket.'

'Under your head, genius.'

Cadmus sat up. He'd been using the leather bag as a pillow. She was talking about the Golden Fleece.

'I can't use that as a blanket!' he said.

'Why not?' said Tog. 'If it's as magical as you say it is, I'm sure it'll stop the cold.'

'I didn't say it *was* magical. That's just the story.'

'And you don't believe the story?'

Cadmus withdrew the fleece from his bag and unrolled it. It glittered beautifully in the dying fire.

'I don't know what I believe any more.'

He pulled it up over his body, fleecy side down, and the thick, golden wool warmed quickly against his skin. There was a pleasing heaviness about it that made him feel safe and instantly ready to sleep.

'It's good,' he murmured.

'Told you,' said Tog.

Warm and with a full belly, Cadmus felt unexpectedly hopeful. He closed his eyes and listened to the wind in the tops of the pines. From somewhere deeper in the forest an owl hooted – a baleful sound, if the poets were to be believed – but from where he lay it sounded more like a lullaby than a bad omen.

XIII

When Cadmus woke, his tunic was wet and heavy with dew, and his body was as cold as the ground he was lying on. The sky among the leaves was a weak, leaden grey. Early morning. For a few moments his head was blissfully empty, before he remembered the events of the previous night; before he remembered that he was a dead man walking.

He rolled over to where Tog was lying. She had taken the fleece and wrapped it around herself. She must have dropped off before waking him. Her mouse was running circuits around her, experimentally sniffing at the fallen leaves but reluctant to stray too far from the warmth and shelter of her body. She was muttering in her sleep again.

'Tog,' he said quietly, tentatively, remembering how violently she had woken last time.

A noise escaped her lips.

'Tog, we should keep moving.'

A groan, and her eyelids fluttered.

'Tog . . .'

This time she didn't swing her arms at Cadmus but flipped herself on to her stomach and began clawing the ground. Her legs thrashed as well, and for a few moments she arched and twisted like some giant fish tossed on to a riverbank, hissing through her teeth. The fleece was thrown to the floor. Her mouse watched her curiously.

'Tog, wake up!' said Cadmus. 'You're safe.' And then, more quietly: 'Sort of.'

He put a hand on the top of her silver head. She turned and looked at him wildly, then at the trees, and realized where she was. Despite the cold, she was sweating.

Her great shoulders rose and fell as she calmed herself with several deep breaths. 'Sorry,' she said, after a moment.

'It's all right,' said Cadmus. 'I'm sorry I woke you.'

'I'm glad you did.' She picked at something on the back of her hand. She seemed embarrassed.

'We should get going,' he said. 'It won't be difficult

for Nero to track us, if he wants to.'

Tog nodded. She brushed the soil and leaves and insects out of the folds in the Golden Fleece and pushed it into her bag. Then she carefully picked up her mouse from the floor and let him run up on to her shoulder.

'Ready,' she said.

They emerged from the woodland on to some gently sloping hills, Tog leading the way. There were slaves working in the fields, driving cattle under the yoke of a plough and churning the earth for sowing. Next to the farmhouse someone was saddling a horse. They kept to the edge of the trees so as not to be seen.

Once the estate was behind them, they stopped by a stream. Tog knelt and cupped her hands for a drink of water. Cadmus did the same. It tasted as sweet as meadow flowers.

'Remind me what our plan is?' said Tog, wiping her mouth with the back of her hand.

'Escape the people trying to kill us,' he said.

'Good.'

'Then get to the port at Ostia. South-west.' He pointed.

'That's north-east,' said Tog.

'Is it? Oh. Well.' He turned in the opposite direction. 'That way. To the sea.'

'And then?'

'And then when we get to Ostia, I suppose we could try and meet up with Tullus again. He'll be getting a boat from there if he's going to Greece. All we have to do is wait for him to turn up.'

'Eh? That doesn't make sense,' she said. 'He'll be with the emperor's people. They're the ones who're trying to kill us.'

'Yes,' Cadmus admitted, 'but Tullus is the only person who might be able to *stop* them trying to kill us. Or at least he could give us some money to get by. It's find Tullus, or go it alone.'

'Then we go it alone.'

She hopped to the other side of the stream. Cadmus stayed where he was.

'Don't be stupid, Tog,' he said. One of her eyes twitched with annoyance. 'Where would we go? We have no money, no food, no clothes.'

'I can look after myself, thank you,' she said defiantly.

'I see. And where are you planning on going?'

'Back to Britannia.'

'How, may I ask?'

'I'll get a boat.'

'There aren't any boats that go all the way to Britannia from Italy,' he said. 'You'll need to go to Sardinia, or Corsica, then Transalpine Gaul, then

Jupiter knows where.'

'Fine. I'll work it out. I'm in no rush.'

'And how far do you think you'll get with that collar on?'

'I'll take it off.'

'How? With all those blacksmith's tools you carry around with you?'

She frowned. Her huge brow gathered like a storm, and it was terrifying.

'Are you making fun of me?'

'No,' said Cadmus, hearing how weak his voice sounded, almost drowned by the noise of the stream. 'I'm just trying to be sensible.'

'You're not. You're being the opposite. Going back to the old man will take us exactly where we don't want to go.'

'We don't have a *choice*. We're slaves, Tog, in case you hadn't noticed. No one else will look after us.'

'You're also being selfish,' she said, ignoring him. 'You want to go on adventures. You want to find these heroes. I heard what your master said at the dinner party.'

Cadmus shook his head, but his silence just seemed to confirm his guilt. He really *did* think that Tullus would be able to help them, and, perhaps even more importantly, he wanted to help Tullus.

But Tog was right. Against Cadmus's better judgement, thoughts of Silvanus's notes kept coming back to him. He could picture the map perfectly. He'd never seen a real-life Sibyl. What secrets did she hold? If the Golden Fleece was real, what else was out there, buried by the centuries?

'It's fine if you want to go after those old things,' Tog said, in a tone so reasonable it made Cadmus feel slightly ashamed of himself. 'But I don't need to go with you. Tullus is your master, not mine. Athens is your home, not mine. You're the one who cares about Silveranus—'

'Silvanus.'

'—not me. I've delivered your letter. I've got the fleece for you. Now I may as well go.'

The heat of Cadmus's frustration was met with a cold, creeping worry. She really didn't need to stay with him, he realized. She was free in that respect. He couldn't make her stay, and if she left, he would be alone again.

'Let's just get to Ostia,' he said. 'Then we can decide.'

She shrugged. '*You* can decide. I've already made up my mind.'

They walked on in silence. At least, Tog walked. Cadmus half-walked, half-ran, always a few paces behind her, struggling to keep up with her huge strides. To make matters worse he seemed to land on a stone or a thorn every three steps. Tog waited for him to catch up. She wasn't impatient, but neither was she sympathetic. She was just Tog.

It was midday when they began to smell salt on the air, and the ridges of the hills were replaced with a deep blue haze where the sky met the sea. They came upon the Tiber again, winding lazily towards the coast, and joined the Via Ostiensis, straight as a legionary's spear and heavy with traffic from the port to the capital.

They kept to one side of the road and tried to look inconspicuous, as far as that was possible with Tog. When they finally saw the walls of Ostia, and the cluster of ships' masts around the mouth of the Tiber, Cadmus's hopes were fading. No one left port this late in the afternoon. Unless the whole project had been delayed by the commotion in the palace, Tullus was long gone.

Ostia was the most important harbour in Italy. The city itself was much smaller than Rome, but busier. More dangerous too. The place seemed populated exclusively with thieves and stowaways. Here, everyone held on to their purses with white knuckles, and walked more quickly than they needed to. Cadmus saw faces from all over the empire – Romans, Greeks, Gauls, Syrians, Egyptians, Ethiopians – each watching the others from the corners of their eyes. In the middle of all these different peoples no one even looked at Tog twice – that was a small blessing.

They followed the sound of the gulls and the smell of fish going bad until they reached the harbour. They emerged from among the warehouses and suddenly the mouth of the Tiber was glittering before them. Four vast merchant ships were moored in the river, with a flotilla of smaller rowing boats bobbing around them.

Cadmus looked along the quayside. Sailors and dockhands trooped up and down the gangplanks like ants, carrying bags of grain, jars of wine and oil and fish sauce, rolls of linen, spices, dyes, mountainous iron strongboxes that no doubt contained enough valuables to buy a hundred of him. Some of the sailors lounged in heaps next to their cargo, drinking and playing dice.

Cadmus froze. At the far end, he saw the slim, unmistakable figure of Epaphroditus. His toga hung slackly around him, like it was draped over a ship's mast. There were two of the *heroidai* standing with him, and a handful of slaves. The whole group turned, and Nero's secretary began to wander away from the seafront. No doubt he was returning to his master.

Tog had her eyes closed and was taking deep breaths of sea air. Cadmus grabbed her arm and hid behind a pile of grain sacks.

'They're here,' he said.

'Who?'

'Nero's people.'

'Then where's Tullus?'

Cadmus popped up from behind their hiding place. Epaphroditus was getting closer.

'I can't see him,' he said, squatting down again. 'I can't see his ship either. These are all trading vessels. Nero wouldn't use them for official business. And he definitely wouldn't use them for secret business.'

'What would he use?'

'Something smaller. Faster.'

'Like that one?'

Tog pointed out over the estuary to the open sea, where a warship had just raised its sail and was carving a swift path through the waves.

Cadmus's shoulders sagged. 'Yes. Just like that one.'

They were too late. Tullus had already left, and now they were trapped within the walls of Ostia with the men who wanted to kill them. Just as Tog had said.

He peeked around the corner of the grain sacks, too afraid to stand up. Epaphroditus and the two enormous guards were still heading their way. If they made a run for the warehouses, they would almost certainly be seen.

Tog herself didn't seem especially worried. 'Oh, well,' she said. 'Looks like you're coming to Britannia with me, after all.'

'Tog, I've told you, it's not as *simple* as that.'

'But one of these ships will take me in the right direction, won't it?'

Cadmus listened to the sailors and the merchants yelling to each other in Latin, and a plan started to form. He looked at Tog's open, guileless face and knew he was about to do something he would regret. He could feel himself pulled towards it, with all the irresistible power of Fate.

'That one,' he said, gesturing in the direction of the boat nearest to them. Its owner was standing at the bottom of the gangplank, arms folded on his vast stomach, nodding with satisfaction as his wares were loaded into the hold. Business seemed to be going well. It looked like he ate five or six meals a day.

'Really?'

'The captain said they're taking the goods north. To Gaul. That's half the journey done.' The words seemed to form a millstone that hung around his neck.

'Good,' said Tog. 'And you're coming with me?'

'Nowhere else to go,' said Cadmus, and smiled weakly. He leant out and looked down the quayside again. Epaphroditus's party were a few paces away.

'So what do we do?'

'They're nearly here. Grab a bag of grain. Put it on

your left shoulder. Then they won't be able to see your face.'

She lifted one of the sacks like it was full of goose feathers and held it in place with one arm. Cadmus tried to do the same, but found he had to carry the weight on his back, like a snail, his spine bowed and knees shaking.

They came out into the open and walked to the edge of the quay. Cadmus strained under his burden. His ears were filled with the sound of his own blood, but Epaphroditus's high voice cut through it like broken glass. He must have been just behind them. What if he recognized them?

Cadmus staggered past the merchant and up on to the gangplank, which groaned and twisted under their feet. He couldn't see the merchant, or the other dockworkers. He just caught glimpses of Tog's heels a few paces in front of him.

He listened hard through his deafening pulse. No one seemed to have noticed them.

Once they were on board, they made their way down some steps into the ship's cavernous hold. Cadmus dumped his sack of grain along with the others, but still felt weighed down. He squinted in the darkness and saw Tog returning to the deck.

'What are you doing?' he hissed.

'Going to get another bag.'

'Why?' said Cadmus, wanting to laugh. 'You know we're not actually employed by this man . . . ?'

'Just thought I'd help out. If he's going to be taking me home.'

Cadmus swallowed guiltily.

'We should find somewhere to hide now, while no one else is around. We might not get another chance.'

Tog looked into the daylight, then into the shadows of the hold, then back to the daylight.

'Fine,' she said.

They barricaded themselves into the bows of the ship with boxes of olives and jars of wine. There they waited, like trapped rats, listening to the irregular tattoo of the waves, and the thump of the sailors' feet overhead. There was the rattle of the anchor being raised and the creak of rigging, and then Cadmus felt the ship bob out into the open sea, tugged by a fleet of rowing boats.

He looked at Tog.

'We're away,' he said.

She didn't reply. She crouched in the corner, hugging her knees. Her hair looked luminous, like the fleece itself. Words that Cadmus didn't understand drifted quietly from her lips.

How was he going to explain himself? After all this, Tog was going right back where she'd come from. She'd been right. He was selfish. He'd heard what the merchant had said to the ship's captain, and had lied to her, lied openly, after all she had done to help him. It was Cadmus who was going home, not Tog. The ship was destined for Athens.

XIV

The weather held for the first five days. They survived in the gloom, eating olives and grains and drinking nothing but wine, which left them light-headed and somehow thirstier than if they hadn't drunk anything at all. They called into two more ports along the way. When night fell and everyone had gone ashore, they would both creep up to the deck to eat and drink from the crew's supplies.

While they sailed, Tog was even more taciturn than usual. Cadmus could see her grinding her teeth from the way her cheeks twitched. Her mouse still scurried along her shoulders, and up and down her arms, but she'd stopped speaking even to him. Cadmus did his best to look after her, wrapping her in the Golden

Fleece and exploring the treasure trove of the ship's hold for food and drink and clean clothes.

It looked like this particular merchant bought and sold anything he could get his hands on. A particularly good find, tucked into the stern of the ship, was several boxes of woven goods, including tunics and togas of impressive quality. While Tog had the fleece, he stole a gleaming white *toga virilis* to use as a blanket, and finally got himself a new pair of sandals.

On the sixth day the heavens opened. For what seemed like an eternity the ship was battered by high winds and higher waves, pitching and yawing, the skies roaring down at them and the sailors roaring back. What little food they ate that day they couldn't keep down. The smell in their little corner of the ship became intolerable. They clung to each other in the dark and where his cheek met hers, Cadmus could feel the warm ridges of her scars.

The last three days were clear, and then the ship stopped for longer than usual. Cadmus could hear crowds outside but thought he might have just been delirious from hunger and thirst. Finally the sailors came tramping down into the hold and began unpacking the merchant's goods.

'Cor, *stinks* down here!' shouted one.

'What *is* that? We're not carrying livestock, are we?' said another, spitting.

The rest swore and cursed in their colourful Roman dialect.

Escaping the ship was not going to be easy. He watched the sailors working in groups of three or four, got a feel for the rhythms of their comings and goings, but there was never a big enough window for them to slip off the ship unseen.

He clutched at the edge of his stolen toga anxiously. What had been the pristine attire of a Roman citizen was now damp and faintly brown, bunched between his knuckles. Then it struck him: maybe he was thinking about this all wrong. Maybe he didn't need to escape unseen. In fact – and he was fully aware that this might have been his delirium speaking – he *wanted* to be seen.

'We need to leave the ship,' he whispered to Tog, 'or they're going to find us.'

She nodded. 'We take a bag of grain each again?'

Cadmus sucked his lip nervously. 'No,' he said. 'I've got a better idea.'

He handed the bag with the fleece inside to Tog. Then, before he'd really thought the plan through, he stepped out from behind the amphorae, wrapped in the dirty toga, in full view of the sailors. If talking was all he could do, he thought, then he would talk their way out of this.

'Who the—'

One of them tapped his shipmate on the shoulder, and they both stared at the stowaway. Cadmus pulled himself up to his full height, five and a bit feet of skin and bones, and walked as steadily as he could towards them.

'I need to see the pro-praetor,' he said, in the best Latin he could muster. His voice hoarse and phlegmy.

The sailors turned to each other.

'What's he talking about? Who the hell is he? And who's the girl?'

Cadmus could feel Tog's anxiety radiating from behind him. She wouldn't understand anything he was saying. He took a deep breath and half-closed his left eye, in case its strange appearance undermined his character.

'Listen to me, plebs. I am Quintus Domitius Tullus, son of Gaius, senator and – ' yes, why not, they wouldn't know any better – '*consul of Rome*, and I *demand* to see the governor.'

'What are you doing here? Where's your own ship, if you're so high and mighty?'

'I don't think you're listening to me.' Cadmus stepped forward. His nose came up to the man's chest. 'My father is *very* important.'

'But—'

'What's going on down there, sluggards?' The merchant appeared above them and hefted himself down into the hold one step at a time. 'I'm not paying you to— Who is this?'

Cadmus repeated himself. Gods, he was tired. Every word felt like it was being dredged up from the seabed.

'I am Quintus Domitius Tullus, *citizen*.' He shook a fistful of his toga as if to prove it. 'I was taken prisoner by pirates in Sicily – I only escaped their clutches thanks to my faithful slave here. We jumped overboard and joined your ship at Segesta.'

The merchant looked at the sailors. All three were baffled.

'I don't understand—'

'I don't *care* if you understand or not. Are you going to help me, or aren't you?'

'How did you get aboard without us knowing?'

'Listen. My father is a consul and could very easily revoke your licence to use these trade routes, my good man.' Cadmus thought of all the obnoxious aristocratic teenagers he'd overheard when he was in Rome, tried to remember their turns of phrase. 'On the other hand, I'm sure he would also reward anyone who aided in my rescue.'

The merchant's tiny eyes sparkled in the darkness. 'Reward?'

'Very handsomely, no doubt. Now let me off this stinking boat of yours, so I can see the pro-praetor and send a message to Rome.'

For a moment, the merchant was frozen; then he gave a sudden, bulging nod, and extended an arm to show 'Quintus' and Tog the way out of the hold.

When Cadmus reached the top of the steps, his feet and heart stopped on the same beat. Beyond the warehouses of the harbour he saw it, distant but unmistakeable: the vast painted columns of the Parthenon, overlooking the city from the top of the Acropolis. He was looking at Athens.

'Is something wrong?' asked the merchant.

Cadmus blinked. 'Only the delay,' he said. 'I trust you can find me adequate transportation from Piraeus to Athens?'

'Of course, I—'

'Good. A litter?'

The merchant winced. 'I can't be sure if—'

'I would also appreciate a loan of a few denarii. I can hardly be expected to meet the praetor looking like this, can I?' He gestured to his dirty toga.

'No. Of course.' The man eyed him for a moment, and Cadmus's skin briefly prickled. Maybe he'd gone too far. Maybe the merchant had seen through him. His Roman accent was pretty good, but it wasn't perfect. And the story he'd concocted – well, it didn't make any sense. Everything was riding on his bravado.

'Ten should do it.'

Without reply, the merchant handed him a pouch of coins from his belt.

'Blessings upon you,' said Cadmus. 'My father will repay this many thousands of times over.'

'But how will you find me? You don't even—'

'Do not worry yourself,' said Cadmus. 'A man of your impressive stature is very difficult to miss.'

The man looked down at his paunch, unsure whether he was being paid a compliment or not. Cadmus shook his hand and marched off down the gangplank as quickly as he could, his toga billowing impressively. Tog was so quiet he'd almost forgotten she was there.

XV

They made their way along the waterfront, which was crowded with sailors and slaves and seagulls picking at the remains of the day's catch. The air was humid and briny, the buildings salt-caked, as though it were low tide and the harbour had just emerged from the water. As soon as they were out of sight of the fat merchant they stopped at a fountain where a group of mule drivers were lazing on their wagons, waiting to take passengers into Athens.

Cadmus turned to Tog and grinned. She was not smiling. The exhilaration of his performance on the boat evaporated all at once.

'This isn't Gaul,' she said. 'It's Athens.'

'Well, it's Piraeus, actually. The port of Athens.'

He shrank under the look she gave him.

'No, you're right, it's not Gaul,' he said. 'I suppose the captain must have changed his mind.'

'You knew all along, didn't you? It was never going to Britannia.'

'I thought it was.'

'You think I'm stupid.'

'That's not true.'

'You think you can use your words to fool me,' she said. 'But I *see* you. I can see you're lying.'

Cadmus's shame returned in a hot flush. He was silent for a moment.

'You never would have made it to Britannia,' he said at last. 'It's much safer if we stick together.'

'For you, maybe. I'm right back where I started. Do you realize how lucky I was to escape from here in the first place?'

'I know,' he said, and hung his head. 'I'm sorry.'

He suddenly noticed that the mule drivers were all watching him. Some were laughing. He had forgotten he was meant to be a Roman citizen, and here he was, in his toga, being chastized by his own slave. He looked around nervously, feeling a fraud in more ways than one.

'Sorry won't get me home, Cadmus.' There was no anger in her voice. It was as deep as steady as ever. If anything that made her seem even more pitiable, and made Cadmus feel even worse. The heat of guilt spread slowly across his chest.

'Tullus can help both of us. I promise. I know this seems counter-intuitive—'

Tog's nostril twitched, a tic he had noticed whenever he used words she didn't understand.

'I know this seems like the wrong thing to do,' he corrected himself. 'But trust me. Maybe my master has friends here who can look after us. Or he can lend us some money. Or he'll know someone heading north. Or something.'

Tog looked unconvinced. He cleared his throat and tried to feign a confident tone.

'First thing's first, though,' he said. 'We need to get into the city.'

Cadmus felt small and a little stupid now in his huge, dirty toga. The mule drivers were still chuckling and elbowing each other in the ribs. He summoned the character of Quintus Domitius Tullus again, walked straight over to them, plucked a denarius out of the purse he had been given, and held it in his palm. There were several pairs of raised eyebrows. It was more than a day's wage. That shut them up.

'I need passage for two to Athens,' he said. 'And I want some information.'

There was a general clamour. One of the drivers

leapt down from his carriage before the others. He was a stocky man, not much taller than Cadmus, whose whole body was carpeted in a wiry black hair. Cadmus closed his fingers.

'What kind of information?' the man said.

'About some people who landed here. Important people. In the last few days.'

'I see everyone that comes through here. I reckon I can help.'

Cadmus handed him the silver denarius. 'We'll talk on the way,' he said. 'And if you can tell me what I need to know I'll double it.'

The man whistled to himself, and then got up into his wagon. Cadmus sat next to him, while Tog climbed into the back. The wood of the seat was baking hot. The driver made a clicking noise and the mule woke from its snooze, flapping its ears. Then he plied the reins and they made their way out of the harbour.

They only had a few miles to travel once they were on the open road. Cadmus watched the city grow ahead of him, his heart swelling. It was exactly as he'd imagined it.

Athens had a radiance all of its own. Here, the air felt cleaner, the light clearer. Rome was a grubby imitation, draped haphazardly over seven hills and slumped into the valleys between. Athens, on the other hand, congregated around just one hill, which put all of Rome's to shame: the Acropolis, an imposing, precipitous crag topped with the enormous Parthenon, the temple of Athena Nike, and the great statue of Athena Promachos, standing sentinel over her people with her spear in hand.

The feeling of homecoming was bittersweet, though. The more joy he felt, the more shame he felt for depriving Tog of that very same feeling. He tried to reassure himself, loudly, in his head, that he had made the right decision; that Tog wouldn't have been able to get to Britannia on her own; that Tullus would be able to help Tog get to her destination. But Tog didn't need anyone's help. Cadmus needed hers.

'Who are these important people, then?' said the driver when they were halfway there. 'Romans, like you?'

Cadmus suppressed a smile. If he'd known it was this easy to disguise himself as a freeborn citizen he would have done it years ago.

'A warship should have arrived in Piraeus a few days ago,' he said. 'It was carrying an elderly Roman senator, and several guards. Probably slaves as well. The guards you couldn't have missed. Very tall. Coloured, enamelled armour.'

The driver was already nodding. 'I seen 'em. Masks? All painted, like?'

'That's right.'

'Thought they were heading for the theatre, to be honest with you. There was a priest with 'em too. Cripple.'

Cadmus swallowed hard. The soothsayer, Polydamas. He didn't relish the prospect of running into him again. Worse than that: knowing that the ancient creature was lurking somewhere in Athens made it feel like he was already being watched.

'They went to the governor's residence,' the driver said. He chuckled. 'I'll tell you something for free, young man: you ain't getting in there looking like that. Or smelling like that either.'

By rights, Quintus Domitius Tullus should have slapped the man for his insolence, but Cadmus was too lost in his thoughts. And, by the gods, it was *tiring* being so arrogant all the time. He didn't know how most aristocratic Romans managed it.

When they pulled up outside the Piraean Gate, Cadmus paid the driver and left him tending to his mule beside one of the huge stone water troughs. Tog disembarked behind him and the cart sprang up into the air. She stood in the hot sun, watching the crowds like a cornered but defiant animal.

'They're here,' said Cadmus. 'And their priest is with them.'

'Hm.'

'They're staying at the pro-praetor's residence. That's going to be almost as difficult to get into as Nero's palace.'

'I see,' she said, and continued her slow survey of the city, as though she was looking for something or someone specific. She obviously hadn't forgiven Cadmus, and the feeling was like a fist clenched around his heart.

'I mean,' he said, trying to sound upbeat, 'I can fool a mule driver, but it'll take more than an old toga to fit in among the friends of a Roman magistrate.'

Nothing from Tog this time.

'I say we go to the baths first. If I clean myself up a bit I might stand a better chance of mingling with the governor's friends. They'll sell food and drink there too.'

She shrugged, which Cadmus took to mean agreement.

They took a series of cool alleyways that led to the Agora, in the centre of the city. They passed rows of artisans, their chisels clinking on marble, boys carrying boxes of scrolls, old, bearded men talking in earnest tones that reminded Cadmus of his master. Only the occasional pair of Roman legionaries reminded him that the city was not entirely free.

By the time they reached the baths, in the south-west corner of the Agora, the silence between them was leaden.

'We won't be able to go in together,' Cadmus said at last. 'Men and women have different baths, and one of us will need to look after the fleece.' He paused and pointed at her collar. 'And I'm not sure how they'll feel about that.'

'So?'

'Well.' He lowered his voice. 'It would probably make sense if I go first and see if anyone is going to cause a fuss. You can pretend to be my slave and watch over my clothes.'

'You want me to be *your* slave?'

'Just pretend!' he said quickly. This was the last thing he wanted, given how guilty he already felt. 'Then you can go in after me.'

Tog thought for a moment, and Cadmus saw a few expressions drift across her face like ripples on a pond.

'I can do that,' she said, with a curious stiffness.

He nodded and tried to smile.

Cadmus went up the steps and through the pillared facade of the bathhouse. He left Tog in the changing room with their possessions. The old men muttered their disapproval, the young men whistled sarcastically. He apologized again for abandoning her, but she seemed not to mind any of it.

The baths were a vast complex of chambers, the vapours so thick they concealed Cadmus's hand in front of his face. It felt like he was navigating the Underworld. Occasionally a figure would emerge from the clouds of steam, or a lonely shout would reverberate among the pillars. Sometimes he would catch a fleeting glimpse of one of the baths' brightly coloured mosaics and frescoes, only for it to disappear again in the mist.

He spent a few moments in the warmth of the *tepidarium* then moved on to the hotter pool of the *caldarium*. The water had the greyish tinge of thin soup. He sat here, thinking and thinking until he could feel his blood boiling between his ears.

When he was about to leave for the cold pool, he heard someone climbing clumsily into the far end of the bath. Then he heard a familiar sigh.

Cadmus felt his way around the edge until he saw an old man's head, pink and glistening in the vapours.

'Master?' he whispered.

There was a tiny squawk of surprise. It was Tullus. His master turned and looked at him, eyes bulging.

'Cadmus? What in *Jupiter's name* are you doing here?'

Cadmus grinned. 'I came to find you, Master.'

His master didn't return the smile.

'I told you to stay in Rome, boy. I expressly *forbade* you to come here. It is too dangerous. Especially since your stupidity in the palace.'

It was bad enough that Tog was angry at him. This didn't make Cadmus feel any better about himself.

'That wasn't my fault!' he protested. 'She was the one who stole the fleece! And if you'd bought me better quality sandals, Nero would never have said a thing.'

He knew he'd overstepped the mark. Tullus's jaw twitched, but he didn't rise to the provocation.

'Is she here too?'

'She's outside.'

'Does she have the fleece?'

Cadmus nodded.

'You must give it to me. And then you must go home, and keep out of sight.'

'Why?'

'Please, Cadmus, hand it back. Nero isn't easily appeased, but we may as well try.'

'But—'

'*Cadmus.* I will beg if I must.'

He looked into his master's sad, grey eyes. They were the same colour as the bathwater.

'It's in the changing room. She's looking after it.'

'Good. I shall take it from her when we leave. And then you must embark on the first boat back to Rome. No, Antium. Go to my country house, it'll be safer than the capital. I'll give you any money you need. For the gods' sake, just keep yourself out of trouble. Heaven knows I have enough blood on my hands as it is.'

That caught Cadmus by surprise. 'Blood, Master? Whose blood?'

His master looked at him, pained, like he was swallowing something very sharp, very slowly. He looked down into bathwater miserably, condensation dripping from the end of his long nose.

Suddenly there was an almighty splash from the opposite side, which sent a tide of warm scum floating towards them both. An enormously fat man had thrown himself into the bath, and a pair of slaves proceeded to scrub his back and shoulders with pumice stones.

Cadmus's blood ran strangely cold in the hot water. He recognized the newcomer at once. It was the merchant from the ship.

'We should go somewhere more private, I think,' Tullus said quietly.

Cadmus nodded wordlessly and glanced at the merchant. The huge man was reclining with his eyes closed, the bathwater lapping at him like some vast, flabby island. His slaves looked faintly sick.

Just as they were about to leave, Tullus stubbed his toe on something at the bottom of the bath and cried out in pain. The merchant's tiny eyes snapped open. He looked at Cadmus, then at Tullus, then at Cadmus again. His face already showed that he knew something was amiss.

'You?'

Cadmus tried to summon the character of Quintus Domitius Tullus, but the cocky young Roman had abandoned him.

'Hello, my, er, good man.' No, not convincing at all. 'A pleasant surprise.'

Tullus screwed up his face. 'Don't be insolent, Cadmus! Why are you talking like that?'

'Cadmus?' said the merchant.

'A nickname my father gives me,' said Cadmus, laughing uneasily.

'This is your father?'

'Er. Yes?'

'No!' said Tullus.

Cadmus looked at him with desperate, pleading eyes, but it was too late. The charade was over.

'Of course you're not his father,' said the merchant. A smile spread over his face, and Cadmus could sense him going in for the kill. 'His father is a consul of Rome. Isn't that right?'

'Er.'

'Can someone *please* explain to me what's going on . . .'

'This reprobate conned me out of ten denarii. No doubt he is planning to do the same to you.'

'This is *my* slave,' said Tullus, his eyes going wide at the man's forwardness. 'He is as honest as they come!'

'He is a thief!'

'How dare you? Where are your witnesses?'

'I own half of this city. I don't need witnesses.'

A third shadow fell over the water.

'I can be your witness,' said a familiar, unctuous voice. 'The boy is most definitely a thief. I saw him steal from the emperor himself.'

Epaphroditus stood above them, flanked by two of his own slaves. The secretary must have come on a separate ship. And if he was here, there was a good chance Nero himself had come with him.

'Seize him,' said Epaphroditus, waving his hand nonchalantly.

His slaves began to make their way around the edge of the bath. Cadmus jumped up, wriggled on to the grimy floor, and set off at a run.

The steam was as thick as it had been when he'd arrived, and he found himself colliding with the other bathers every five or six steps. The sweat poured down him. At some point he must have taken a wrong turn among the columns, because he found himself looking across the *palaestra*, in blinding sunlight, where men were wrestling and throwing discuses and lifting weights. They all looked around in surprise. Behind him he heard the slap of the slaves' feet.

Naked as a baby, he sprinted around the colonnade of the exercise yard and re-entered the baths via a different doorway. He passed the massage rooms, the snack sellers, the cold plunge pool, and skidded to a halt in the changing room.

Tog was gone.

He went to the alcove where he had left his possessions. His toga, his tunic, his sandals, the fleece, even the little bag of coins he had taken from the merchant. Everything was there, apart from Tog.

He heard the shouts and footsteps of his pursuers echoing down the passage behind him. He threw on his tunic and sandals, grabbed the fleece and the purse, and fled across the mosaic floor. Just as he reached the steps of the baths, he felt something tug on his shoulder. One of the other slaves had taken hold of the bag with the fleece inside. Cadmus spun and let the strap fall from his arm, then kicked his assailant hard in the shin and half-staggered into the street.

Outside everything was too bright, too loud. His head was still hot and fuzzy from too long spent stewing in the *caldarium*. He felt almost as naked as he had in the baths. No toga. No Golden Fleece. He was just a slave now, and a small and feeble one at that.

He set off at a run, hardly knowing what direction he was heading in.

XVI

Cadmus was on the other side of the city before he was sure he was no longer being followed. At the Diomeian Gate, in the eastern wall of the city, he slumped behind a watering trough and caught his breath. The afternoon was drawing on, and the area to the north of the Acropolis was lost under a landslide of shadow.

A stray, flea-bitten dog came nosing along the wall and looked up in surprise, as though he hadn't been expecting Cadmus to be there. He began sniffing around Cadmus's lap, and then pushed his wet muzzle into his face.

'Go *away*!' Cadmus said miserably. He swatted him with the back of his hand. 'I don't have any food. And if I did, I wouldn't give you any.'

The dog lowered its ears, but didn't move.

'Leave me alone!'

He raked in the dirt for a stone to throw, but the thought of Tog stopped him. She would never have done that. If she were here, she would probably have wanted to take the dog with them.

He wondered where she'd got to. Of course she'd run away. Good on her. She deserved to be rid of him, after the way he'd treated her.

Perhaps, he thought, he should return to Italy after all. He wasn't doing any good here. He'd lost Tog. He'd lost the fleece. He'd probably landed Tullus in all kinds of trouble. The dog was still staring at him, his eyes strangely judgemental.

'I *know*,' said Cadmus. 'I'm *useless*.'

Going back seemed impossible, though. There wasn't enough money in his ill-gotten purse to pay for a journey of that distance. If he didn't pay his way, he hardly fancied trying to slip aboard a ship in secret *again* – he knew Fortune didn't favour him that much.

He was completely at a loss. Perhaps now was the time to turn to the gods in earnest. Perhaps he should go to a temple, make an offering, pray to Apollo for guidance.

Suddenly he sat up, and made a faint, mocking

smile. He didn't need to pray to Apollo, he realized. He could talk to him directly.

Cadmus's memory was one of few gifts the gods had granted him, and one that had never ceased to amaze Tullus. He could transcribe an entire session of the Senate – a whole day's worth of speeches – without any notes, hours after the event, if the need arose. On the rare occasions that Tullus attended a dinner party, Cadmus was able to remember the names and faces and careers of men he had met years ago.

When it came to Silvanus's map, he only needed to think of it and it was as though he were holding the papyrus in front of him. If he went to the Sibyl's shrine, he was bound to meet up with Nero's party sooner or later, and hopefully Tullus would be with them. But there was more to it than that. He wanted to meet the Sibyl herself.

He scooped a few mouthfuls of water from the trough and set out on foot. To his annoyance, the dog insisted on accompanying him.

He didn't really know what he was looking for. The longer he walked, the more foolish he felt. The prophets and prophetesses in Rome were charlatans, for the most part, out to make a quick couple of sesterces by exploiting the hopes and the fears of the poor. There was the famous prophetess at Delphi, but he'd always thought of her as little more than a tourist attraction. The Sibyls – priestesses of Apollo, divinely elected women who spoke with voice of the god himself – were the stuff of poetry and myth.

But then, so was the Golden Fleece, and he had seen that with his own eyes. Seen it, held it, lost it again.

Cadmus trudged on, the dog still trotting happily beside him. The city receded and the day waned. Behind him, atop the Acropolis, the massive bronze statue of Athena Promachos raised her spear in challenge to the setting sun. He passed beyond the roadside tombs into the olive groves and the farmhouses, disordered and scattered like chips off a sculptor's block. The chatter of the crowds disappeared and was replaced with the burr of cicadas. The sky in the east turned the colour of a ripe peach.

Then he saw it. A farmhouse, set back from the road, burnt out, half-demolished. Its roof had caved in, and one of its walls was a mound of blackened stones. This was the spot that had been marked on the map, he was sure of it. It didn't look much like a shrine to Apollo.

He walked up to the farmhouse through the short, brittle grass and scattered stones. A few goats emerged from behind the walls and then ran away into the olive trees, followed by the lonely clang of the bells around their necks. The dog chased after them and disappeared from sight.

Cadmus felt as though he was in a dream. There was something unsettling about the house, but he was drawn to it all the same. The half-light of dusk only made the scene feel more unreal.

Everything was very quiet. He wished Tog was with him.

There was a courtyard at the front of the house. Charcoal and bones and bits of pottery cracked under his sandals as he made his way across to the rooms at the rear. They were empty of furniture, and what remained of the walls and ceiling was stained with soot. He couldn't see into the gloom of the kitchen and the storerooms, but they smelt of death – dust and blood and rotten eggs. There were stairs up the other side of the building, but the upper floor had completely collapsed, and the room beneath was half-exposed to the sky. He went back across the courtyard to investigate. The threshold was covered with bits of broken timber. It took a moment for his eyes to adjust to the darkness.

'Gods below . . .' he muttered.

The floor was covered with the burnt remains of animals. In the middle of the room, illuminated by a single shaft of dull light, was an altar. It was smeared with ash and blood, and on top of its feebly glowing embers rested a large bronze dish. Hanging from the ceiling were bunches of dried herbs and flowers. At the rear, in the deepest darkness, Cadmus could just make out a table and a chest, both of them black and cracked and strangely glossy from the ravages of a fire. When he got closer he saw the tabletop was scattered with glass bottles, a tiny bronze tripod, an oyster shell, and the wrinkled form of something that Cadmus thought was a fig, but found was in fact a desiccated, headless frog. There was, tantalizingly, a box of half-charred scrolls underneath the table.

From the doorway came a noise that sounded like a sneeze. Cadmus whirled around. The dog was there again, sitting on his haunches in the doorway. He barked, and it seemed to split the twilight in two.

'Shush, Orthus . . .'

An airy voice drifted into the farmhouse from the courtyard. Someone was following the animal. Cadmus leapt through a hole in the opposite wall and crouched behind it, trying not to breathe.

The dog sat for a moment, watching the space where he had just been. The voice came again.

'*Orthus!*'

Behind the dog a woman appeared, dimly silhouetted against the doorway. Her voice had sounded young, but from where Cadmus sat it was impossible to tell her age. Her hair was unbound and so dirty it was clinging together in thick strands the size of her fingers, like tree roots growing from the top of her head. She also seemed to be wearing a toga; or rather several togas, layered over each other, crimson, purple, black, hanging in countless folds around her body. She was shorter than Cadmus, and slight under all of her robes.

In one hand, at waist height, she held one of the goats by its horns.

The priestess led the animal to the altar a little unsteadily, the blackened carcasses snapping under her bare feet. When she fanned the embers and the orange light was cast on her face, Cadmus saw why. A piece of rough-spun fabric concealed her eyes. She was completely blind.

He watched her shuffle around. She piled up the fire with sticks bundled next to the altar, and then, still holding on to one of the goat's horns, felt her way slowly to the table where Cadmus had been nosing around her possessions. She led the animal back to the fire. She began to chant, her song matched by the victim's bleating.

Cadmus looked away, as he always did at public sacrifices. He heard the familiar sounds – the rough slice of the blade, the slop and spatter as the animal was gutted, the hiss as its insides were heaped on to the blazing altar – and didn't turn back until he was sure the whole ritual was complete, and the body was spitted and roasting over the flames.

'Come,' said the priestess suddenly. 'Eat.'

Cadmus froze.

'Aha. I know you're there.'

He peeped through a gap in the stones. She was facing him.

'You have been witness to the sacrifice, so it is only right that you eat the sacrificial meat and take the Hecate's blessing.'

She beckoned in his direction.

The Hecate. Goddess of the dead, of night, of magic. This woman wasn't a Sibyl. She could hardly even be called a priestess. She was a witch.

Cadmus came out slowly, his muscles stiff from crouching for so long, his heart rattling behind his ribs.

The priestess tore off strips of meat with her curved knife and held them blindly in front of her. Cadmus took a piece and nibbled it tentatively. The dog, Orthus, again began sniffing around his knees with great interest.

'He likes you,' said the woman. 'He doesn't usually like anyone.'

Even though her eyes were covered, she seemed to be staring at him, frowning, as if trying to picture him through force of will alone. The fabric of the blindfold twitched erratically. She took a couple of paces towards him and then laid her hands upon his face. Her fingers were cold and calloused. Cadmus shivered, despite the heat from the fire.

'I like you too,' she said. She caressed him a moment longer and then withdrew her hands. 'But then, I already know you.'

It took him a moment to compose himself.

'You know me?'

'Mmm hmm.' She felt her way around the room with surprising ease and selected herbs and powders and unguents. She began mixing them in a small clay crucible. 'I have seen you a thousand, thousand times. In the vapours. They come from below, below, below . . .'

She threw the contents of the crucible into the bronze dish and set it on the fire. It sent up plumes of acrid, sea-green smoke.

Cadmus didn't know what to say. She didn't seem entirely sane.

'Yes, we like you. Much more than the other one.'

'The other one?'

'You're not going to shout at us, are you? Like he did?'

'Do you mean Silvanus?'

'I tried to help him. I tried to steer him from his fate. But he was stubborn, and the fleece blinded him.

Like it always has done. And now his thread is severed, and he has gone below.'

Cadmus watched her face twitching in the firelight. Her skin was white and unblemished as Parian marble – she couldn't have been much older than him, he thought. As she nodded, a thick loop of hair fell from her head and swayed heavily in front of him. He looked closer and saw the glint of a tiny polished eye. It wasn't hair. It was a snake, binding her tresses in its muscular coils.

She kissed it lightly on its head and gently pushed it out of the way. Cadmus's skin broke out in gooseflesh.

'Did you kill him?'

The priestess inhaled the bitter-smelling fumes rising from the altar. She inclined her head as though lost in thought, or perhaps listening carefully for something beyond Cadmus's senses.

'Mmm,' she said.

Not for the first time, Cadmus began to wish he had never come. To the house. To Athens. He wished he'd stayed at home under his blanket.

He swallowed drily, and when he next spoke his voice was hoarse. 'Why?'

'He came to us twice,' she said. 'He was looking for things that didn't belong to him.' Her voice was calm and distant. 'Sacred things. Sacred places. A tomb. I told him what he needed to hear and sent him on his way. But he returned, some days later. He was angry. He had followed my directions, but did not find what he needed to find. It was in front of him, and he did not see it.'

'The Golden Fleece?' said Cadmus.

'That was what he *wanted*. Not what he *needed*.' She chuckled quietly. 'He wanted me to tell him exactly where it was. He said he wanted to keep it safe, but I could read his heart. He desired the fleece for himself, like all men do. He tried to force the answers from me, but the goddess refused to speak. Fool. He should have known what happens when an asp is cornered.'

She stroked the snake again, whispering something under her breath, and it slithered back into the masses of her hair.

So Silvanus hadn't died of fever at all. He had been bitten. Poisoned.

'Well,' he said. 'Killing him didn't solve anything. They found the fleece, after all.'

'Hmmm,' she said again.

Cadmus wasn't sure how he felt. He didn't like the idea that Silvanus had threatened the young woman – and he knew the man sometimes had a short temper – but surely that wasn't reason to kill him?

'I don't understand. The shrine you sent him to – are you saying it *was* Medea's grave? Or not?'

She didn't reply to that.

'Do you know where the other heroes are buried? And the other relics?'

More silence. Orthus had lain down next to the altar, nose on his paws, basking in its warmth. The embers popped occasionally.

'Maybe I didn't say that right,' Cadmus corrected himself. 'I mean, can you *see* them?'

'See?' The priestess cocked her head, faintly amused.

'I don't mean see with your eyes. I mean *see*. Into the future. Isn't that why people come here? There are some people who call you a—'

He broke off.

'What?' she said. 'What do they call me?'

'They say you're a Sibyl.'

She broke into raucous laughter, so loud and jarring it made Cadmus wince.

'A Sibyl? Oh dear, oh dear, oh dear, oh dear.' Her laugh dwindled to a gurgle in the back of her throat. 'There hasn't been a true Sibyl among mortals for hundreds of years. This is an age of iron, an age of dark – the Olympians abandoned us long ago.'

There was a pause that lasted so long Cadmus thought she had forgotten he was there, or perhaps had fallen asleep. Her snake curled lazily around her shoulders.

'No,' she continued. 'I am not a Sibyl. You might say I am the kind of Sibyl the world deserves these days. I am a handmaiden. I serve the Hecate, our Lady of the Crossroads. Like my mother did. Like all of my ancestors have done. We have all had the gift.'

'The gift?'

'Of, as you say, *seeing.*' The priestess frowned suddenly, as though physically pained. 'Only my sight is not as clear as theirs. Pieces. Fragments. Past and present and future. And the flames. Always the flames.' She paused. 'So many people come to me for answers, but the goddess shows me many things I do not fully understand.'

Her tone had changed. It sounded more human now – the voice of a young girl more than of a prophetess. Cadmus felt unexpectedly sorry for her. She seemed a different species from the prophets and astrologers who loitered in the Roman Forum, making money from the hopes and fears of the unwary. She seemed to carry a terrible burden.

'But you've seen me before?'

'Oh, yes,' she said. 'Many times. Only glimpses. But enough to know you.'

'I don't suppose you could . . . share some of what you've seen? Knowing my future would be very, *very* helpful right now. I'm in quite a lot of trouble.'

A frail smile suddenly formed on her face, like a

crack shivering across a vase.

'You have the fleece, don't you?'

How did she know? He hadn't mentioned that he'd taken it from Nero. He also hadn't mentioned that he'd promptly lost it on his way out of the baths. An age seemed to pass before he spoke again.

'I used to have it,' he said.

'What?'

'I had it this morning. Then someone took it from me.'

'Took it? Who?'

'A slave.'

She shook her head violently. 'No, no, no, no, no. You were meant to bring the fleece to me. You are bound to it. Your fate . . . the thread . . . I can't see the thread . . .' She plucked at the air blindly with thumb and forefinger.

'I'm sorry,' said Cadmus, feeling stupider than ever. 'I had to let it go. Nero would have caught me and killed me.'

The priestess suddenly became perfectly still. Cadmus watched the snake tighten its coils through her hair. It was probably the last thing Silvanus had seen before those fangs found their way into his flesh.

'Nero,' she said.

'That's right. I stole it from him.'

'And what did this fleece look like?'

Cadmus was baffled. 'Golden. Fleecy. What else would it look like?'

To his surprise, the priestess smiled again.

'Ah,' she said. 'Interesting.'

Suddenly she sat up very straight. She cocked her head on one side, then the other, like a bird listening for something.

Then he heard it too. Footsteps, voices, out on the road. He went to the door of the farmhouse and peered around the edge of the broken frame. Outside, lights bobbed in the darkness like boats far out to sea. He saw the outlines of giant men. The *heroidai* had arrived.

'It's him, isn't it?'

'I'm sorry,' said Cadmus, for what felt like the fiftieth time that day. His heart felt like it was pumping nothing but air. 'I knew they were coming. I should have told you.'

'I should have seen it myself.'

'We need to go. They're looking for a lot more than just the fleece, and they'll be a lot less polite than Silvanus.'

She didn't move.

'Don't worry,' she said. 'I know how to deal with unwelcome visitors.'

XVII

Cadmus quickly climbed through the hole in the wall and went around the back of the farmhouse. The priestess didn't follow him.

Where the main portion of the building had been demolished there were several large piles of rubble, where he could hide and watch the courtyard. The dog joined him, panting quietly. Cadmus could feel his warm, thin ribs pressed against his thigh.

The *heroidai* emerged from the night, moonlit and fire-lit and weirdly iridescent. There was one who stood out among them. He wore the Golden Fleece over his shoulders, and a mask of gold to match it. He was a good head shorter than the others. He also wore a set of armour that had been specially contoured to accommodate his considerable gut. Nero had come in person.

The emperor and his *heroidai* were followed by perhaps twenty slaves and two old men. Cadmus recognized both of them, too.

The first loitered at the back of the group, scroll in hand, his face somehow grey despite the red pulse of the torches. However much he tried to hide himself, he was unmistakably Gaius Domitius Tullus. Chastened, but alive, Cadmus was glad to see. He was staring at his sandals and seemed to be deliberately avoiding looking at the priestess.

The second man was even older than Tullus. He arrived several moments after everyone else had assembled, bent almost double, propped up on two slaves. His head was veiled, as it had been before, and all Cadmus saw was the man's chin, tufted and greenish like fruit left to rot. It was Polydamas. Cadmus found himself thinking of the cranes he'd seen on Roman building sites, or water pumps, or siege weaponry – there was something mechanical and angular about the way the soothsayer moved, like he had been poorly engineered and might fall apart at any moment.

The priestess came out of the doorway and stood before the assembled men. She looked so small, swaddled in her many robes. A child, almost.

Polydamas limped over to the emperor and spoke something into his ear. His lips curled like leaves in winter, then he withdrew. Nero lifted his mask.

'Good evening, my dear,' he said. He licked his lips. 'Perhaps I should offer you my thanks, first of all. For helping me to find my inheritance.'

He gave the fleece a little flourish. The priestess said nothing. Nero stepped closer. Uncomfortably close.

'Of course,' he said, waving his fingers in front of her blindfold. 'You cannot even see it. You don't even know who I am! Or maybe – ' he leant into her ear – 'you know me by the sweetness of my voice?'

From where he was crouching, Cadmus saw the priestess's snake twitch underneath the mounds of her hair. It slithered down her neck and began winding its way up Nero's bronze-clad forearm.

It was a moment before the emperor himself realized. He jerked backwards, squealing and swinging his arms wildly. He hurled the snake over the wall of the farmhouse, and fell over with the momentum. The snake landed a little way away from Orthus, hissing furiously. Cadmus froze and nervously watched it trying to untangle itself. The dog didn't seem at all concerned.

Nero picked himself up from the floor, the fleece wrapped around his head. Even with masks on, the *heroidai* looked faintly embarrassed.

'Now listen,' Nero said, trying to free his mouth from the folds. '*Listen to me.* You will tell me what I want to know. You will tell me where to find all the things that are *rightfully* mine. You will speak when I command you to speak. Do you understand?'

The priestess shook her head fractionally.

'No.'

'No?'

'The goddess does not speak on demand. There are rites to perform. You must purify yourselves.' She paused. 'You are unclean.'

'Unclean?'

She bowed a little. The emperor stared at her. A grin grew upon his face, wide and ugly and fixed as his mask. He took two steps forward and seized her around the throat. He forced the fingers of his other hand into her mouth.

'You will deliver the goddess's words to me,' he seethed, 'if I have to pull them *one by one from your lungs.*'

Orthus, who had been growling softly since Nero's arrival, suddenly stood up. Before Cadmus could stop him, he lurched through the broken walls and went bounding towards the emperor. Nero shrieked and released the priestess as the dog jumped up at him. The *heroidai* still seemed faintly bemused.

Orthus barked and snapped, prancing this way and

that and flinging strings of saliva from his muzzle. Nero straightened up and drew his sword, a gold, bejewelled trinket that hung from his belt. He advanced cautiously, as though unsure of his invulnerability, and directed the point of the steel at the dog's jaws. The dog feinted left, then right, then sunk his teeth into the emperor's arm.

Cadmus barely saw what happened in the ensuing scrap. He still had one eye on the snake. Nero howled in pain, and the dog came at him again. Somehow the two of them ended up rolling in the dirt of the courtyard, and the Golden Fleece became tangled in their flailing limbs. Nero tried to tug it back with his one uninjured hand, but the other end was clamped in the dog's jaws.

Cadmus heard a drawn-out whine, but he couldn't be sure whether it was the man or the animal. Then, beneath that, a tearing. The sound was short and irregular to begin with, then it suddenly widened. Nero held one half of the fleece in his fist. Orthus held the other in his mouth. Even after that, the dog continued snapping at the fabric, tossing it with his whole head, until in the space of a few heartbeats the fleece was in shreds on the floor.

The rest of the party looked on, motionless, unsure of what this meant. Cadmus held his breath. A real animal hide wouldn't have torn like that.

'What are you waiting for?' screamed Nero. 'Kill it! *Kill it!*'

One of the *heroidai* eventually stepped forward. Orthus quickly realized he was outnumbered, and after a few more defiant barks, ran off into the shadows. The priestess also bolted and stumbled blindly back into the house. Two of the *heroidai* caught her as she reached the threshold of her ruined shrine and dragged her back to the emperor with her arms pinned to her waist.

Nero shook with rage. He picked up the torn fragments of the Golden Fleece and shook them in her face. Even from where Cadmus was crouching, he could see the frayed edges catch the firelight. It wasn't a hide at all. It had been *woven*. The fleece was a fake.

'What is *this*?' Nero screamed. 'What is this piece of trash? Where is the real thing?'

He rounded on Polydamas.

'You knew, didn't you? You knew it was a trick and you didn't *tell* me!'

The soothsayer bowed low and wrung his hands.

'Tullus?' The emperor spun again. 'Is this your doing? Yes, yes, you planned it with Silvanus, didn't you?'

'I, ah, assure you, Caesar, I knew nothing—'

'Or did you plot it with the boy?'

'There was no plot—'

'If this is a fakery,' said Nero, 'then the Golden Fleece is still to be claimed. *And the boy is still out there to claim it.*'

Cadmus's whole body was getting cramps, he'd been still for so long. All he wanted to do was run, but that would only have drawn attention to him. He glanced beside him. The snake had gone, but he had no idea where.

Nero turned back to the priestess.

'You're going to tell me *everything*,' he said quietly.

She didn't move.

'Let me guess, the goddess doesn't feel like talking? Well, let's see if we can't encourage her a little.' He nodded to Polydamas. 'You. Wretch. Redeem yourself.'

The soothsayer bowed again and spoke a handful of rasping words to the slaves. They disappeared into the room with the altar and emerged carrying the priestess's bronze dish and tripod, which they set up in the courtyard. Others went to the fringes of the farmhouse and began hacking down the olive trees and piling them at the woman's feet.

When all was ready Polydamas lit the kindling and placed the tripod over the flames, then seesawed his way around the fire on legs that seemed to be of wildly different lengths. He threw handfuls of herbs into the bronze dish, and lastly produced a small clay phial that he had tied around his wrist. He pulled out the stopper and emptied its contents, and the dish coughed up gouts of dirty smoke.

The soothsayer leant into the fire and picked up the bronze dish with his bare hands. Cadmus could see every bone standing out in the soothsayer's skeletal hands, could see the smoke where his white skin was burning, but the man never flinched. He brought the bowl around to where the priestess was standing. She was tensed now. She tried to pull back from what Polydamas was offering her.

One of the men holding her put a hand to the back of her head and forced it over the blue-green vapours. Her body shuddered for a moment as she tried to resist. The rest of the *heroidai* looked on with their blank, bronze faces.

The farmhouse went quiet. No cicadas, no birds, no wind in the trees. Nero stepped forward and addressed her.

'Now, my dear. Perhaps you might like to tell us the truth. All of it.'

Polydamas muttered something in the emperor's ear, but he swatted him away.

'*Shut up!* You're like my mother all over again! I will ask whatever questions I like!'

The priestess went slack suddenly, and for a moment Cadmus thought she had been put to sleep.

Then, from her feet to the top of her head, she stiffened, as though in agony. She threw off the two men grasping her arms and they staggered back as she went raving around the courtyard, eyes rolling in her head, white foam flecking her lips.

When she spoke, the sound that left her mouth was not a human voice. It was as though the earth itself were speaking. The ruins of the farmhouse shook, and the vault of the sky and the caverns of the Underworld echoed her words back at her. Cadmus had never seen or heard anything like it.

'*The bearer of the Golden Fleece, sacred to the Sun, and to Ares, and to Poseidon, and to Hermes above all, shall have dominion without limits of time and space; all peoples shall kneel to him, and as the generations grow and die like leaves on the trees he shall not fade, but ever grow in strength and wisdom and enjoy green old age, and youthful vigour without end.*'

Cadmus listened closely. This was the same oracle that Tullus had mentioned when they were in Nero's palace, but he felt much less inclined to dismiss it as fantasy when it came from the priestess's lips. The words resonated through the earth and boomed around the inside of his skull, as though she was talking to him and him alone.

'I *know* all of this,' said Nero irritably. 'Tell me where the damn thing *is* or I'll have you spitted like a pig!'

The priestess went on whirling around the fire like a spinning top, writhing, jerking, clawing at her hair and clothes.

'*You will travel far from this country, to the very edge of the world, where the land breaks and breaks again, and the pieces are devoured by the cold and frothing sea; by a great voyage, and through many trials, will the bearer of the fleece prove himself worthy of his inheritance. On the island of Mona you will find her, Medea, descended from the Sun, in a grove of oak, under a crown of stone. The thing you seek is in her grave.*'

The priestess suddenly pulled a grotesque smile, then slumped to the floor, her mouth still foaming. The courtyard was swallowed in silence. The *heroidai* creaked awkwardly in their armour.

'Is that it?' said Nero after a moment. 'Is that what I came all of this way for?'

He took a few steps forward and nudged the priestess's body with his foot. When she didn't respond, he bent down and began violently shaking her limp form.

'*Speak to me!* I am your emperor! I am the heir to the fleece! It belongs to *me!*'

Nero finally grew tired and flung her body to the floor. He rounded on Tullus.

'Mona? Did she say *Mona*?'

Tullus looked up, startled. 'Ah, I believe, Caesar, it is

an island in Britannia.'

Britannia. Cadmus's heart leapt with excitement on Tog's behalf, before he realized that she wasn't there and he had no way of telling her.

'I know the bounds of my own empire, you old fool,' Nero snarled. 'What does Britannia have to do with any of this?'

'Well,' said Tullus, wringing his hands. 'She spoke of Medea. It would seem that the fleece is buried with her, as we thought. But her grave is not where we thought it was. At least, not where Silvanus thought it was.'

Thoughts and memories of Tog quickly faded as the logical gears of Cadmus's mind began to whir. This was all new to him. He didn't know of any versions of the myths in which Medea ended up in Britannia. Even if Medea had really existed, the details of the end of her life were very thin. Some said she stayed in Athens. Some said she returned to the east, to Colchis. But most simply never mentioned how or where she died.

If she were a fugitive, though, it made sense that she would flee to the furthest ends of the earth. And Mona was renowned for the magic of its inhabitants.

Nero was still staring at the fragments of the counterfeit fleece.

'Britannia,' he said again. 'I can't go all the way

there. It is a land of savages. Besides, think how my people would despair if I was away from Rome for so long!' He turned to Tullus again. 'You shall go. With Polydamas. With my *heroidai*. Not as our guest, or our advisor, but as our prisoner. I still do not trust you, but I recognize your usefulness. If you do not cooperate, you will find yourself crucified alongside your boy, when we find him.'

He jerked his thumb at the lifeless form of the priestess.

'You'll take her with you too. I'm sure the goddess can provide more specific answers if we *really push her*.'

One of the giants came forward and slung the young woman over his back. The slaves collected the other items they had pilfered from the shrine, and the whole party melted one by one into the darkness. Tullus was the last to go, prodded by one of the *heroidai*. He looked over the ruins of the farmhouse one last time, and Cadmus could see his eyes were shining with tears. Then he too disappeared with a slow and lonely trudge.

Cadmus came out from behind the piles of stones and stood in the light of the dying fire. He picked up the pieces of the fleece and inspected them. The craftsmanship was incredibly fine. Who could have made such a thing? Surely not the priestess? He cursed himself for not recognizing it was counterfeit earlier – it plainly hadn't come from an animal.

He suddenly realized he was holding an armful of spun gold. Frayed and dirty as it was, there was a good chance it would fetch an extraordinary price. That kind of money could get him far. He went and found a leather bag from among the priestess's possessions and bundled it inside.

In the middle of the courtyard the bronze dish was still smouldering with oddly coloured smoke. He stared into the fumes and shivered. He'd never seen or heard anything like it. Of course, he told himself, it was probably quite easy to find an unguent or a herb that induced hysteria. It was probably quite easy to *fake* a divinely inspired 'fit', as he was sure most prophets did.

But even so, everything he had just witnessed seemed very real. The priestess had spoken with a voice not of this world. A huge, dark question reared up before him, one that he had only glimpsed until now and had tried to ignore: what, exactly, *did* he believe?

While he was lost in thought, there was a rattling sound from the corner of the courtyard. He looked up and squinted into the darkness. His heart leapt into his throat.

Polydamas was looking straight at him. The ancient

figure had never left. He began to cackle, and then scuttled off with surprising speed.

Cadmus ran. He was barely out of the grounds of the farmhouse before he heard shouting. He looked behind him, down the hill, and saw the torches of the *heroidai* dancing like fireflies against the night.

He wove through the olive groves, the dry air scouring his throat. When limestone reared up out of the ground he climbed until his hands and feet bled. He tumbled down the other side of the ridge and came to a stop, dust-caked and panting, next to an outcrop of overhanging rock that formed a shallow cave. It smelt of wild animals.

With the shouts of his pursuers still echoing around the other valley, he climbed inside and prayed to Hermes to shroud him in darkness.

XVIII

Cadmus was woken by a warm tongue rasping over his face. He spluttered and flailed his arms, then sat up too quickly and banged his head on the roof of the cave. That knocked the sleep out of him. He muttered some words that Tullus didn't allow in his household, and rubbed the dirt and sweat from his eyes.

Silhouetted against the half-light was Orthus. The dog was watching him without a huge amount of sympathy.

'Oh,' said Cadmus. 'It's you.'

The dog came towards him on slender, delicate paws. He was old, Cadmus noticed, a beard at the end of his muzzle that was almost white.

'What are you doing here?' he said, crawling out of the cave and dragging his bag behind him. 'Shouldn't you be protecting your mistress?'

The dog wagged his tail and followed him.

Cadmus stood up and stretched, clicking from his neck to his knees. It was cold, and the earth was blue in the dawn. He strained his ears. All he could hear was the twitter of the birds, the occasional tiny rock-falls dislodged by goats who had ventured up this far.

The hill was not especially high, but it gave him a good view of the city. The walls and the Acropolis were still dotted with torches and small fires. The peace and quiet did little to calm Cadmus's nerves, though. For all he knew, the *heroidai* were still scouring the hills and the plains for him.

'Any ideas about what I should do now?' he asked Orthus. The dog slumped to the ground and scratched behind one of his ears. 'No, I thought not.'

His first thought was to go back and find Tullus, but returning to Athens was out of the question. It wasn't just Nero he was worried about. He was thinking of the merchant too, whose network of friends and associates no doubt included some unpleasant types. Cadmus knew how men like that operated. In fact, he could imagine the merchant and Epaphroditus striking a lucrative deal after the incident at the baths.

Cadmus racked his brains. The towns of Eleusis and

Megara seemed too close for comfort. But beyond them, about fifty miles from Athens, was Corinth.

Corinth was almost as famous and prosperous as Athens. It was a major port too, which meant two things: first, he could probably find a merchant to buy the remains of the fake fleece from him; second, there would be plenty of ships to take him away from Greece. Where exactly he planned on sailing to was still a matter of debate. Rome? Antium? Britannia? Everywhere seemed equally dangerous.

The sun rose and the mountains took on their hard white edges. Within an hour, the earth was hot as griddle. Cadmus set off on foot towards the coast road, hoping to find a driver willing to take him as far as Corinth.

He wished he could talk to Tullus, to Tog, to anyone. So he discussed his predicament with the dog. To his credit, Orthus listened patiently and attentively and never interrupted. Cadmus was glad for that much.

At Eleusis, Cadmus found a man heading to Corinth with a wagonload of amphorae, and after a little haggling and a few sideways glances at the dog, he agreed to let them ride in the back with his wares.

They spent two days on the road, perched uncomfortably on the hard, clay wine jugs. Cadmus had plenty of time to think about what had happened back at the farmhouse. The priestess's words had worked their way into the marrow of his bones. He usually set little store by prophecies, but hearing it from the priestess's foaming mouth was different from reading about it in a book.

Dominion without limits of time and space. Youthful vigour without end.

If this was truly what the real Golden Fleece promised, then handing it to Nero really would be as catastrophic as Tullus made out. As they rattled along the coast road, Cadmus came to the slow, cold realization that he was the only person outside of the emperor's circle who knew about any of this. Which meant that he was the only person who could stop it. Which meant that, by the time he arrived at Corinth, he had made up his mind. He had to go to Britannia.

At midday on the second day, they pulled up outside the city walls. Cadmus thanked the driver and paid him from his ever-diminishing purse, then made his way to the agora for something to eat and drink. The centre of Corinth was similar to Athens, lined with temples and porticos, although both the buildings and the people seemed a little rougher around the edges.

Cadmus kept to the shadows of the north stoa, scanning the marketplace for any sign of Nero's men.

His heart nearly stopped when he saw a tall, muscular man loitering on the steps of the sacred spring. He looked like he could be one of the *heroidai*, minus the gaudy uniform.

Cadmus tried to laugh off his paranoia. Just being tall didn't make him an agent of the emperor. Still, he moved as far as he could from the man's line of sight.

He skirted to the south side of the agora where there was a row of shops and bought two cups of well-watered wine. Orthus immediately knocked his over with his long nose, but didn't seem to mind licking it off the paving slabs. Cadmus smiled and sipped his own cup. It was strangely reassuring having the dog around.

In front of the shops, a slave auction was taking place. He watched for a moment as a boy with enormous, dark eyes – Egyptian, Cadmus thought – was paraded in front of the clamouring crowd with a tablet hung around his neck. He was younger than Cadmus. A man in a toga stepped up on to the platform, checked the boy's teeth, slapped his flanks like he was a horse, and then returned to the crowd, shaking his head and chuckling. This happened several more times until the boy was led from the stage without a buyer.

That was when he saw her. Unlike the others, she wore manacles on her hands and feet, and these were connected to the collar she already had. She didn't seem at all pained, but wore her usual expression of complete boredom. As alarming as it was to see Tog chained and subdued, Cadmus couldn't help smiling.

He had to help her. She was standing behind four or five other slaves, but the queue didn't seem particularly orderly, so he couldn't tell when she would be beckoned to the platform. If he didn't act quickly she would be sold right there in front of him.

There were five denarii left in the merchant's purse, hardly enough to purchase another human being. Then he remembered: he still had the fake fleece in his bag. At least one *libra* of woven gold. He ran along the row of shops with Orthus until he found a Syrian selling jewellery. He was talking to a wealthy Roman *matrona* who was already wearing so much gold she seemed to be struggling to stay upright.

'Please,' Cadmus interrupted, 'how much will you give me for gold thread?'

'*Excuse me?*' said the woman, turning very slowly under her necklaces and circlets and earrings. Her eyes flicked to Orthus.

The shopkeeper didn't look at either of them.

'Ignore him, my lady. As I was saying, these pearls come from the Euxine Sea, there are no others like them in all the world . . .'

'I have lots of it,' Cadmus blurted. He looked behind him to the auction. There were now only two individuals between Tog and the platform.

'I don't *care*,' hissed the Syrian. 'I don't want some dirty piece of thread you have found on the streets, you brat! I am dealing with a *real* customer.'

Cadmus pulled the scraps of the counterfeit fleece out of the bag and threw them on to the table between them, which was spread with bangles and rings.

Buyer and seller fell completely silent. Cadmus watched with satisfaction as both sets of eyes bulged. There were gasps from the other shoppers.

The Syrian picked up the remains of the fleece with his thumbs and forefingers and scrutinized the weave very closely. He held it up to the light; then compared it with a headdress, which was also threaded with gold; then held it to the light again; then looked at Cadmus.

'Twenty,' he said.

Twenty denarii was more money than he had ever seen in his life, but it still wouldn't come close to paying for Tog. He looked over his shoulder again but the auction was now concealed by the crowd that had gathered around the merchant's stall. Among them was the tall, tanned man he had seen earlier. Whereas everyone else was trying to get a glimpse of the fleece, he was looking straight at Cadmus. The man's gaze fell on him like a slab of granite.

Cadmus turned back to the stall, unsettled.

The Syrian was still inspecting the pieces of the fleece. He extracted a single thread, and grinned. The woman huffed with impatience as the shopkeeper turned, slowly unlocked a strongbox behind his stall and began to count out twenty coins. He straightened up and placed them one by one into Cadmus's palm. Cadmus almost wept. They weren't silver, but gold. Twenty aurei. That was *five hundred* denarii.

He thanked the man and apologized to the woman, then thanked the woman and apologized to the man, before sprinting across the agora with the heavy bag of gold. He joined the back of the auction crowd and tried to squeeze his way to the front. Tog was on the platform now. The auctioneer was just getting warmed up.

'One thousand,' he called. 'Do I hear one thousand denarii?'

Cadmus's blood ran cold. Double what he had! And the price was only going to go up. Tog hadn't seen him – she was staring out over the heads of the crowd as though she could see the shores of her home from the top of the platform. He felt the hand of the man next to him twitch and then fly up into the air.

'Does she speak Latin?' he asked.

'Um, well,' said the auctioneer, a tiny Greek man with a bulbous, plum-like nose. 'No. But she speaks Greek very well. For a barbarian, I mean. And Gaulish. I think. Don't you?'

Tog stared at him and said nothing. The auctioneer gave her the briefest of glances and turned back to his audience. He was scared of his own merchandise.

'And *physically* she is without compare,' he said, trying to pique the crowd's interest again. 'Wouldn't you say? Look at the size of her!'

'Why's she got all those scars?' asked another potential buyer. 'Looks like her other masters had reason to punish her.'

'Trouble written all over her,' agreed another.

Tog yawned, and Cadmus laughed to himself. It was a spectacular performance.

'Well, she used to work in the mines . . .' The auctioneer stopped, knowing immediately he had misspoken.

'The *mines*?'

'I give her two days before she's stone dead!'

'Very well, eight hundred denarii,' said the auctioneer, plainly flustered. Cadmus's spirits rose a little. *Keep it up, old friend*, he thought.

'She seems a little slow to me,' said the man next to Cadmus, who had asked about what languages

Tog spoke.

'Yes,' Cadmus chipped in, hoping to drive the price down further. 'I don't think she's all there. Mentally.'

Tog saw him. Her face was not so much one of surprise as curiosity. Cadmus grinned back at her.

Down went the price. 'Six hundred denarii . . .'

'What's that on her shoulder?' someone shouted.

Tog's mouse was poking its head out from under the cascade of her hair.

'Is that a *rat*?'

'Is she diseased or something?'

The little man moved to swat the mouse away, but Tog took a particularly menacing breath and he decided to keep his hands to himself.

There were general noises of disgust from everyone, and Cadmus could have sworn the auctioneer's nose began to glow with embarrassment.

'Five hundred denarii?'

'Yes!' Cadmus threw his hand into the air and pushed his way to the front of the stage. The auctioneer looked at him in surprise. There was laughter from some of the other men in the crowd.

'Serious bids only, young sir . . .'

'I am serious.'

Cadmus came up on to the platform, not caring who saw him. He handed his coin pouch over to the auctioneer, who peered inside and then looked over at a much larger, burlier man who was standing with the rest of the slaves. He must have been the slave dealer who had actually captured Tog in the first place – though how he had achieved that, Cadmus did not know.

The two men nodded to each other, and the auctioneer announced, with some relief:

'Sold.'

XIX

The slave dealer grudgingly removed Tog's manacles, with the exception of her old collar, which was still locked and keyless. The rest of the crowd watched in bemusement as Cadmus led her away – or rather, as was always the case, she led Cadmus. The first thing he did was to buy her a new tunic. Then they left the agora as quickly as possible.

In the shadow of the basilica, Tog finally stopped and spoke.

'You've got a dog,' she said.

Cadmus looked at Orthus, then at Tog. He knew not to expect a great outpouring of emotion or affection from her, but even by her standards this remark seemed a little flat given what had just happened.

'Um. Yes?'

'What's his name?' she said, crouching down and putting her arms around the dog's neck.

'Orthus.'

'I like him,' she said.

Cadmus watched them both. Tog pressed her face against the dog's muzzle, and he wriggled like a fish out of her embrace.

'Aren't you going to thank me for saving you?' said Cadmus.

'I wouldn't have needed saving if you hadn't brought me back to Athens,' she said matter-of-factly.

'Oh.' She had a point there. 'Are you still angry with me?'

She shook her head. 'I was never angry with you.'

'You were. With good reason.'

'I was not. How would that have helped our situation?'

Cadmus shrugged. 'I suppose it wouldn't. Doesn't look like running away helped either, though.'

'Leaving you was better for both of us.'

'I wouldn't say that . . .'

Tog looked him up and down. 'You seem fine.'

'Well. I'm tired, and confused, and very, very badly sunburnt. But I'm all the better for seeing you again.'

'Hmmm.' She took a moment to decide whether she was pleased to see him. Then at last she nodded.

'Yes. It's good to see you too.'

Just that was enough to make Cadmus glow. His smile turned into a full-blown belly-laugh. He wanted to throw his arms around her like she had done to Orthus, but knew she probably wouldn't appreciate it.

'What happened?' he asked. 'How did you end up here?'

She stopped trying to snatch another cuddle from Orthus and stood up. 'They caught me while I was asleep. They must have heard me talking . . . I thought I was far enough from the road, but obviously not. I was so tired they had the chains on me before I was awake.' She offered a finger to the mouse on her shoulder. 'Embarrassing,' she added.

'You're lucky I was here,' said Cadmus. 'What are the chances?'

She shrugged. 'What happens, happens.'

'Spoken like a true Stoic,' he laughed. 'But this feels like more than coincidence.'

'Why do you say that?'

'Our fates have aligned, it seems. We're *both* heading to Britannia now.'

Tog raised one eyebrow, which was perhaps the most expressive gesture he'd ever seen her make. He told her everything that had happened since she had abandoned him in the baths. When he reached the part about the priestess's prophecy, Tog stopped him.

'I know Mona,' she said. 'It's where fugitives go. All the people who ran from the Romans. The last of the druids live there.'

The druids. Cadmus had read about this Gaulish religion. Their priests were sorcerers, necromancers, men who dabbled in human sacrifice. The Romans had been so appalled by their practices that they'd trapped them on their island and massacred them only two years previously.

But as much as they were feared and hated by Romans, the druids sounded like perfect company for someone like Medea. And she was definitely a fugitive . . . It seemed to fit quite nicely.

'I don't know how we'll get there before Nero and Tullus,' he said. 'I don't know how we'll get there at all, in fact. Even if we find the fleece—'

Cadmus was suddenly aware of a presence a little behind him. Taller than him. Taller even than Tog. When he turned he saw the tanned, leathery man who had been watching him earlier. Orthus started barking,

'Shut him up,' he said in a rough and earthy voice. 'You've made enough of a scene as it is.'

Cadmus patted Orthus and drew him to his side. He looked at the man. Beneath his great beard his face was seamed and craggy, and his tunic was not woven but stitched together out of animal skin. He almost seemed in costume, an ancient tragic hero ready to take to the stage.

'Where did you get it?' the man said, once Orthus was calm.

'What?'

'Where did you get the fleece?'

'I don't know what you're talking about . . .'

'Don't play stupid with me. I saw you selling it to the Syrian. Where did you find it?'

'It's . . . difficult to explain . . .'

'Did you get it from Eriopis?'

The man stepped forward and completely over-shadowed Cadmus. Tog watched him carefully, her fingers curling slowly into fists.

'Eriopis? I don't know who that is.'

'The witch.'

Cadmus paused for a moment. He looked at Tog, then back at the bearded man. It wasn't worth his while starting a fight.

'Yes. In Athens. She called herself a priestess of the Hecate.'

'Then you have spoken to her?'

'Well. Yes. But—' He stopped. 'Why are you look-ing at me like that?'

The man was staring intently into Cadmus's eyes, almost like he was trying to see *past* them. Cadmus closed his one yellow eye self-consciously.

'How do you know Eriopis?' he said.

'I told you, I *don't* know her. That's the first time I've heard that name – we only spoke very briefly. And she spoke mostly in riddles.'

'What did she say?'

'She said she'd seen me before.'

'And?'

'She said . . .' His thoughts were fuzzy. The man was intimidating. 'She thought I had the fleece. But I didn't.'

'What else?'

'She made a prophecy. About what the fleece could do. And where to find it.'

The man scrutinized him carefully, as though trying to discover the truth of what he was saying.

'She mentioned the grave?' he said after a moment.

Cadmus nodded. How did the man know these things? These were secrets it had taken Tullus his entire life to uncover.

The man straightened up and looked around. 'We should not talk of such things in public,' he said. 'Come with me. We may be able to help each other.'

As he turned to go, a pained cry that resounded around the agora.

'Ah,' he said. 'It seems our Syrian friend has realized he is missing something.'

Smiling, the man pulled back his tunic of animal hide and revealed a mass of golden thread beneath.

'You know,' said Cadmus tentatively, 'that's not the real thing?'

'Of course I know,' the man said. 'I was the one who made it.'

Corinth occupied a narrow strip of land separating seas to the north and south. To the west of the city the land curved round in a long, mountainous peninsula, creating a safe harbour for ships entering from the gulf. The man led them out of Corinth and along the bay, until they reached a small shrine to Fons. Here, a small stream emerged from the rocks and tumbled down towards the sea. The mixed scents of sea air and pine resin were suddenly replaced with something less pleasant.

'Smells like eggs,' Tog complained.

'Sulphur,' said Cadmus. 'There must be a hot spring here.'

A few paces ahead of them, the man bent, cupped the water with his hands, and drank.

'Who is he?' said Tog a little too loudly.

'I am Thoas,' he said, standing.

'How do you know about the priestess?'

'Eriopis is one of us,' he said. 'Broadly speaking.'

'Who is "us"?'

'That will be answered in good time,' said Thoas. 'Now. We are entering a sacred place. Drink your fill from the spring. It is long way to the heart of the mountains.'

Cadmus quickly found himself at the rear of the group, Orthus at his side. The ground was steep and uneven, and every one of Tog's giant steps sent rock and grit sliding down behind her. They scrambled higher and higher into the scrubland, Thoas never speaking, never even glancing over his shoulder. Cadmus began to wonder if they'd made a terrible mistake. Without the sea breeze the sun was brutally hot. The trees here were sparse and stunted, barely higher than Cadmus's head, and offered no shade whatsoever.

He'd lagged far behind on an uphill stretch when Tog's voice suddenly rolled around the mountainside.

'Cadmus,' she said. 'Look at this.'

He climbed a landslide of broken rocks, spitting dust and muttering to himself.

And then he saw the view. What little breath he had left in his dry and creaking lungs was quite taken away.

From the top of the mountain he could see almost all the way back to Athens, the land folded and creased like old leather. To the north was the expanse of the sea, hazy and no longer glittering now the sun was directly overhead. To the west and the south were the high, pale mountains of the Peloponnese, their foothills cloaked in a thick mist that seemed to suggest they were not just in a different place, but a different time altogether.

'It's beautiful,' he said.

On this side of the mountain, facing away from the sea and the city, the trees and bushes were suddenly vastly more numerous – not only pine, but also oak, plane and myrtle. On the slopes of the next ridge were grasses and a thick forest. It was like stumbling upon a lost world.

Tog stood a few paces ahead of him with her arms folded and nodded with satisfaction. Thoas was already striding down the other side of the ridge.

Orthus suddenly stiffened like a hare disturbed from its burrow. He turned an ear in the direction of the trees a little further down the mountain.

The first spear narrowly missed Tog's shoulder and planted in the ground between Cadmus's feet. He had just enough time to see a dozen or so men and women springing from among the pines in animal skins, when the second spear came whistling at him. He turned his back and the point clipped the edge of his tunic and clattered among the stones.

'Stop,' Thoas said loudly. 'They're with me.'

Cadmus came out from behind a rock, and saw the

men and women advancing from among the trees. They looked very similar to Thoas – almost primitive, some of them bare-skinned above and below the waist, others in animal hides. Many were armed, spears in hand, shields slung upon their backs. One man wore a lion skin and held a club in his right hand. One carried a lyre. They were all, men and women, dark and muscular and proportioned like no human beings Cadmus had ever seen, except, perhaps, Tog herself. They looked as though they had escaped from the design of a Greek urn.

They formed a circle around the newcomers, their eyes narrow and suspicious. Cadmus did his best to calm Orthus, who was still growling and barking.

'I found him in the agora,' said Thoas. 'He was carrying this.'

He pulled the fake fleece out from underneath his tunic. There were gasps from the others.

'His eye,' said the one in the lion skin.

'Yes,' said Thoas. 'I know.'

'Does he?'

Thoas shook his head.

Before Cadmus could ask what they meant, he and Tog were thrust together and led down a narrow, stony path through the trees. Orthus stayed close to him. It was good to feel the dog's muzzle brushing his calves. They descended the eastern side of the mountain and went up the opposite ridge, where the woods were thicker. They walked in silence, swatting mosquitoes from their faces. The air among the trees was hot and thick, like the inside of the baths.

Cadmus's head swam in the heat. The man had said they could help each other, but now he felt more like his prisoner. He wondered why the man in the lion skin had mentioned his eye. He wondered who any of these people were, and how they knew everything about the fleece already. He looked round at Tog, but as usual she seemed unruffled by the situation. Perhaps her head was spinning as much as his, and she just didn't show it.

As they walked on, Cadmus saw a dark shape further up the mountainside. He squinted but could make no sense of it – there were strange angles and lines that did not belong in a forest. At first he thought it was a strangely shaped boulder, but as they got closer he realized that it was not a work of nature. It was something that had been built, long, long ago.

After a hundred paces the trunks of the trees thinned and they entered a theatre of rock, an uneven semicircle hollowed out of the mountain and fringed with trees. At its centre, miles from the sea and sunk into the earth, was a boat. It was rotten and ruined and overgrown with twisted bushes, but the name on its prow was still visible even from where Cadmus stood:

$$APΓΩ$$

They were standing in the shadow of the *Argo*.

XX

They sat in the broken hull of the ship, on benches that had been built for the oarsmen, while their captors talked in low voices in the bows. Cadmus and Tog had each been given a cup of warm, sulphurous spring water, but aside from that they had been ignored since their arrival. Orthus had been forbidden from entering the shrine, and Cadmus was surprised by how much he noticed his companion's absence.

The only light came in thin, yellow shafts through the gaps in the decking, but Cadmus could see the boat was richly decorated. Inside and out, the ancient timbers were painted with scenes from Jason's quest: the defeat of the fire-breathing bulls, the soldiers sprung from the ground, the great serpent put to sleep; his long journey home and his meetings with the witch Circe, with the Sirens, with Talos the bronze giant; his triumphant return to Corinth and the reclaiming of his kingdom. Medea, Cadmus noticed, hardly featured in these pictures – her role in the story had been almost entirely erased.

Piled up beneath these designs were gifts that the cult had dedicated to their hero. There were urns, tripods, statues, all cast in gold and silver. Enough to buy Tog and himself several hundred times over.

Cadmus shook his head. 'I don't believe it,' he said.

'You don't believe anything,' said Tog.

'It can't be *the Argo*. Lots of ships are called the *Argo*.' He rubbed his hands over the wood, which was smooth with age. 'Still. It does look very old.'

'Why can't it be what they say it is? What's so special about it?'

'It depends on which version of the myth you read,' he said, 'but some people say the *Argo* was the first ship to ever sail the seas.'

'Ever?'

'Ever. Another story says one of the timbers –' again he rubbed a hand over the warped bench – 'came from Zeus's sacred grove at Dodona and could speak prophecies.'

'A piece of wood could tell the future?'

Cadmus smiled and nodded. 'Who's the unbeliever now?'

'Just seems strange.'

'At any rate, the *Argo* was the ship that carried Jason and the Argonauts to Colchis and back again. It survived all of the trials you can see painted here, and then it was consecrated to Poseidon when it finally returned to Corinth. So we are at least in the right part of the world . . . Another part of the myth says that the ship killed Jason much later on in his life. He was sleeping underneath it, and a rotten piece of the mast fell and hit him on the head.'

'Now that I *can* believe in,' she said, and started picking at the hull with her finger. 'This thing is falling apart.'

The group suddenly split and Thoas walked down the length of the boat.

'I have convinced them not to kill you,' he announced.

Cadmus blinked. 'Um. Thank you?' he said.

'On the condition that you tell us everything. Starting with who you are.'

Cadmus paused before speaking, looking from face to face, scanning the length of the ship. He gathered what little courage he felt.

'You first,' he said.

'Excuse me?'

'If you want to talk about the fleece, you need to tell me who you are. Prove to me you're not just another treasure hunter.'

Thoas gave a little smile. 'He is pious,' he said over his shoulder to the others. 'That's good.'

'Well?'

'You needn't have any fear about our intentions, boy. We seek only to honour the relics. To keep them out of the wrong hands.'

'But why?'

'It is our duty. Has always been our duty. We are the *heroidai*.'

Cadmus jerked his head involuntarily. That didn't make sense.

'No, you're not,' he said.

'Yes,' the man said slowly. 'We are.'

'You're *not*.'

'We are!'

'Well, you're not the only ones. I should know, they've nearly killed me twice. I think they're just gladiators in fancy-coloured armour, but Nero calls them his *heroidai*.'

Thoas grimaced and spat.

'As if Nero, or anyone who associates with him, is pure enough to claim that name. We are the *true* sons and daughters of the heroes. There are more of us in the world, but most of us have made this holy site our home. To preserve and defend our heritage. To keep the secrets of our ancestors and—' He stopped. 'Please ask your friend to stop that.'

Cadmus looked to where he was pointing. Tog had got bored and was picking a chunk of wood the size of her fist out of the hull. She looked up, saw them both staring at her, and let it fall to the floor.

The man looked at her for a moment before continuing.

'Each and every one of us can trace our lineage back to one of the Argonauts,' he said. 'Many of us have divine blood in our veins. My name is Thoas, son of Jason.' He pointed to the man in the lion skin. 'Hyllus, of the line of Heracles. Linus, of the line of Orpheus. Meleagra, daughter of Atalanta . . .'

A hero cult. Cadmus drifted into his own thoughts as the list went on. Plenty of people claimed descent from gods – all of the emperors had asserted with a straight face that the goddess Venus was the fountainhead of their family – but no one took such things literally. These people, though, really *looked* like the heroes they said they were descended from.

Something suddenly made sense. A comment Silvanus had made in his letter.

'Is that how you know Eriopis? The witch? Are you both descended from the children of Jason and Medea?'

Thoas spat again.

'The witch has none of Jason's blood in her. She is all poison, like her mother, and her grandmother, and the rest of her lineage. All of them deceitful, dangerous women.'

Cadmus swallowed. The old grudges obviously still ran deep.

'You still hate her? Because of what Medea did to Jason?'

'Her debt will never be repaid,' he said. 'And she continues to wrong us. Her family have always known the secrets of the Golden Fleece. They know where Medea is buried. They know where the fleece is. And yet they keep the knowledge to themselves. It was Jason who rightfully claimed the fleece. It was never Medea's. It belongs here, among us, with the *Argo*.'

Cadmus looked at Tog. He began to feel uncomfortable. Unwittingly he had wandered into a centuries-old family feud.

'I see,' he said. 'So you've had to make do with the fake all this time.'

'It is not a *fake*,' Thoas bristled. 'It is a faithful replica of the original. But Eriopis wouldn't even allow us that much.'

'What do you mean?'

'She had the nerve to come to us and take it for herself. She spun us lies about Romans searching for the heroes' relics. She said it was in all of our interests, and in the interests of the fleece itself, to satisfy them with the replica. We refused, obviously. So she *stole* it, from this very altar.' He pointed at the prow and then turned back to Cadmus. 'You see? Deceitful, danger-ous woman. You did well to escape from her.'

Cadmus chewed his lips for a moment.

'I understand why it might be difficult to forgive Medea,' he said, 'but Eriopis wasn't lying to you . . .'

The inside of the *Argo* fell silent. The other *heroidai* seemed to lean in to listen.

'Nero really is looking for the Golden Fleece. And the *Argo*. And any other heroic artefact you care to mention.'

'That is no concern of ours,' said Thoas. 'We know what kind of man rules the Romans. He is a moron. He wouldn't know where to begin looking.'

'He *has* already begun looking,' Cadmus said. 'He has found Eriopis. He has taken her. And he has ways of forcing oracles from her lips, whether she wishes to speak or not.'

Thoas frowned, his great brow cracking like a slab of limestone.

'Forcing?'

'She has already told him where Medea's remains can be found. No doubt she will speak just as readily when they ask her where the *Argo* is.'

The descendant of Jason took several deep breaths, holding Cadmus in his gaze.

'You said you heard the oracle. You said you knew where Medea was buried.'

'I do.'

'Then tell us.'

Cadmus didn't know what to think. He didn't much like the way these *heroidai* spoke about the priestess. She was strange, certainly, but that didn't make her dangerous. If he told them what she had said in her prophecy, he felt like he would be betraying her. And from what he'd seen, it looked like she had suffered enough in her short life.

But then again, it sounded like they would bend every effort to finding the fleece. It would surely be better for a hero cult to have the Golden Fleece than Nero. At least they seemed to respect the artefact itself, even if they were a little on the fanatical side.

He suddenly realized Tog was looking at him. Anyone else would have found her expression completely blank, but he had spent enough time around her to read the subtleties in her various kinds of blankness. He knew what she wanted.

'If I tell you,' he said, 'will you take us with you?'

Thoas nodded. 'Of course.'

He looked at Tog again. Her silence screamed at him. He took a deep breath.

'It's in Britannia. On the island of Mona.'

There were excited mutterings from the gathered *heroidai*. Thoas himself grinned so broadly Cadmus immediately wondered whether he had made a mistake.

'Athena bless you,' he said, standing. 'You have done us a great service. You have done yourself a great service also.'

'When do we leave?' asked Tog.

'As soon as we have permission.'

'Permission?' said Cadmus. 'From whom?'

'The ship.'

XXI

The *heroidai* had dug themselves well into the mountainside, in a labyrinth of caves and tunnels with the *Argo* at its centre. Lean-to shelters had been erected along the sides of the ship, and huge squares of canvas had been stretched between the edge of the boat and the mountainside to keep off the sun and the rain. There were tents on the deck, an altar erected on the prow, and rope ladders strung haphazardly around the clearing.

The community was larger than Cadmus had first thought. There were families here, grandparents, children, mothers still clutching babies to their breasts. He wondered how they had remained undisturbed for so long, but then remembered the reception he had received when he had arrived – they probably had been discovered, many times, but whoever had found them hadn't lived to tell the tale.

It was evening by the time they left the ship. Thoas led them to one of the caves, and the other *heroidai* watched them go with narrow-eyed suspicion. Their leader ignored Cadmus's constant stream of questions and left them in the darkness with two rough-spun blankets and a dish of old fruit. Tog fell straight to sleep, as usual, but Cadmus's thoughts chased themselves around his head until he didn't know where one ended and another began. It was only when Orthus slunk back to the camp and bedded down beside him that he at last closed his eyes and fell into an exhausted stupor.

In the morning he was woken by a flood of daylight against the cave wall. Tog's bedroll was empty, and there was no sign of the *heroidai*. Only Orthus kept him company, his muzzle resting on his paws, his brow twitching with whatever dog-dream he was having.

Cadmus got up and wandered blearily out into the hollow in the mountainside. Between the canvas awnings the sun was blindingly white. He squinted at a tall figure striding towards him.

'You're late,' the figure said. 'Or were you hoping to get out of doing any work?'

Cadmus squinted. 'Tog?' He rubbed his eyes for the third or fourth time. 'You look different. You sound different too.'

He couldn't put his finger on it. If anything, she was even taller than usual, and her voice seemed louder and clearer.

'I asked them for some clothes,' she said. 'And they gave me some. Look, it's got a little pocket for the mouse.'

She was wearing a sheep's skin over her back, and a tunic stitched together from old, supple hides. She had a new pair of boots on her feet, tightly bound with leather straps. But there was something else too that changed her completely.

'Your collar,' he said. 'It's gone.'

As his eyes adjusted to the sunlight, he saw that the skin around her neck was so pale it was almost green. Without the iron collar, and wearing her hunter's garb, it was like Cadmus was seeing her for the first time; like she had only been disguised as a slave up to this point, and she had flung that disguise triumphantly aside to reveal her true identity.

'They have a smith here,' she said. 'He said he'd remove it for me. Two taps with a hammer. All done.'

'If I'd known it was that simple, I would have tried to do it earlier.'

Tog pointed at his biceps. 'With these little things?

You probably would have missed and killed me.'

Thoas suddenly appeared behind her, holding a mallet in one hand and an axe in the other. He had stitched most of the pieces of the fake fleece back together, and was wearing it over his shoulders.

'Are we ready?' he said.

'Ready for what?'

'Thestor, son of Idmon, has spoken with the sacred timber. The omens are good, but we have a few repairs to make before the *Argo* is seaworthy. Come, the work has already started.'

Cadmus ran down the dusty slope after Thoas, with Tog a few paces behind him. The sun had only just flooded the valley; the earth was still cool and the pines cast thick bars of shadow over the path. Around them the *heroidai* were already making the first axe strokes into the trees' trunks.

'Um ... Can I ask some questions?' he said, drawing level with Thoas's elbow.

The man said nothing.

'How are going to get that ship down to the water?'

Again Thoas ignored Cadmus, moving between his people and giving them instructions.

'Even if we make the *Argo* watertight,' Cadmus pressed, 'surely it won't survive a journey to Britannia? In fact, travelling by boat is pretty much the *slowest* way to get there. Have you looked at the maps? We'll need to go all the way along *Mare Nostrum* – which, incidentally, is infested with pirates – around Hispania, up the coast of Gaul. We'll never catch Nero's team. If you read the accounts of anyone who has been there, the quickest way is over land—'

Thoas finally turned and spoke to him.

'Not everything can be learnt from books and maps, boy.'

'Yes, it can!' Cadmus cried, feeling like the man was stabbing at the heart of his very being. 'This is completely irrational! I may as well get an oxcart all the way there!'

'You are welcome to,' said Thoas. 'The oracles state that the *Argo* will make a second journey, to reclaim the fleece from Medea's remains. You can come with us, or you can stay here with our wives and children.'

He smiled a smile that brought Cadmus's blood to boiling point, and then handed the axe to Tog.

The *heroidai* worked for a day and a night, felling trees, hewing and shaping timbers, patching the holes in the ship's flanks. The structures that had grown up around the *Argo* were dismantled and the canvasses were stitched into an enormous sail. They fashioned new oars and a new mast and laid them in the aisle between the rowers' benches.

Cadmus tried to offer them advice on the best proportions for the cross-bracing; he made calculations about the length of the oars and the heights of the oar-locks; he explained to them about the dangers of shrinkage in various types of wood; he told them about the best way to weight the ship, based on Archimedes's principles of buoyancy. It made him feel useful. Grounded. Sane.

The *heroidai* ignored all of this, of course.

By midday, Cadmus had taken the hint and retreated to the coolness of the caves. He could still work out the route. Tullus owned a map of the empire that he could recall in minute detail, and he had a fairly good knowledge of the climate and the winds around Italy and Greece. Unfortunately, the sons and daughters of the heroes had no need for writing implements. There were no tablets, no scrolls, no pens or ink. He could do a lot in his head, but nothing so complex as an entire journey to Britannia. Despite all his learning, Cadmus ended up feeling completely redundant – and all the while Tog was chopping down trees twice as fast as anyone else, and gaining wide-eyed admiration from all who saw her at work.

At dawn on the second day Cadmus was still awake, trying to calculate the minimum wind speed required to get them to Britannia before Nero. He was writing his figures in the dust with a stick, Orthus looking on, as though checking his arithmetic. Thoas entered the cave and erased them with two of his giant footsteps.

'It is ready,' he announced.

Cadmus sighed and got up from his haunches. He followed Thoas into the clearing.

The sun had just risen, and it illuminated every flaw in the ship with excruciating clarity. The hull was a patchwork of old and new timber, shot through with wooden pegs and spattered with black tar. The prow was at very odd angle. It somehow looked even more of a wreck, and even less watertight, than it had done when they first arrived. Cadmus went and stood next to Tog and gave her a doubtful look. She just nodded. He didn't know whether that meant she shared his lack of optimism or not.

The largest stones and bushes were cleared away from the ship, and the treasures inside were removed and piled up in the mouth of one of the caves. All of the *heroidai*, men, women and children, assembled in a large circle around the landlocked vessel. Thoas stood before them in the remains of the fake fleece.

'Today,' he said, 'the *Argo* will feel the salt of the ocean upon her sides for the first time since she returned from Colchis with her precious cargo. We honour our ancestors in seeking that divine relic again, to save it from the hands of the unworthy, and the unholy.'

'I still don't understand how we're going to get to the sea,' Cadmus interrupted.

Thoas gave him a hard stare.

'The ship is blessed by Athena,' he said. 'She will lend us her strength.'

Cadmus turned back around to see the circle of men and women close slowly upon the ship until they were crowded around its hull. They held out their hands and took hold of timbers where they could. Some scurried underneath the keel where it protruded from the earth, squatted and pushed their backs against it. Only the very young and the very old hung back, and even some of them tried to volunteer.

'They're not going to *carry* it?'

There was a combined groan, and the grind of stones underneath the ship. It rocked slightly to one side, and the prow wobbled violently. Then it rolled back again, there were more cries of exertion, and the whole thing settled back in the same hollow it had sat in for centuries.

'This is ridiculous!' said Cadmus.

Tog didn't reply. She marched forward and got into position at the stern of the boat, gripping the hole left for the oars.

Thoas, underneath the prow, gave the sign and again the members of the cult strained, their arms and thighs and backs shuddering, to lift the ship out of its grave. Again it leant to one side; again there were shouts of pain and frustration; again it rolled, like a lazy sow, back into the dust.

When Cadmus looked along the lines of the *heroidai* and saw Tog, she was staring at him. He knew what that look meant.

Feeling more than a little stupid, he went around to the far side of the ship, muttering to himself. Orthus accompanied him, weaving happily around his legs. He took up a position opposite Tog. When he passed her he saw she was sweating heavily, and she had been pushing so hard her feet were buried into the earth.

Cadmus squeezed himself between a woman in a leopard skin and an old man who smelt of goat, and managed to fit his fingers under the spine of the boat's hull. A splinter jabbed into his palm and he hissed between his teeth.

Thoas called down the line again. The old man grunted and wheezed. The woman in the leopard skin spat with effort. Cadmus strained and strained under the shadow of the boat, arms burning, knees shaking. His pulse pressed against the inside of his ears, like his head was moments from exploding.

There was a roar from the front, different in tone from the previous ones. It wasn't the sound of exhaustion or frustration, but of surprise, and then, as the noise swelled, of triumph. Cadmus felt his legs straighten, heard oaths and prayers fluttering around him from the other members of the cult. He looked down and saw daylight shining on the ground where the keel had just been. Orthus ran happily from one side to the other, underneath the ship's massive bulk. It swayed a little, but didn't return to the earth. The *Argo* was moving.

XXII

The route down the mountain was even slower and more painful than Cadmus had expected it to be. They carried the ship with tiny shuffling steps, stopping every time someone tripped or fell or became ensnared in the bushes. Not far out of the clearing, the *Argo* became wedged in between two trees, and it groaned ominously while two scouts were sent to clear a path through the forest. Further down the mountain, the hull ran aground on a sharp spur of rock, where it teetered for a few moments until the *heroidai* at the back were able to heave it free. When it came loose, those at the front were nearly crushed beneath the boat's keel, and several men had to be carried back to the settlement to tend to their injuries.

On they went, into the valley and over the next ridge. Down in the foothills the fug of hot sulphur began to be rent by cold gusts of sea air, and Cadmus knew they were nearing the coast.

Thoas had chosen a secluded cove for their departure, concealed from the residents of Corinth. Cadmus ran ahead with Orthus and watched the boat come crawling down the side of the mountain. The *heroidai* were concealed completely in its shadow, giving the impression that it was being drawn to the sea of its own accord. On either side, trailing back up to the forest, it left a bow-wave of swirling yellow dust.

And finally there it was, in front of him, crunching over the pebbles of the shoreline. The *heroidai* heaved as one, and with an almighty splash the *Argo*'s keel forged into the waves, and the seawater wetted its ancient timbers.

The men and women followed the boat into the water, where they washed off the dirt and sweat and blood. Some attached mooring ropes to rocks and trees.

Cadmus went over to where Tog sat in the shallows, bathing her face and arms. They watched the waves breaking against the prow for a moment.

'See?' she said. 'It's not sinking.'

'That's because it's still touching the bottom,' said Cadmus. 'The tide is low. Wait till we're out in the middle of the Gulf – then I'll be more confident.'

The afternoon stretched on, and the sea crept up the beach. The *heroidai* came and went, loading the ship with provisions. A pair of oxen were sacrificed to Apollo Embasios, on an altar built from sea-smoothed stones. Cadmus, as always, chose not to observe the rites but took the sacrificial meat when it was offered to him. Took more than he should have. Gorged himself, even. He wondered grimly if this meal might be his last.

While he and Tog ate, the priest, Thestor, stared into the flames of the altar. He muttered and chanted. When the sun had gone beneath the earth, and the sky and the sea were black, he finally stood up and declared that the omens from Apollo were favourable, and the wind was at their backs.

'We're leaving *now*?' Cadmus said to Tog, as the *heroidai* began to wade out to the ship. 'In the middle of the night?'

Tog shrugged and got to her feet. She lifted her mouse on to the top of her head. They followed the other *heroidai* through the breakers, Cadmus gasping as the cold water reached his waist. Tog climbed aboard the *Argo* first, while Orthus scrabbled inelegantly up the prow. Cadmus was last on deck. He stood in the breeze, dripping and shivering. The night had deepened. The stars glittered like the fires of an army camped out across the heavens.

Some of the *heroidai* took to their benches, while others severed the mooring ropes. With a groan, the rowers leant on their oars, and the *Argo* lurched forward over the wine-dark sea.

When they were out of the bay, and Corinth was the faintest smudge of orange on the horizon, the steady beat of the oars stopped. The sailors raised the mast and hauled on the rigging, and the sail filled with a noise like a thunderclap.

Cadmus stared into the night, listening to the hiss of the sea around the ship's keel. He wasn't sure if he was asleep or awake. Nothing seemed quite real, and it made him fearful and fearless at the same time. Behind him, Tog was babbling something to Orthus. When he turned around he saw her trying to introduce the dog and the mouse, but they didn't seem to be getting on with each other. He smiled at her and turned back to the empty air. How was she always so calm?

'How long will it take?'

She was beside him all of a sudden.

'Honestly?' he said. 'Even with favourable winds, a month and a half.'

'Hmm. And how long will it take the others?'

'It depends,' he said. 'If they really flog the horses they'll be there in a month.'

'But they might be slower than that?'

'Possibly.'

'That's not so bad. Some good luck for us, some bad luck for them – we can make up a few days. And when you get to Britannia you'll have the advantage over them. It's my land, my people. I can talk to people. I can help you get to Mona, or wherever you're going.'

Cadmus wanted to point out that this didn't necessarily give them the upper hand. Many of the British chieftains were now on the Romans' payroll, and Nero's men would have no problems finding natives to help them. A bribe is bribe, in any language. But he didn't mention that. Besides, there was something about the way she was talking that unsettled him.

'Wherever *I'm* going?' he said.

Tog nodded.

'I take it, then, you're not coming with me?'

She frowned a little. 'No. I'm going home, remember?'

And that was all she said. Cadmus felt angry with himself for being even the slightest bit surprised. Of course she was leaving him. What did she care about the Golden Fleece? About the ambitions of a foreign emperor a thousand miles away?

'I'm going to try and get some sleep,' he said.

'Good,' she said, and turned back to the darkness.

Cadmus went down through the narrow cutaway in the deck and Orthus followed him. He found a vacant bench and tried to get comfortable on the hard, smooth wood. He looked around the hull at the paintings of Jason and his triumphs. Seawater was already dribbling through the cracks in the planks, causing the colours and the lines to run. As sleep came over him, Cadmus thought, distantly, that it looked like the great hero was weeping.

When he woke up, he could see a thick shaft of light falling through the gap in the deck. He swung his feet off the bench, nearly treading on Orthus, and wandered drunkenly down the length of the boat. Some of the crew were also sleeping down here; the rest he could hear thumping about overhead.

He climbed the steps and warm sunshine washed over him. On all sides of the *Argo* the sea was spread out like a vast tapestry threaded with gold. Thoas had the helm and Tog was at the prow, shielding her eyes against the glare. Her mouse was back on her shoulder.

'Hello,' Cadmus said with a yawn. 'Where are we?'

'I don't know,' she said. 'I thought you could tell me that.'

Cadmus looked around. Not a landmark in sight.

'I'm not sure,' he said. 'But let's not forget, you're talking to the boy who didn't know east from west.'

She looked out over the glittering waves and sighed.

'Then where do you *think* we are?' she asked.

'Best guess . . . somewhere just past Zakynthos, or Cephalonia. But I can't see either of them.'

'So?'

'So . . . either we're way off course or we are making much better time than I expected.'

'I thought so,' said Tog. 'I told you we could catch up a few days.'

'I admire your optimism,' said Cadmus, 'but we've got a *very* long way to go yet. I hope the gods are as favourable as Thoas seems to think – if the wind isn't with us, this journey could be ten times as long as the one from Rome to Athens.'

The hours and waves and the high clouds passed them by, and it seemed that the gods were indeed on their side. They saw nothing but flat ocean and occasional schools of dolphin, which had Tog yelping with delight. The weather remained hot and fine, and the breeze was at their backs even after nightfall. Linus, the man descended from Orpheus, played songs for them on his lyre. It was almost idyllic.

The following day, a rugged blue landmass appeared on the horizon, rising to a distinctive peak at one end. Cadmus ran to Thoas, who was guiding the two steering paddles at the rear of the ship.

'That's Mount Etna,' he said.

Thoas nodded.

'But it can't be. We can't have reached Sicily already. We've only been at sea for two days.'

'As I have told you,' Thoas replied, 'the *Argo* is blessed by Athena. And Apollo has shown us the way.'

He gave his patronizing smile again.

Cadmus turned away and scowled at the horizon. Growing up with Tullus made him wary of any good luck. If his master had been there, he would have reminded Cadmus daily to beware of Fortune's fickleness: *At Jupiter's door*, he would have said, *stand two urns, of good and evil gifts, and he deals from them equally . . .*

After Sicily, Jupiter began to dig particularly deep in the second of those two urns. The winds remained favourable, but even on calm seas the *Argo* barely held together. Every time Cadmus awoke on his bench, he noticed a little more seawater lapping at his feet. The crew tried carving wooden staves and pegs out of one of the oars, which they used to plug the holes, but still the water came in. At Hippo Regius, part of the decking collapsed, and two men fell through on to the rowers beneath them. One of the steering paddles broke on a reef two days later, and they were forced to zigzag for the best part of a day before they could fashion a new one.

And it wasn't just parts of the ship they lost. When they stopped at Tipasa, Hyllus, the man in the lion skin, went hunting and never returned. At Thoas's command, they left without him.

Still the *Argo* limped on, as far as the Pillars of Heracles and the edge of what Cadmus knew as *Mare Nostrum*: 'Our Sea'. Here – he told Tog – Heracles had single-handedly narrowed the gap between Hispania and Africa, to prevent monsters from the ocean entering the seas of Italy and Greece. As they passed through into the vast blue beyond, Cadmus hoped that was one myth that wasn't true.

Sea monsters, it turned out, were the least of their worries. All the way up the coast of Hispania they were battered by storms, and the *Argo* was tossed like driftwood on the towering, bristling waves. After a month at sea, Cadmus found himself going below decks to pray to the gods, regularly and without embarrassment. There really was nothing else he could do. It was just as Thoas had said – everything Cadmus had ever read and learnt counted for nothing when the powers of heaven were turned so fiercely against him.

In the middle of one of these tempests, crouched with Orthus in the darkness of the hull, he felt an arm around his shoulders. He looked up and was surprised to see Tog beside him. He hurriedly wiped the tears from his cheeks.

'Don't worry,' she said, and her voice was so calm and deep that it seemed to quell the shrieking winds.

'I want to go home,' he said, and as soon as he gave his thoughts words, he started to cry again.

'I know,' said Tog.

He waited a moment to compose himself, sniffing loudly. 'I should never have left Rome. I shouldn't have gone looking for the fleece. I'm not made for this sort of thing. I'm not a hero. I'm an idiot. I'll get to Britannia, and then what? Defeat Nero and the empire on my own?' He took several deep, shuddering breaths. 'What am I going to do?'

She looked at him seriously, her blonde hair like an aurora in the gloom.

'Endure,' she said.

Cadmus opened his mouth but sensed she had more to say. The ship rose into the air and crashed into the trough between waves, sending Cadmus's stomach into the roof of his skull. She spoke again.

'That is all we can do. All we have ever been able to do. We cannot change what the world gives us. We cannot hope to have control over Fate, or Fortune, or the gods. If you try, that will only cause you more pain. Right now, there are two storms, Cadmus. One out there, and one – ' she pointed to Cadmus's heart – 'in there. There is only one that you can hope to put a stop to. You cannot choose whether you suffer, or how you suffer, but you can choose what you think and what you feel about suffering. You can fight against it, little Cadmus against the universe; or you can accept it. Think of your heroes. Did Jason *want* to go looking for his special blanket? No. He was forced to by his uncle, and he endured what was given to him. Did this man Heracles *want* to do his labours? No. He would rather have stayed at home, I am sure. This is how a hero is made. They are made in hardship, like a sword forged under a hammer. So. Endure for now. One day, you might enjoy remembering all this.'

Cadmus just stared at her. It was the most Tog had ever said. It was also everything Tullus had tried and failed to teach him from his philosophical dialogues. This kind of Stoicism always seemed such an easy thing to advocate if you were a wealthy Roman senator. Coming from Tog, Cadmus thought for the first time there might be some truth to it.

'I'm glad you're here,' he said.

Tog nodded, suddenly awkward. There were shouts from above, and she went back up to help bring the *Argo*'s sail under control.

To Cadmus, sitting in the darkness, the storm seemed suddenly quieter.

XXIII

When he woke up, the ship was rocking Cadmus slowly from side to side, like a mother with her child. Water was still dribbling through the seams between the old and new timbers, the crew were endlessly bailing, but it remained afloat. Just.

Tog was standing next to him, shaking his shoulder.

'Cadmus! Wake up! Come and see!'

She didn't wait for him, but ran back up the steps into the daylight. He rolled off his bench and followed her up on to the deck.

The sail was in tatters overhead, and the boat was strewn with debris. It was a floating shipwreck. Tog was leaning over the rail around the ship. Her mass of blonde hair blew crazily around her ears, and the waves threw spray into her closed eyes.

In front of them were miles of colossal white cliffs, topped with green so vivid it made Cadmus's eyes hurt. The weather had cleared, and the sky was not one he had seen before. Tufts and whorls of cloud broke and merged and broke again, giving glimpses of pale blue beyond. The spring sun came and went, and the cliffs shimmered in its cold light, higher than any he had seen in Italy or Greece.

'Britannia,' he said.

She turned and gave a wide smile.

'I know these cliffs,' she said. 'My grandfather conquered some of these lands. If we continue around this headland we'll enter the mouth of the river, and that'll take us into Catuvellauni territory. I know where to go from there.'

The *Argo* drifted towards the beaches, its crew staring open-mouthed at this new and strange land. As the cliffs rose and fell and crumbled in places, they were given tantalizing glimpses of the mysterious world beyond, lush and green and swollen with rainfall. Then, as suddenly as it had been revealed, the clouds massed ranks and the sun began to sink and the island was lost in shadow.

'What's he doing?' said Tog, pointing to the front of the ship. The priest, Thestor, wasn't looking at the land but into the air high above him.

'He's reading the skies,' Cadmus explained. 'Looking for omens in the flight of birds.'

Just as he said this a pair of white gulls flew west of the mast, and Thestor gave a shout. He went and spoke to Thoas at the helm, and Thoas bellowed his orders.

'To the oars, men!'

The *heroidai* went noisily below decks and the oars appeared from the sides of the *Argo* like the legs of a spider. As they swept the sea, Thoas pulled hard on the new steering paddle, and the ship began to crawl slowly in the opposite direction. Tog frowned and ran to the back, followed by Cadmus and Orthus.

'What are you doing?' she demanded.

'We have drifted too far to the east. But Apollo has shown us the way. The fleece lies to the west and the north.'

'But my home is east.'

Thoas just looked at her with disinterest and strained on the tiller again.

'We are not here to take you home.'

'Then I'm going,' said Tog defiantly.

'If you wish,' said Thoas. 'I will not stop you. We have no need of you.'

'Is that so? Well, good luck talking to the druids without me. Good luck with the local tribes. Good luck finding your way through the forests and the marshes.' She brought herself closer to him. 'You are far from home,' she said, in a voice that made Cadmus's hairs stand on end. 'Your gods hold no power here.'

Thoas ignored her and set his eyes on the horizon. Tog turned to Cadmus.

'Are you coming?' she said.

'Coming?'

'If you really want to find your special blanket, you need to be with me, not them.'

'But . . . how . . .'

'Don't listen to her, boy. You are surrounded by the blood of the heroes. We are the only ones who can rightfully claim the Golden Fleece. Stay with us and you will be honoured to the heavens.'

Tog already had a foot on the balustrade of the ship. Cadmus looked around. The few *heroidai* who weren't rowing were watching the scene unfold.

'I can't . . .' he began.

Tog looked a little disappointed, but no less determined. He watched her tucking her mouse into the inside of her tunic.

'That's all right,' she said. 'I understand.'

Before Cadmus could say another word, she dived from the side of the boat into the white water churned by the oars.

Cadmus watched her blonde head disappear beneath the waves and reappear, darker, in the ship's wake. The cliffs were perhaps two hundred feet away. He had no doubt she could make the distance easily.

He needed more time to think. Always thinking, never just doing. Same old Cadmus.

'We are better without her,' said Thoas. 'Athena has guided your decision well.'

Cadmus looked at Tog, paddling to shore so steadily she looked almost lazy. She seemed to draw him with her on an invisible thread. No more thinking, then.

'Sorry,' he said to Thoas. 'I'm going to take my chances with her.' Then he turned to Orthus. 'I hope you're a better swimmer than me.'

He went to the edge of the boat, held his nose, and jumped.

A calm, yellow light. The ground cold, gritty, but not uncomfortable after so long sitting and sleeping on a wooden bench. A fine rain, like a mist, tickling the skin.

Cadmus propped himself up on one elbow, took a deep breath, choked, gagged, and was violently sick on the sand. He collapsed again into the shallow pool of water beneath him, which was slightly warm from the heat of his body.

He took a few more tentative breaths, keeping his

eyes tightly shut. There was a tang of salt and seaweed that made his nose sting.

He sat up again. His head spun for a moment, and then stopped. He opened his eyes.

'You might not be able to swim,' said a voice, 'but at least you float.'

Tog cast a long shadow over him. He shielded his eyes against the low sun and saw her standing a little to one side, a bedraggled-looking Orthus at her feet. Cadmus coughed again and spat a mouthful of seawater on to the sand.

'What happened?'

'I wish you'd said you were coming. I had to swim back and fish you out.'

'Oh. Sorry.'

'No. You made the right choice.'

The top of her hair twitched, and her mouse peered out of a thick blonde nest.

'He made it!' Cadmus exclaimed.

Tog nodded. 'He got a bit wet,' she said. 'I'm trying to dry him out.'

He looked out to sea. 'Where's the *Argo*?'

'Gone.'

That made Cadmus feel strangely tense. If the *heroidai* found the fleece first, it wouldn't matter. Keeping it out of Nero's hands was the important thing . . .

Only it *did* matter. After all he had been through, he thought that he deserved to find it first. He wanted to see it, to hold it, to know the truth of it. Not just wanted to. Needed to.

'Come on,' she said. 'I know where we are. If we can get ourselves some horses we can be at my village tomorrow.'

Cadmus wondered where Tullus was at this exact moment. They had been at sea for thirty-five days, unless he had miscounted – which was, in fact, highly likely. But for all their misfortune, they had been faster than he had predicted. If Tullus's group had suffered any setbacks of their own, there was a good chance Cadmus and Tog were ahead of them. For the *heroidai*, sailing around the west of Britannia would be hard work, especially given the state of the *Argo*.

He had already come further than he ever expected. Britannia was beneath his feet. He had a guide. He might just make it, with Tog's help. The glimmer of hope was a new and unusual feeling.

At the top of the cliffs the air was fresher and greener. Tog set off across the grass towards some thick woodland, looking taller and more upright than ever now she was in her own territory. Cadmus still felt weak and nauseous from his time at sea, but she never let up the pace. She reached the woods and disappeared into the sodden darkness, but Cadmus and Orthus loitered for a moment on the edges, peering among the dripping branches.

'What's wrong?' Tog called back to him. 'They're just trees.'

But they weren't *just* trees. These were larger and older than any Cadmus had ever seen, their cracked and moss-covered bark knotted into faces that seemed to watch them as they passed. Things moved in the undergrowth and the canopy that he had no names for. He could well understand why the first Romans to land here believed Britannia was an island of monsters.

They walked on, taking deep lungfuls of peaty air. It couldn't have been further from the atmosphere of Athens and Corinth, which scoured the throat with dust and heat. Cadmus began to understand what Tog had been talking about, all those weeks ago, when they walked among the tombs of the Via Appia. The woods were alive.

Every now and again Tog would stop, prod the ground, inspect the undergrowth. Sometimes she put a finger to her mouth and tasted the soil. Then she would point and set off in a new direction.

When they emerged from the trees they were faced with a rolling meadow. Perhaps a dozen horses were cropping the long grass.

'*There* you are,' said Tog, apparently to the horses.

She turned to Cadmus. 'Wait here.'

Even after all her feats of strength and endurance, watching Tog approach and tame one of the horses was a wonder to behold. She selected a shaggy-looking brown mare and followed it at a respectful distance. She spoke to it softly, making several laps of the meadow, stepping gradually closer each time. By the time she was finished, the horse let her place a hand on its long nose, and she effortlessly leapt up on to its back.

She trotted back to Cadmus and extended a hand.

'Is it . . . safe?' he said.

'She's not wild. Some tribes let their horses go when they get old. But she's got good spirit. She'll see us through.'

Tog pulled Cadmus up and sat him behind her. He held on to her waist, his mouth and nose full of the smell of her hair and her sweat. He was nervous in a way he couldn't explain. Pleasantly nervous.

'Where are we going?' he asked.

'North,' she said. 'Londinion.'

XXIV

The next day, when the sun had almost completed its course across the sky, they found themselves standing on the south bank of the River Tamesis. On the other side of the broad, brown flood was 'Londinion' – Londinium, as Cadmus knew it.

'This is the only bridge across for miles,' Tog said. 'I wanted to avoid the Roman towns, but we'll have to pass through to get to my home.'

'Is it much further?' asked Cadmus, bleary with tiredness. His thighs had been rubbed raw. He wondered if he'd ever walk again.

'No,' said Tog. 'Stop complaining.'

'I'm just thinking of the fleece . . .'

'So am I. My family will be able to help you. Give you provisions, directions. Be patient.'

Across the bridge, the town was in bad shape. It was laid out in a far more orderly way than Rome or Athens, with a simple grid of wide and straight streets, but half of the buildings were still under construction and in places there were piles of burnt wood and rubble. The whole place seemed to rattle when the wind blew through it.

'Who did this?' Tog asked.

'Your hero. Boudicca. She destroyed the whole town.'

Tog smiled.

Inside the walls, they dismounted. They made a strange pair – Tog leading her horse, Cadmus leading his dog – and there were more than a few curious looks from the passers-by.

Londinium's forum was busy but looked as decrepit as the rest of the town. In its current state it was little more than a large square of bare earth, with long wooden shelters built along three sides. Most of the stalls were selling wares imported from the rest of the empire, and groups of pinched and cold-looking Romans wandered the marketplace looking to buy a piece of home – jars of wine, sacks of olives and figs, fine and colourful fabrics. A pair of soldiers surveyed the square from the corner, one of them sniffing incessantly.

'So much for the glory of Rome,' muttered Cadmus.

Tog didn't reply. She was staring at one of the legionaries. And he was staring back.

'Come on, Tog,' he said. 'We don't want to make a scene here.'

The soldier said something to his companion – he of the runny nose – and then came over to Tog.

He planted his feet in front of her. They looked each other over. Then Tog punched him squarely in the face.

The Romans doing their shopping gasped and clutched their togas to their chests; a handful of Britons laughed. The man fell to the floor, helmet askew, holding his nose and crying out. Tog was shouting too, but neither of them made sounds that were Greek or Roman. They were both speaking in Britonnic.

Meanwhile, the other legionary had dashed forward and pointed his sword at Tog's throat. She knocked it from his hand and pushed him away as though swatting at a bothersome child. Orthus barked and pranced. The horse whinnied and reared, until Tog put a hand on her mane to calm her.

The legionary with the bloodied nose got to his feet. They continued to talk in that lilting voice that Tog used to speak to her mouse, animated but no longer angry, it seemed. The other soldier looked between the two of them in confusion, and then at Cadmus. The Roman shoppers stared at the two pairs, fright turned to fascination.

Cadmus was totally bewildered.

Tog's mood seemed to change. Her face turned stony. She spoke less and less, until it was the legionary doing all of the talking. She began shaking her head, and then she suddenly jumped up on to her horse. She would have left without Cadmus, he was sure of it, had he not grabbed hold of her calf and thrown himself over the horse's rump like an empty sack.

His nostrils were filled with the strong, slightly sweet smell of the animal's hide, and its body was hot beneath his. He turned to see if the soldiers were in pursuit, but the world was all askew, bouncing and rattling in time with the horse's hooves. Tog rode as fast as she could right through the centre of the town, Orthus bounding alongside them, men and women shouting and scattering in their path.

They raced out of a gate in the north wall and took a Roman road that carved through a thick forest. Cadmus gradually righted himself and put his arms around Tog. She was still muttering something in her own tongue, and Cadmus could hear something in her voice that had never been there, not once since he had known her. She was scared.

'Can you slow down?'

She didn't reply.

'What did the soldier say?'

Still nothing.

At a point on the road that seemed significant only to her, Tog dismounted and ran into the trees. Orthus ran with her excitedly, misjudging the mood of the situation; Cadmus trailed behind, tripped by roots and slapped in the face with wet branches.

'Tog? Where are we going?'

She didn't answer. Cadmus had never seen her really stretch her legs, and by the gods she *flew*, over the earth and over the undergrowth and leaving not a single leaf broken by her footfall. He nearly lost her several times, and was only prompted in the right direction by Orthus's barking.

He finally caught up with her in a clearing. There was an earthwork at its centre. It was the perfect site for a settlement. Only there was no settlement.

On top of the hill the ground was completely charred, and he could see the low circles of ash that had once been roundhouses. There were the blackened remains of a loom sticking out of the mud, and a few pieces of furniture that had not been fully consumed by flames. There was no sign it had ever been lived in. The place had been burnt to the ground.

Tog walked slowly from one end of the village to the other. Then she turned and came face to face with Cadmus.

'It's all gone,' she said. 'After everything I've been through. There's nothing left.'

The sun was setting now, a fierce orange globe behind the clouds. The wind had picked up too, and blew Tog's hair around her. She had a face as grim as the Furies.

'I'm sorry,' said Cadmus. It sounded so feeble. 'It must have happened after your rebellion. After Boudicca. The Romans were . . . uncompromising in their reprisals.'

'Smaller words, Cadmus.'

He swallowed. 'They punished your people. Badly.'

She looked out over the golden treetops and took several deep, steadying breaths.

'My aunt and uncle lived there,' she said, pointing to a mound of charred wood. 'My uncle's forge was on the far side. And this was where I played with my cousin. We used to roll down the hill.'

'Maybe your family got out?'

'No. He said my aunt and uncle were killed.'

'Who said?'

'The soldier.'

'How did he know?'

She looked at him squarely, and then spat on the

ground. 'Because he was my cousin.'

Cadmus didn't know what to say. It wasn't a surprise to him. It was common for the Roman army to accept auxiliaries from the peoples they captured. In fact, it was key to keeping order, and minimizing chances of rebellion. But for Tog to see him in the uniform of her oppressors . . .

'We can't judge him,' he said. 'War always gives us difficult choices.'

'I can judge him,' Tog said bitterly. 'And I will. We used to talk *all the time* about fighting off the Romans. He joined Boudicca's rebellion with me. And now he's with the enemy.'

'He may have had no choice about joining the army,' said Cadmus. 'Remember what you told me on the boat? Sometimes Fate deals you things you cannot avoid.'

'He had a choice.' She spat again. '*The pay is good.* That was his defence! Money!'

'Maybe we can look around. Go back to Londinium, see if there are any more of your people who survived. Make peace with your cousin.'

'No,' she said. 'There's nothing to be done here.' She started walking down the slope again. 'We should get moving. We should find the fleece.'

'Oh.' Cadmus hadn't been expecting that. He found himself lost for words again. He caught up with her at the edge of the trees. 'Are you sure?'

'Yes. And when we have found it, I get to keep it.'

Cadmus frowned. 'You?'

'If it is as powerful as everyone says, then my people need it more than any Romans.'

'Um. I'm not sure I can—'

'That's the deal. I'll continue to help you, in return for the fleece. Otherwise you're on your own.'

Cadmus thought for a moment. He hadn't fully considered what would happen to the Golden Fleece if they actually found it. No doubt the *heroidai* would stake their claim to it. Eriopis too, probably. For his own part, he wanted to *see* the artefact, and he wanted to stop Nero from having it, but he wasn't sure he wanted to keep it. If he did he would be running for the rest of his life.

Perhaps this was the perfect solution. The fleece would be removed to the furthest reaches of the empire, perhaps out of the empire entirely, in the hands of an unknown British girl. There would be no way of tracking it. And maybe, after all she had suffered, Tog really did deserve whatever blessings it bestowed upon the owner.

Besides, he didn't really have a choice. He needed her.

'Agreed.'

'You swear?'

'I swear. By my gods and yours.'

He held out his right hand. She shook it so firmly he thought his arm might break.

XXV

They rode for a week, sleeping in caves and under fallen trees and in the dens of animals. Tog taught him how to hunt for their food; how to skin, gut and butcher an animal; how to build a camp and make a fire; how to find herbs and plants to help them sleep, to soothe scratches and burns, to settle their stomachs when the water was not as fresh as it should have been. She even let him take control of the horse for some of the way.

They didn't follow any of the Roman roads but wound through fens and forests and streams that Tog seemed to navigate by smell. They didn't see another soul. While they rode those ancient green paths, Cadmus could believe they were the only two human beings left in the world.

On the seventh day since leaving Londinium, they emerged from among the trees to see a broad estuary, slate-grey and flat, broken here and there by sharp, white wave-peaks. They could smell the sea. A flock of gulls was sitting calmly amidst the pebbles, and Orthus wasted no time in racing down the shore and scaring them all into flight.

'There,' said Tog, pointing to the other bank. 'That's it.'

'Mona?' said Cadmus.

She nodded.

They dismounted from the horse, and Cadmus went to the water's edge. He wet his finger and tasted it. Sure enough, the water was salty.

The island – although it didn't look like an island from where they were standing – was low and thinly wooded, like the terrain they had just passed through. Cadmus had been expecting high cliffs and a mountainous interior, snarled with strange trees and wild animals, but in fact Mona seemed quiet and nondescript. All along that grey shoreline there was evidence of the Roman invasion – remains of cook-fires, broken spears and shields, scraps of cloth and leather and abandoned sandals, weathered by the three intervening winters. The failing sun contributed to the feeling of emptiness and abandonment.

Cadmus felt a chill in his marrow, and it was not simply from the cold sea air.

The tide was low enough for them to ford the inlet with their horse, and Orthus seemed more than happy to swim. As they rode west across the island, they didn't have to look hard to see more signs of Roman devastation. The whole place seemed frozen in time at the point of the Romans' departure, now nearly three years ago. Copses and groves had been hewn or burnt to the ground; the remains of settlements, reduced to uneven piles of ash, could be seen on higher ground; a pyre for mass cremation was heaped up in a hollow, but whether it was for Romans or Britons Cadmus didn't know. The flatness of the island only made it seem more barren. There were no hills to make an obstacle to the wind, and it howled and whispered like the ghosts of those who had lived and died here.

Tog pulled their horse up and surveyed the land.

'Look at what they did,' she said. 'So much death.'

Cadmus's heart had sunk too. If all the inhabitants really had been killed, who was going to point them to the tomb? They could hardly scour the entire island. A grove of oak, a crown of stone . . . It could be anywhere.

'There must be *somebody* here,' he muttered.

She squinted at the horizon and pointed suddenly.

'Look. Smoke.'

That wasn't necessarily good news, Cadmus thought, but she had already spurred them onwards.

The horse cantered up a gentle slope, until they found themselves looking down on a grove of oak filling a hollow. A little to one side, arranged into neat rows, was a Roman camp. The smoke was coming from the soldiers' cook-fires.

'We're too late,' said Cadmus. Of course they were too late. Why would he have expected anything different?

'Are you sure they're the emperor's men?'

'Who else would they be?'

They had seen no signs of the *Argo* or the *heroidai* on their ride across the island. They were on their own. He wondered if Tullus was down there somewhere. That would at least give him some consolation, knowing that his master was safe.

Orthus suddenly pricked up his ears, nose quivering. He looked at the camp for a moment, then raced off down the ridge.

'Where's he going?' said Tog.

Cadmus shrugged. The dog hadn't left his side in weeks. It seemed odd that he would abandon Cadmus now, after all they had been through, in their hour of need. Then he realized: there was only one other person who Orthus showed greater loyalty towards.

'I think I know,' Cadmus said. 'Follow him. Quietly.'

They skirted the oak woods until they reached the fringes of the encampment. It was still under construction – a temporary, marching camp – but it was already surrounded by sharp wooden stakes and watched over by several pairs of legionaries. Cadmus could hear the gruff voices of the soldiers within and the dull, wet thud of axes on new timber.

Before they came within sight of the sentries, Orthus slipped into the trees, stopping occasionally to let Cadmus and Tog catch up. When they reached the far side of the camp they found a baggage train being unloaded. At the front were a pair of rather more comfortable *carpenta*, and at the rear was a wagon that was hardly more than a cage on wheels. The dog waited until the slaves and the soldiers had left with their equipment, and then pointed his keen-scented nose towards the mobile prison. Cadmus and Tog kept low and followed, hidden by the long shadows of the evening.

'Hello, old friend,' said a voice like the wind in the trees. A thin white hand emerged from the cage and stroked Orthus's head.

Cadmus put his fingers to the wooden bars of the cage and felt something cold and smooth constrict around his wrist. Every part of him wanted to scream out in terror, but he bit his lip for fear that he would bring the whole camp down on them.

It was a snake. The same snake that Nero had hurled into the grass beside Cadmus when he was hiding in the ruins of the farmhouse. Somehow it had found its way back to its mistress.

'Thank you for looking after him,' said the priestess. 'I knew you would come back. I knew I wasn't mistaken.'

Tog was staring at her in disbelief.

'She looks like a druid,' she said, not half as quietly as Cadmus would have liked.

'Some would say I am different only in name,' said the priestess. 'Medea taught the druids their first rites when she fled here. Two streams from the same fountainhead.'

So it was true. Medea was buried here. And Cadmus's hunch had been right: there *was* a connection between her and the druids. His heart thumped uncomfortably, excitement mounting on fear mounting on plain old exhaustion. Things were connecting. Things were making sense. The shadows of myth and history retreated before him.

'Is the grave nearby?'

'Very near.'

'And have they found the fleece?'

'No,' she said. 'There is a delay. They are scared to enter the grove. The old man, he has put such fear into the Romans.'

Another rush of excitement.

'Which old man? Do you mean my master? Is Tullus here?'

'He has told them of the trials within. Traps. Deadly sorcery.'

Cadmus laughed. *Well done, Tullus. What a good idea, to play upon Nero's superstitions.*

'You will pass through them untouched, though,' she said. 'I have seen it.'

He looked at Tog, then back at the priestess. 'Wait,' he said slowly. 'You mean there really are traps?'

'Oh, yes, yes, yes.' Eriopis swayed where she sat, and then flung herself against the bars suddenly. 'Fearsome trials await you, just as they did Jason. But you know this. Hmmm. That is why you are here, is it not? You heard the Hecate's words, when we last met.'

Something vast began to shift in Cadmus's thoughts. Another retreating shadow. A misunderstanding so huge he could only just begin to discern its edges.

'What do you mean?'

She pressed her blindfolded face through the gap in the lattice. Cadmus could feel the snake tightening itself around his hand even further. 'The Golden Fleece belongs to you,' she said.

'But ... Nero ... the oracle ...'

'The oracle was for you, boy, not Nero. The goddess knew you were listening. The pig emperor isn't even here.' She pointed a slender finger at him. 'You were the one who was meant to come here. You are the one who will make his way through the trials of Medea's tomb. You are the one who will lay eyes upon her body and claim your inheritance.'

Cadmus stared at her dumbly. She whispered something he couldn't quite hear, and her snake slithered back into the cage with her.

'These trials . . .' he began.

There was the sound of heavy footsteps and raucous laughter from the entrance to the camp. The soldiers were returning to the baggage train.

'I cannot say any more,' Eriopis said. She grabbed him by his wrist. 'Go quickly. Go lightly. And go alone.'

Cadmus made his way into the darkness of the sacred grove, following Tog. He could see why the legionaries were afraid to enter. There was a strange energy about the place. The noises of the camp seemed to have disappeared completely, but he thought he heard voices among the trees, whispering the priestess's words back to him. *Go quickly. Go lightly. Go alone.* He turned to Orthus for reassurance, but the dog was nowhere to be seen.

While he was lost in his thoughts he wasn't watching where he was putting his feet, and abruptly tripped over a tree stump. He looked up from where he lay prone in the soil and saw several more ahead, misshapen and bulbous.

'We must be close,' said Tog from up front. 'The druids put these here.'

Cadmus squinted in the gloom. Only when he got to his feet and put a hand on one of them did he discover what they really were. He jerked back like he'd stuck his hand in a fire.

They were skulls. Human skulls, stacked on top of each other and pierced through with a stake. There were more of them, leading in a line towards the centre of the grove. When he looked up he saw bones suspended from the boughs of the oak trees, and small human figures made from twigs and grass hung alongside them.

More dark shapes loomed beyond the woods, monumental things with corners and hard edges. They came to a clearing in the trees and found stones, at least three times as tall as Cadmus was, carved into rectangular slabs and arranged in a circle. On top of these, more slabs had been laid horizontally, and there were more skulls and bones tucked into alcoves in the rock. In the centre of the circle was some form of altar, flat and circular like a millstone. Here was one druid shrine, it seemed, that the Romans hadn't destroyed.

It was unnaturally quiet in the centre. The ashes on the altar were cold and damp.

On the other side of the clearing, beyond one of the stone arches, was a flight of shallow, uneven steps leading to a narrow crevasse. At the bottom was the mouth of a cave, a vertical slash like a wound in the rocks. Cadmus went to the top of the steps and stared into the chasm. The sun was beneath the sea now, and the druid shrine was cloaked in purple twilight. The cave was darker still. A deep, living blackness.

'This must be it.'

'Let me go first,' said Tog.

'No,' Cadmus said, more firmly than he had been expecting. 'She said I had to go alone. I'm not putting you in any more danger. I'll need a lookout anyway.'

Tog made a face that didn't fill him with confidence. He went to one of the strange hanging totems, yanked one of the bones free and wrapped it in some material torn from his cloak. Then he collected some tinder and returned to the mouth of the cave.

'Do you remember what my master looks like?' he said to Tog.

'From the dinner? I think so. Old. No hair.'

'That's close enough,' said Cadmus with a sad smile.

'Why?'

'If things go wrong and I don't come back, go and find him. I want him to know what happened.'

Tog nodded.

'Thank you.' He looked into the abyss. '*Audentis fortuna iuvat*,' he muttered, and before Tog could ask what he meant, he disappeared under the earth.

XXVI

Stepping into the cave felt like sinking to the bottom of a deep, cold lake.

Once inside, Cadmus set about lighting a small fire with flints, as Tog had shown him. From this he lit the material he had wrapped around the end of the bone to make a torch. Its light licked feebly over the walls of the cave. The jagged and broken shapes of the rock passed just over his head, glistening with moisture, and his breath echoed back at him from the walls. Even if Tog had been able to come with him, Cadmus thought, there was a good chance she wouldn't have fitted through this narrow fissure in the earth.

Go quickly. Go lightly. Go alone.

All the things that Eriopis had said swarmed in the

darkness with him. What if she was right, and Fate had always been pulling him towards this point, to this corner of the earth, to this dark, oppressive tomb? What if his missing sandal really had marked him out as the inheritor of the fleece? What if he'd had no choice over anything in his life, since the day he was abandoned by his parents? That was a bleak thought.

The tunnel opened up. The shapes of the rocks changed. They no longer looked natural and chaotic, but carved and ordered. Cadmus caught a glimpse of four huge, horned heads, grotesque in the firelight. He cried out, dropping the torch and cowering in the wet sand.

A hero indeed.

When he heard nothing but the trickle of moisture from the rocks and the hiss of the flames on the floor, he retrieved the torch and held it up to what he had seen.

They were carved from the cave wall, four colossal bulls, eyes rolling and mouths gaping in terror and exhaustion. They towered above him, so tall that Cadmus could only reach up to touch their open mouths when he was on tiptoes. When he did, something black came off on his fingers. They were coated in soot.

In the story of the Argonauts, Jason's first challenge had been to master King Aeëtes's fire-breathing cattle and use them to plough one of his fields. Here they were again, carved with exquisite menace into the wall of the chamber. It seemed fire had passed from the statues' lips at some point, but their throats had long since gone cold. He looked around the cave to see if there was some sort of trigger he had missed. The floor was just sand, with a few uneven rocks making a path towards another cleft in the cave wall. Nothing to trip on, nothing concealed under the earth. A strange trial, if that was what it was. Or perhaps it was simply so old that it no longer worked.

Eager to escape from under the bulls' wild eyes, he picked his way over the path on tiptoes and reached the entrance to the next passageway. Nothing happened. That didn't make him feel any better. He *wanted* something to happen. His body was as tense as a primed catapult.

He felt his way along the damp rocks and into the next chamber. At first he thought it was empty, but as he came forward the flames of the torch danced off something laid out in rows on the floor. The sight was somehow more unsettling than the monstrous statues of the last chamber. Hundreds of helmets, half-buried in the sand. Their plumes had mostly rotted, and the bronze was patched with dull green, but they filled the entire chamber from one wall to the other.

Cadmus tentatively nudged one of them with his

foot. There was a head beneath it. The helmet belonged to a man, buried standing upright, as far as his empty eye sockets. When he looked closer, Cadmus saw that next to each head was the very tip of a spear, protruding from the earth.

A phalanx of soldiers, born from the earth. In the story, Jason had defeated these men by throwing a rock among them and causing such confusion that they turned upon themselves. But the warriors in front of Cadmus were dead and buried and perfectly still. Again he scanned the cave for something he hadn't seen, but there was no clue as to the dead men's purpose.

Ahead the walls narrowed. A cold, sour-smelling draught passed from one end of the cave, whispering of the secrets yet to be found. He moved carefully among the helmets and the spearheads and squeezed through the fissure into the third chamber.

This was where the path ended. It was smaller than the previous two rooms. In the centre was a deep stone sarcophagus, covered with intricately engraved symbols and lines of text that seemed to be some ancient, corrupted form of Doric Greek. Hanging above it, only visible when he brought the torch into the middle of the chamber, was a huge serpentine head, fangs bared, eyes shining with something that seemed more alive than stone or marble.

Cadmus had seen pictures of Jason's final trial, reproduced on urns and frescoes. He could clearly remember the image of a man's torso hanging limply from the snake's mouth while Athena looked on. The snake here was easily large enough to swallow a man.

He came around the side of the coffin, one eye on the gaping maw above him, and tried to read the inscriptions carved into the stone. He set the torch in the earth and got down on his hands and knees. Some of the words were indecipherable, but he understood enough.

It was the story of Medea's life, but it bore little resemblance to the myths he had learnt growing up. He scanned over the lines and matched the words he recognized with the pictures above. Here she was, spurned by Jason and hated by his people. Here she was, reclaiming her 'dowry' after Jason's betrayal, and taking the Golden Fleece for her own. Here she was, not murdering her children, but escaping with them to Athens. The final piece of the inscription told of how she had exiled herself to the edge of the world, and how the Golden Fleece 'resided for ever with her remains'.

He lingered on that last word for a moment, then stood up and looked over the huge stone box. If her remains were inside, the fleece would be with them.

He felt for the edges of the sarcophagus's lid,

jammed his fingers underneath, and pulled. It was unspeakably heavy. He strained until his fingertips were white and raw, but it wouldn't move.

Just as he collapsed from the effort, there was a noise from one of the other chambers. A voice, perhaps, but so distant and distorted he couldn't tell if it was man or woman or animal. Had Tog followed him inside? Or Orthus? Perhaps it was his own voice, echoing back at him? He sat on the damp ground and listened, heart trembling with more than just exhaustion.

The cave was silent again.

Cadmus got to his feet and set to his task once more. The sooner he got the sarcophagus open, the sooner he could escape this grim underworld. He gritted his teeth and hauled with all of his body-weight, but the thick stone lid must have been at least two or three times as heavy as him. He strained until he was deafened by the blood in his ears. Then, just as his limbs felt ready to burst, it moved.

Slowly, bit by grinding bit, he shifted the slab to one side. It teetered on the edge for a moment and fell to the earth with a thud. The sarcophagus exhaled. A cloud arose from inside, thick with dust and incense. There was no smell of rot. It was the smell of the temple, of the shrine, not of the grave.

He peered into its depths.

The body that lay before him seemed to be of a woman who had died only a few hours earlier. In fact, it hardly looked like she had died at all. Her skin was dove-white, and just as soft, plump, even; by contrast, her hair was black as Hades, thick and unbound. The resemblance to Eriopis was easy to see. Even her robes looked similar, shrouded as she was in layers of vivid crimson, and she wore the same assortment of golden pendants and bracelets.

It was true. All of it.

As he stared, he was drawn to Medea's eyes. They were wide open. In the centre of the left eye there seemed to be a circle of amber, or gold, or newly beaten bronze. It shone with a light of its own. His thoughts jarred. He had seen those eyes a thousand times. They were his own.

Time seemed to stop. Various half-conceived notions came together, theories formed and evaporated. He was brought back to himself by another echo from the chamber behind him. A voice, he was sure of it. Footsteps too.

Then there was a *whoosh* that sounded like the squalls he had endured on the *Argo*. Shrieks and cries. A crackling like a bonfire catching light. What had happened? What if he was trapped?

Cadmus had forgotten why he had come to the grave in the first place. The Golden Fleece. It was nowhere to be seen. He ran his hands along the inside of the sarcophagus. Nothing. He tried, gingerly, to feel beneath Medea's body, but at the slightest touch her perfectly preserved form collapsed into dust and only her faded robes and tarnished jewellery remained in the bottom of the casket. It was as though she had never been there at all.

The voices grew louder. They were in the next chamber along now. There was another unexpected sound – the grind of metal on rusted metal, followed by a crash of sand, like a wave hitting the shore. What was *happening* back there?

There was nowhere for Cadmus to go. The walls of the cave were completely smooth, no nooks or crannies to hide in. Featureless, with the exception of the stone snake and its giant fanged head.

The footsteps came closer. Twenty or more, he estimated.

Cadmus did the only thing he could. He extinguished his torch and climbed up on to the edge of the sarcophagus. From there he could just reach the neck of the snake, protruding like a tree trunk from the rocks. He swung himself up on to its back, then shimmied up to its head. There he waited, listening to his heartbeat, trying not to cough.

Torchlight licked over the cave walls, followed by shadows of men. He could hear their breath. There was a pained wheezing from one of the intruders, a gurgling of fluid-filled lungs. Erratic, shuffling steps. Cadmus knew who it was even before his bent silhouette emerged from the passageway.

Polydamas paused on the threshold of the chamber and leant heavily on his stick. Then he came forward a single step, and did the same. And again, and again. The soothsayer wasn't just tired, Cadmus thought. He was probing the ground for something.

After half a dozen paces, the stick knocked against something hard. Polydamas hissed and pushed down with all his weight. There was a dull *clunk*, like someone hitting two stones together.

Go quickly. Go lightly. Go alone.

Cadmus suddenly realized how he had passed through the trials of the tomb unscathed. There were traps set into the floor, and he was simply too light to set them off. A grown man would have triggered them. So would Tog. So would an average-sized boy of his age. Only the puniest of heroes could have made it through each chamber.

He was still grinning in the darkness when this last trap began to operate. A few moments after Polydamas had pressed on the stone, the snake's head began to shudder. Behind him, where the statue met the cave wall, the rock cracked and the statue began to sway like a felled tree. Cadmus's stomach flew up into his ribs as he tumbled down from his perch, clinging to the stone head. The huge fangs struck the ground right where Polydamas had pressed with his stick, sending up a cloud of dust on either side. The rest of the snake's body shattered and filled Medea's open sarcophagus with rubble.

Cadmus rolled forward and found himself at the feet of Polydamas. He looked up, spitting dirt. For the first time, he could see under the soothsayer's veil. The man's head looked like a walnut, or a swelling fungus, his wrinkles so deep and thick they almost covered his eyes completely.

The ancient creature smiled slowly. Cadmus thought he could *hear* the skin around his mouth creaking. Then he drew his familiar rattling breath, and extended his arm as though to help Cadmus up from the floor.

Cadmus ran, and collided head first with a vast, immovable body. One of the *heroidai* – not the real Sons of the Heroes, but Nero's imitations in their brightly coloured masks and armour. A thick pair of arms grasped him around the waist, and suddenly he was being carried back out of the cave, kicking and screaming like a wayward child.

XXVII

As he was dragged back to the world above, Cadmus passed through the other two chambers and saw that their traps had also been set off. In the second, the dead men had erupted out of the ground and now stood to attention in rows, weapons pointing at the ceiling. If he had been a little heavier, the rusted spearheads would have passed straight through him. The first chamber was now unbearably hot, and two of Nero's guards had removed their masks and were tending to burns. The bulls, it seemed, still worked perfectly.

The cool night air was a relief when they emerged from the mouth of the cave. The druids' shrine looked very different now. A detachment of Roman legionaries, perhaps as many as fifty, were standing in a semicircle around the altar. They were plainly ill at ease to be in such an unholy place. Some moved their lips in silent prayer.

There was no Tog. No Tullus either.

The giant pushed Cadmus towards a pair of the soldiers.

'Is this him?' one of them said. 'I thought we were here to butcher a few barbarians.'

The giant stared at him.

'Throw him in prison with the other one,' he said from behind his mask. 'The emperor wants him.'

For a moment it looked like the legionaries might disobey him, or at least offer a retort. But they just sighed, bound Cadmus's hands, and led him back through the grove. As they went, the trees seemed to lurch and writhe in the light of their torches.

'Since when do we take orders from gladiators?' one of them grumbled.

'Since now,' said the other. 'Don't complain, at least we're out of that place. Bloody horrible. Don't want to know what sorts of things happen in there, but I can guess.'

'Who's the runt, then?'

'Search me.'

'We haven't come all this way for *him*, have we?'

'I don't *know*.'

'Who are you, runt?' said the first one.

Cadmus played dumb.

'Oi! Who are you? What were you doing in that cave?'

'He's British, you idiot, he doesn't understand you.'

'Well, I wish someone would tell me what we're doing here. I'm frozen stiff. I need a proper meal. Biscuits for breakfast, biscuits for dinner. Last time I had a proper cup of wine we were in Rome.'

'You had wine last night.'

'I said proper wine. Italian stuff. Falernian.'

'As if you can afford Falernian.'

'What are you saying?'

And so it went on. It appeared the emperor had kept them all in the dark about their purpose in Mona. If he wasn't careful, he'd have a mutiny on his hands.

They led him through the camp, still arguing, to the same wooden cage in which Eriopis had been imprisoned. As they opened the door and threw him inside, he caught a glimpse of Orthus skulking around the other wagons. There was still no sign of Tog. Perhaps she had escaped. Perhaps something much, much worse had happened.

Eriopis sat upright, head thrown back as though sniffing the air. Cadmus watched her closely for a moment. She looked identical to the body he had seen in the sarcophagus. The legionaries wandered back to their tents, still grumbling, and took the light of their torches with them.

The priestess reached out and gently clasped his head in the darkness, as she had when they first met.

'Did you find the tomb?'

'Yes.'

'And you saw her?'

'I did.'

'And the Golden Fleece?'

Cadmus said nothing. Her nails pressed into his skin just a little more.

'Do you have it?'

'No.'

'Do *they* have it?'

'No. It wasn't there.'

Eriopis groaned.

'But . . . it has to be. You must have looked in the wrong place. I *saw* it. The Hecate showed me. The fleece was in your hands.'

'It must have been the fake you saw,' Cadmus suggested. 'The grave was empty. Apart from her.'

He was about to mention about Medea's eyes when a bright, orange blaze suddenly illuminated both of them. One of the tents on the far side of the camp had gone up in flames. Orthus started barking. Eriopis let go of Cadmus.

'What's happened?'

'Fire.'

Another tent began to burn, then another, then the commander's pavilion at the centre was alight. An accident? Perhaps the mutiny had started already. There were confused cries from the legionaries who were still in the camp. Men began running towards the fires with pails of water, and in a few moments the quarters nearest the grove were emptied of men.

Cadmus heard whinnying and an irregular thump of hooves. The silhouettes of a dozen horses galloped in front of him, their slender legs casting a strange and complex dance of shadows. Someone had released them, and they were fleeing from the flames in terror. They split and merged and split again like a flock of birds.

One of the Roman horses made its way towards the prison. There were two people in the saddle.

'Found him,' called a familiar voice.

Cadmus squinted against the glare of the fire.

'Tog?'

'This is him, isn't it?' she said. 'Old and bald?'

'*Master?*'

Clutching Tog around her waist was Tullus, his skinny neck protruding from a thick, fur-lined cloak. He managed a weak smile.

The wave of relief nearly overwhelmed Cadmus. He began laughing when Eriopis's cold hand clasped around his wrist again.

'Beware him,' she said.

'Who? Tullus?'

'I know him.' She sounded frightened. 'I remember now. He comes with murderers, through the flames.'

'Nonsense!' Cadmus tried to laugh again. 'This is my master. He's a good man.'

'I *know* him.' She let go of him and clasped her own head, as she often did. 'The flames . . . He comes through the flames . . .'

'I don't understand,' said Cadmus. 'Master?'

Tullus looked at his hands, then at Cadmus. Whatever he knew, words failed him.

Tog growled in exasperation. 'Are you finished? I am *trying* to rescue you all. Talk later.'

Behind them, the legionaries were still trying to bring the blaze under control. They hadn't noticed the prisoners escaping at the opposite end of the camp, but now more men were beginning to emerge from the woods, drawn away from the shrine by the sight and the sound of the fire.

Tog jumped down from her horse and approached the cage.

'It's only made of wood,' Cadmus said. 'You could break it. Like you broke Tullus's front door.'

His master looked up suddenly and spoke for the first time.

'You broke my front door . . . ?'

Tog threw her shoulder at the cage once, twice, three times. On the fourth try, two of the bars split. She and Cadmus worked together to loosen the others and made a hole large enough for Eriopis to climb out of. Just as Cadmus was helping her down to the ground, he heard another shout from the woods, different in tone and volume. Someone had spotted them.

'I'll take her on the other horse,' Tog said quickly. 'You ride with your master.'

'What?' Tullus spluttered. 'Cadmus can't ride a horse!'

'A few things have changed since we left Rome,' said Cadmus, climbing up into the saddle in front of him.

A handful of soldiers ignored the fire and charged them, swords drawn. Orthus met them head-on, barking and snapping at their legs and arms. Cadmus watched in horror as they took swings at the dog, but he leapt and ducked around their blades and held them at bay long enough to settle the horse.

'If we're going, we're going now!' shouted Tog.

'Wait!' said Tullus. 'I've just remembered! My notes!'

'It's too late,' said Cadmus. 'They'll be up in flames.' It pained him as much as Tullus to think of it. Years of work, gone in an instant.

His master protested, but Cadmus didn't listen to him. He wheeled his horse around, drove his heels into its flanks, and took off into the night.

XXVIII

They flew through the darkness, Tullus gripping Cadmus's waist a little too tightly and complaining frequently about the recklessness of his riding. But Cadmus didn't slow down. The shapes of two horses, four human beings and a dog flitted across the island under the light of a full moon. When they reached the straits between Mona and the mainland, Tog drew up her mount and stared over the water.

'The tide is in,' she said. 'We won't be able to cross.'

Cadmus spoke to Tullus over his shoulder. 'How did you get here? Is there a bridge?'

Tullus shook his head. 'We forded at low tide, but that was a long time ago. Even then, the water nearly swept the wagons away.'

'Then we're trapped.'

Tog thought for a moment. 'We should go as far as we can from the road and find somewhere to hide. I let all their horses go, so they'll be slow looking for us. We can cross in the early morning.' Without waiting for agreement, she turned around and set off along the shore.

They came to the western edge of the island, where the straits opened up to the sea. The full, bright moon was a blessing for finding their way, but also threatened to reveal them to anyone who came looking. Here they found a narrow path down to the beach and huddled in a cave among the cliffs.

They built a small fire, which struggled to produce anything apart from a steady stream of grimy smoke, but the embers glowed enough to reveal the faces of their bedraggled little band. Tog had taken one look at Eriopis's snake and clutched her mouse protectively to her chest. Eriopis had gone completely silent, and visibly winced whenever Tullus spoke. That was odd. What had she meant, back at the camp? Why would she think his master a murderer?

Tullus himself steepled his fingers and looked at nothing in particular.

'Well,' he said. 'Here we are.'

'Here we are,' Cadmus agreed.

In the silence, the hopelessness of the situation settled upon them like a cold, wet blanket.

'I can't believe you came all this way,' said Tullus.

'*I* can't believe I came all this way,' said Cadmus. 'For nothing.'

Tog looked up from her lap, where her mouse was scurrying in the sand. 'What do you mean?'

'The fleece,' he said. 'It wasn't there.'

Her face fell. 'Did someone get there before us?'

Cadmus thought about this. The moment he had touched Medea, she had turned to ash, so the tomb couldn't have been raided earlier. 'I don't think so. The body was undisturbed when I found it. More than that. It was perfectly preserved. *Unnaturally* preserved, I'd say.'

He looked at Eriopis, hoping she might offer some insight. But her face was a mask of confusion. The question that had been pounding the inside of his head since he'd left the tomb was now fighting its way out of him. That shining circle of gold rose before him again.

'I did find something, though,' he said.

The others leant into the dim glow of the fire, and suddenly Cadmus felt nervous.

'Her eyes,' he said.

Tullus and Tog waited quietly for him to elaborate. But the priestess gasped, suddenly brought to life.

'Eyes?' she said. 'What about her eyes?'

'They looked exactly like mine.'

Eriopis shook her head.

'No, no, no, no, no, no . . .'

'I'm telling you,' said Cadmus. 'I've never seen anyone with eyes the same colour as mine. One was dark. One sort of golden. It was like looking in a mirror.'

Eriopis groped blindly for him and grabbed his wrist in her thin, strong fingers.

'Ow! What are you doing?'

Something had changed. The priestess's breath was quick and trembling, and her lips moved in sudden spasms, as though she were mouthing silent words. Tullus got to his feet, unsure of what to do. Tog simply looked on, bemused.

'You never told me . . .' Eriopis said, and seized him by the front of his tunic.

'Let go! You're hurting me!'

'Look at me,' said Eriopis, as he struggled to free himself from the snares of her fingers. '*Look at me.*'

She let go of his wrists and thrust her fingers into her thick, dishevelled hair. Cadmus edged away from her. She began untying the fabric from around her head.

Very slowly she lowered the blindfold. Her eyelids were red and raw, he could see, and fluttered as though the smoke and the light pained her. But even so she drew herself closer to him, and to the flames. Then, for the first time, he saw what had been concealed all this time. They were just like Medea's. Just like his. One dark. One the colour of gold.

'She was descended from the Sun,' she said. 'We all carry a piece of him with us. An echo of his light.'

The fire spat in the darkness.

Cadmus hung his head dumbly. He could barely connect two coherent thoughts. So much information had been thrown at him he felt almost punch-drunk.

'So, what? Are we related?' he said. And then, looking again at her bizarre clothes and the snake coiled around her neck, he added: 'Distantly, I mean?'

'Not just related.'

No one had expected to hear Tullus speak. They all turned to look at him. He was smiling sadly. He had never looked older, Cadmus thought.

His master took a deep breath and spoke again: 'She is your sister.'

There was a moment's silence, broken only by the wet hiss of the embers. Cadmus looked from face to face to face. Then he burst out laughing.

'My *sister*?' He shook his head, and his laughter disappeared as soon as it had come. 'I know we all need cheering up, Master, but that kind of joke is in pretty poor taste.'

'It's not a joke, my boy.'

Cadmus had to close his eyes to try and stop his head from whirling.

'But . . . that's nonsense. How would you know? You'd never seen her before Athens.' A pause. 'Had you?'

Tullus's silence said a great deal.

'You knew I had a sister? You knew I had family and you didn't tell me?'

'I thought she was dead. I thought you were the only one left.'

'What do you *mean*?' Cadmus could feel his confusion turning to pure, hot anger. 'You told me I was abandoned on the side of the road! You said you knew nothing of my family!'

'I know,' said Tullus. 'Because the truth was too awful to even try and explain. I was going to tell you when we were in Nero's palace, because I knew I probably wouldn't get another chance. That was why I summoned you. But, as usual, I spent too long thinking and never got around to it. And now here we are, at the end of everything. It's too late for me to wait for the right time, or the right words.'

'The right words are the simplest, Master,' said Cadmus. 'That's what you always taught me.'

Tullus nodded once. 'Then I shall be plain and clear.'

He spent a while considering where to begin.

'Fourteen years ago,' he said, 'I was asked by the Emperor Claudius to find the Golden Fleece.'

'Claudius? He was looking for it too?'

'Oh, yes. The Sibylline prophecy has been known for decades. Every emperor has tried to get his hands on the fleece – in secret, at least, for fear of public mockery. At the time I was the most able scholar and mythographer in Rome, and I was delighted to accept the emperor's commission. I had a map, just like Silvanus did. The result of years of research. Decades, even. It directed me to a prophetess who lived outside Athens. The prophetess was your mother.'

A sound escaped Eriopis's lips, a murmur of fear relived. It seemed to strike Tullus's heart, and for a moment he closed his eyes and paused.

Cadmus didn't move, didn't speak, didn't blink. His every thought was bent on the old man's next words. Nothing else existed apart from their four souls, in this ring of firelight. Even Orthus was curiously still.

'Believe me – both of you – I approached her with all the respect and courtesy she deserved. You see, I knew of her lineage. I knew she was a descendant of Medea. But most importantly, I knew she had the Golden Fleece itself.'

'He's lying,' said Eriopis. 'Lying, lying, deceitful . . .'

'It is the truth. Your mother probably never told

you. You were only a very young child, and Cadmus here was a baby.'

'But the oracles . . . The goddess told me, the fleece resides with the remains of Medea.'

Cadmus remembered the inscription on Medea's tomb, and something clicked. '*Hoi loipoi*,' he said.

Tullus looked at him. There was a hint of a smile on his weary face.

'Go on,' he said.

'Those were the words on her sarcophagus. Everyone has misunderstood it. It doesn't mean "remains", like a body. It means "that which is left behind". Or rather, "*those* who are left behind". Her children. That means you, Eriopis.' Then he added, very quietly. 'And me.'

'Very good, Cadmus,' Tullus said. 'We'll make a scholar of you yet.'

It was a joke that Tullus had always made when they were at Rome, but now the words sounded foreign and unfamiliar. Sad, not funny. A memory of a past life Cadmus couldn't return to.

'My mother had the fleece, then?'

'She did. It had been passed down every generation since Medea herself.'

'I'm assuming she wasn't happy to just hand it over.'

'No,' said Tullus. 'I wanted to be civil with her. I respected her. But Claudius's men had other ideas.

– 313 –

They thought only of their reward. When your mother didn't give them answers, they threatened to burn her house down, with her children inside. And when she still refused, they went ahead and did it. I was too weak, too much of a coward to stop them.'

Tullus's eyes were shining with tears. He looked at Eriopis.

'Forgive me. I should never have come to the house. But I swear, by all the gods, it was never my intention to harm any of you. When they took your mother away, I stayed behind to try and save you. Both of you. I couldn't find you, my dear, but I heard Cadmus crying. His cradle was devoured by flames, but he – he was unharmed. Wrapped in his blanket. Cool to the touch.'

He looked at Cadmus meaningfully.

And that was when Cadmus saw the truth of it. It was like in the old heroic poems, when the gods remove the mortal veil from the hero's eyes, and showed them the world as it really was.

'It's been in my bedroom all this time, hasn't it?'

Nobody spoke for a few moments. Eriopis was open-mouthed. Tullus looked almost embarrassed. Tog was the one to break the silence. Cadmus's Britonnic hadn't improved much since he had met her, but he was fairly sure he knew when she was swearing.

'I thought it would be the last place anyone would look for it,' Tullus said in a hurry. 'And you deserved to keep it, as the last of Medea's descendants.'

'Why was I the last? Why couldn't you have returned it to my mother?'

He knew he answer before he had even asked the question. But he had to hear it, out loud.

'She died, Cadmus. In captivity. When I returned to Rome I stopped my research and put my efforts into raising you. It was the very least I could do. When Nero forced me into his service, I knew you had to stay behind. I wasn't going to put you in danger. And I certainly wasn't going to take you back to the ruins of your old house.'

They all sat in total silence. Words and tears now seemed a poor and tawdry currency.

'But why come all the way out here?' asked Cadmus, finding safe ground in practicalities.

'To lead them in the wrong direction! I'll admit, the fake had me confused for a while – I thought I had made a mistake, all these years. That was why we went to the library, boy. I needed to know if I had missed something. But once I knew it was counterfeit, I was sure of what I had to do. I encouraged Nero to make every mistake, pursue every misinterpretation. Because I knew every step was taking them further away from you, and keeping you out of harm's way.'

Cadmus stared at Tullus. Again he felt the slow simmer of anger in his stomach. The old man had known all along and had said nothing.

'Well, thank you for filling us in, Master,' he said. 'Your timing has been impeccable.'

'I tried to tell you in Nero's palace,' said Tullus. 'But I couldn't find the words. Then there was the dinner. I would have told you in the baths, but . . . you know what happened. Cadmus, I—'

But Cadmus was on his feet, walking away down the beach. The sea was a sheet of beaten silver under the moonlight. He looked out to the horizon, calmed by the steady *shush* of the waves. The heat of his anger faded. Away from their feeble fire he got very cold very quickly. He should have been happy, he thought. He had found his family. His sister. His master. The fleece. Why this hollowness, then?

A warm tongue rasped over his fingertips. He looked down and saw Orthus's grizzled head at his side.

'He always loved you.' Eriopis's voice floated over his shoulder from nowhere. 'He used to guard your cradle when you were a baby.'

Cadmus scratched Orthus behind his ears, but said nothing. What was there to say?

'I am ashamed,' said the priestess. 'A dog was able to see the truth, and I, a handmaiden of the Hecate, was blind to it. My own brother, hidden from me. I was wrong about everything.'

'Not everything,' he said. 'Back at the farmhouse you said the thing I was seeking was in Medea's grave. You were right about that. I found what I wanted. It just wasn't the fleece.'

He tried to smile. He was glad she couldn't see how forced it looked. They were silent. Under the moon, the sea spread veil after glittering veil over the sand.

'I wish—' She stopped short and chewed her lower lip.

'What?'

'No, it is blasphemous. A terrible thing to say.'

'Tell me.'

She lowered her voice. 'I wish I did not have my gift. I wish I had my old eyes. I wish I could see you, as you see me. Then I would have known straight away, the moment you came to the house.'

Cadmus looked at her, saw himself reflected in her pupils.

'Did you lose your sight in the fire?' he asked.

She nodded.

'How did you survive? Afterwards?'

'There is a group of men and women,' she said, 'who also claim descent from heroes. They knew of my mother's death and looked after me until I was old enough to look after myself. Which was not so old.'

Cadmus didn't need to ask who she meant. He couldn't believe it.

'The *heroidai*,' he said. 'I know them too. They brought me here. They never said anything about raising you.'

'It fills them with shame. They despise our family, Cadmus. Such ancient hatred – gods above! I have no doubt they only took me in because they hoped I would reveal the secrets of the Golden Fleece. But when I was older, I showed too much of our mother in me. I started hearing the Hecate, calling to me, always calling.' She trailed off for a moment. 'So they cast me out again. I followed the goddess's voice and I went to the only place I knew. I went home.'

'The house drew us both back,' said Cadmus.

He moved to hold her hand, but when he drew up next to her the snake slithered over his arm. He yelped in surprise and jumped away from her.

'What is it?' she said.

'Nothing,' he said. 'I—'

'What?' She sounded sadder this time.

'Nothing,' he said again.

His sister bowed her head. Cadmus stared at the sea. They may as well have been standing on opposite shores.

XXIX

At dawn, they saw that the waves had withdrawn, revealing an expanse of wet sand that sparkled in the sunrise. Tog was asleep and snoring. Eriopis sat upright, swaying slightly in the breeze. She was wearing her blindfold again, and it was impossible to tell if she was awake or not.

'The tide has gone down,' Tullus said quietly. 'We should try to cross again.'

'And then what?' said Cadmus. 'Do we have a plan?'

'Well, we, ah, have to get back to Rome somehow,' said his master. 'The fleece can't just stay in the house. We'll have to fetch it and find somewhere new to hide it. Oh, dear. Dear, dear. I'm not sure I can face another month on the road.'

'I'm not sure we can take the roads at all,' said Cadmus. 'They'll send out word to every town. They'll be looking for us.'

'This is true,' said Tullus, his brow collapsing into a deep frown.

'And they'll be watching your house, no doubt.'

Tullus put his head in his hands. 'Oh, gods. This is all such a terrible mess.'

Out of the corner of his eye, Cadmus saw Eriopis stiffen. She jerked her head in the direction of the sea.

'They're coming,' she said.

'Who?' said Tullus. 'Who's coming?'

Cadmus didn't have to wait for the answer. He woke up Tog and started fiddling with the buckles on his saddle, his fingers numb and clumsy from the cold. He could hear the tramp of marching legionaries and the thunder of hooves. The Romans must have recaptured at least a few of their horses.

Tog was the last to wake and the first to be ready. She jumped on top of her horse and watched the others with a look of slight impatience. By the time Cadmus had helped his sister and his master into their saddles, the single rocky path that led down to the beach was blocked with soldiers. On the cliff edge stood a pair of Nero's giants, plate armour like jewels in the sunlight.

'What do we do?' said Tullus nervously.

'Can we outrun them on the beach?' asked Cadmus.

Tog simply watched the assembling force, as though calculating her next move. Behind her, Eriopis continued to squirm and face the sea.

'They're coming,' she said again.

'I know,' said Cadmus, and then softened his tone a little. Sometimes it was easy to forget she was blind. 'They're here. They've blocked the path.'

'No, brother,' she said. That word still sounded odd in Cadmus's ears. 'They're carried by the waves.'

Cadmus turned and squinted. Around the headland, cleaving the morning mist, he saw the bows of a silhouette. Orthus ran to the edge of the beach and pranced in the shallows, barking at the approaching ship. Ahead of them, the legionaries began marching down the cliff path.

'Trapped,' said Tullus miserably.

'No,' said Cadmus. 'Wait.'

He looked more closely at vessel. It was older than a Roman warship, and seemed in terrible condition: the timbers were so rotten and splintered they had an almost furry appearance. The sail hung in tatters from the crossbeam.

'Tog,' he said. 'Is that what I think it is?'

She shifted in her saddle, and her eyes widened.

'I don't believe it.'

Cadmus laughed out loud. It wasn't part of the Roman navy. It was a Greek ship, the most famous in all of history. He could see Thoas manning the tiller and a handful of the other *heroidai* on the prow. Most of the crew were at the oars. The ship glided through the breakers and came to a halt a stone's throw out to sea.

'Who are they?' asked Tullus.

That was a difficult question, Cadmus thought, and one that he couldn't begin to answer with ranks of Roman soldiers advancing upon him. He wasn't even sure he could call the *heroidai* allies – especially now he had Eriopis with him. But they had little choice.

'I'll explain once we're on board,' he said.

'We're getting on that *wreck*?'

'That wreck,' said Cadmus, 'is the *Argo*.'

While Tullus gaped, Cadmus got down from his horse and went to help his sister. Tog stayed in her saddle.

'Go,' she said. 'I'll hold off the soldiers.'

'But—'

'Go,' she said again. 'She is blind. He is old. You'll be slow getting to the ship.'

Before Cadmus could protest any further, she drew the sword she had pilfered from the Roman camp and set off up the path.

Cadmus led his master and Eriopis to the edge of

the water and they waded clumsily through the waves. Tullus cursed and sucked his teeth as the freezing water struck his midriff.

Behind them, Tog was cutting a broad swathe through the column of men, riding back and forth with her silver-gold hair flying behind her. Even from this distance, Cadmus could see her arms were spattered with blood. Whose blood, he did not know.

When they reached the *Argo* his feet were just able to touch the bottom, though the waves were over his shoulders. He hauled himself up the rope ladder, and then helped Eriopis and Tullus up after him. Orthus paddled to the prow, where he climbed on to the bronze ram and then squirmed his way up on to the deck.

Thoas stood over Cadmus, hands on hips, apparently unconcerned by the carnage on the beach. Some of the soldiers had come past Tog, and were running across the sand towards the ship.

'Do you have it?' Thoas said.

Cadmus was shivering so hard he thought his teeth would shatter. 'What?'

'Do you have the fleece?'

'No.'

The man's eyes narrowed. 'Zeus strike you down . . .'

'But we know where it is. It's not here. You have to take us back to Rome.'

'Rome?'

'Yes. I can explain.'

'Swear an oath.'

'I swear,' he said, getting to his feet, 'by all the gods above and below. I can get it.'

Thoas looked at him a moment longer and then shouted his orders.

'*To the oars, men.*'

'No!' shouted Cadmus. 'My friend is still on the beach!'

'There is no time. She has made her choice. *Heave!*'

The deck shifted beneath their feet and Cadmus saw the oars churn the seawater to a murky brown.

'Stop! You've got to wait for her!'

Thoas returned to the tiller. Cadmus ran to the edge of the ship.

'Tog!' he screamed.

But she couldn't hear him, and she was too far away to make it back to ship in time.

As the *Argo* turned and made its way out into the open water, the soldiers dragged Tog from her horse. Cadmus saw one last, wild flick of her hair, and then she was surrounded by bodies. He kept staring as the shore receded, but even if she had reappeared he wouldn't have seen her through the blur of his tears.

Once they were under sail, Tullus suggested they all go below decks to get out of the wind and rain.

Eriopis insisted she wanted to remain on deck, despite the mutterings of the crew, so they left her with Orthus. She cut a miserable figure on the prow, shunned by the other sailors. Cadmus thought about staying with her, but he was so cold he worried he might succumb to fever.

He and his master huddled on one of the rowers' benches and listened to the wind howling overhead. The hull still let water in, which the *heroidai* would occasionally have to bail out.

'I'm sorry about your friend,' said Tullus.

Cadmus just nodded.

'I know you are furious with me,' he said. 'None of this would have happened if I had told you earlier. I am a fool.'

The flame of Cadmus's anger had long since been doused.

'Master,' he said, 'you have nothing to apologize for. You saved me. You raised me. And everything you have done since was done to keep me safe.' He paused and shivered. 'Besides, I probably wouldn't have believed you if you'd just sat me down and told me I was the heir of the Golden Fleece over dinner.'

'That much is true, I suppose,' said Tullus, smiling sadly. 'I still find it hard to believe. And yet, here we are. On the *Argo* itself. Grey-eyed Minerva, protect me.'

He looked around the leaking hull, marvelling at

the paintings of Jason and the Argonauts, now faded and water-stained. Cadmus told him of how he and Tog had found it, of the *heroidai*, of their journey to Mona.

'She sounds an extraordinary soul,' said Tullus. 'She deserved better.'

Cadmus swallowed down the urge to cry. *Endure*, he thought. But that only reminded him of Tog and brought the tears back more fiercely.

While Tullus comforted him, Thoas came down the steps into the bowels of the ship. He stood in front of them awkwardly for a moment, and then offered them a flask of wine.

'Drink,' he said. 'It will lift your spirits.'

To Cadmus's surprise, it did make him feel better. His fingers and toes were still frozen, but it warmed his heart and belly.

'You should not have brought her with you,' said Thoas.

'Who?'

'The witch,' said Thoas. 'She is an ill omen. The men think she will betray us. Be thankful I have not thrown her overboard.'

Whether it was the grief of losing Tog, or a gradual coming to terms with last night's revelations, Cadmus suddenly felt fiercely protective of her.

'She is not an ill omen,' he said. 'She is descended

from heroes, just as much as you are. And she is my *sister*.'

He tried the word for size and found it more comfortable in his mouth than he'd expected. Thoas looked unmoved. Bored, even.

'I know this,' he said. 'Some of the men would like me to throw *you* overboard too. In fact, some wanted you killed the moment they saw you. So that's twice you have to thank me.'

'You knew?' said Cadmus. 'How?'

'Your eyes. You have Medea's blood in your veins. I saw it as soon as we met, but I decided to trust you. It has been a long time since Medea's line produced any male offspring. I thought you might be more trust-worthy for that reason.'

Cadmus clenched his cold fists.

'You knew, and you didn't say anything . . .'

'Why would I? You seemed not to know, and if we had told you, you might have got it into your head that the fleece was your inheritance. You might have sided with your family name against us.' He came closer and bent down. 'But know this, boy: the Golden Fleece belongs with us. With Jason's pure bloodline. Not the poisonous offspring he made with Medea.'

Cadmus stood up and looked the man squarely in the face.

'Then why *haven't* you thrown us overboard?' he said.

Tullus made a gurgling noise as though he were about to intervene, but seemed to not be able to find the words.

'Because—'

'Because you need us,' Cadmus interrupted. 'You always needed us. Just like Jason needed Medea. He wouldn't have been anything without her.'

Thoas bared his teeth.

'The gods will punish you for this sacrilege!' he said.

Cadmus laughed out loud. 'Will they indeed? Have they not punished me enough already? I have lost my mother, my home, and the only friend I ever had. The emperor of the known world wants me dead. I don't know what else the gods can do to me.'

'You do not know real suffering, boy.'

'You don't need to threaten me,' Cadmus said. 'I will get you the fleece, and I will gladly hand it over to you. It's a curse, not a blessing. Perhaps being rid of it will bring some good luck to my poisonous family.'

With that he pushed past the bemused Thoas and went up on deck. There he found his sister, looking blindly into the salt spray. He put his arm around her, and the sailors looked at them from the corners of their eyes.

XXX

After that Cadmus hardly spoke to anyone apart from Eriopis. Tullus was generally too seasick to hold a conversation, and the *heroidai* ignored them. He learnt a little more from his sister every day. He learnt she was a full four years older than him; he had been one year old when the fire had happened; she had no knowledge of their father, since it was traditional among Medea's descendants to not take a husband. Born out of an ancient fear of betrayal, Cadmus guessed.

He also found out his real name. Cadmus was the name Tullus had given to him, borrowed from the hero who brought the written word to Greece. It seemed fitting for a young scholar, his master had said.

But his mother had called him Medus. Son of Medea.

Despite the *Argo*'s ruined state, it still made as good a time as it had on the outward journey. Summer was approaching, and the weather was calmer. After a month at sea, they found themselves skirting the bay of Naples, close enough to see the rows of vines on Mount Vesuvius. They eventually made port at Antium, some eighty miles south of Rome.

As they pulled into the harbour, Thoas found Cadmus and spoke to him for the first time in weeks.

'You and your sister will stay on the ship when we go into the city. Thestor has foreseen a betrayal, so the *heroidai* will go to fetch the fleece alone.'

Cadmus gave a tired smile. 'Good idea,' he said. 'I wouldn't want to jeopardize the mission. I hope Fortune smiles upon you.'

'You mock me.'

'I do nothing of the sort. I wish you every success.'

Thoas left him and gathered a group of six men. They stood at the foot of the gangplank, talking. Cadmus waited. Thoas returned.

'Now,' he said, 'where is the Golden Fleece kept?'

'Oh,' said Cadmus innocently, 'do you need me to tell you?'

'Do not test me.'

'Very well. Our house is on the Caelian Hill.'

A pause.

'Where is this hill?'

'It's easy to find. If you're coming through the Porta Lavernalis, go past the temple of the Good Goddess and it's east of the Palatine.'

He could see Thoas was trying hard to hide his confusion.

'Where on this hill is the house?'

'We're next door to Pollianus.' He paused again to enjoy Thoas's expression. 'You can always just ask for directions from one of Tullus's neighbours. You speak Latin, don't you? They're a snobbish lot, I'm not sure you'll get on their good side if you ask them in Greek.'

'You know very well that we will not speak that barbarian tongue.'

Cadmus made a theatrical frown. 'It sounds to me,' he said, 'like you and your men might not be the best people for the job. And, judging by the reaction to our arrival here, I'd say you're hardly going to slip in and out of Rome unnoticed. Everyone will be talking about you. What happens when Nero finds out you have the fleece and sends his legions to destroy you?'

'He'll never find us.'

'Of course he will. Do you think I'll keep silent under torture? Or Tullus, for that matter?'

Tullus suddenly appeared on the deck again.

'Hm? Torture?' he said.

'Listen,' said Cadmus. 'I have already said I'm not going to keep the fleece for myself. Let me and my master go to Rome alone. We won't arouse suspicion. We can be there and back in a matter of days.'

Thoas stared at him. The rest of the *heroidai* muttered among themselves.

'Swear an oath,' Thoas said. 'In the sight of the gods.'

'I swear,' said Cadmus. 'I will bring the fleece straight back here.'

'And the witch will stay on the boat?'

Cadmus felt a small spark of anger at his dismissive tone, but nodded.

'She would only draw attention to us,' he said.

Again the *heroidai* spoke among themselves in low voices. Thoas eventually turned back to him.

'Very well,' he said. 'But if you have not returned in three days, we will pursue you.'

'If I have not returned within three days, may Zeus strike me down to the deepest pits of Tartarus.'

That seemed to satisfy them. While his master hovered, Cadmus went looking for his sister. He found her below decks, looking like a bundle of dirty washing piled up in the corner. She was talking to Orthus. Cadmus came and laid a hand on her shoulder.

'We're going,' he said. 'I think it would be better if

only my master and I return to the city. It won't be safe for you.'

Her blindfold twitched.

'The flames,' she said.

'The flames? What about them?'

'I see them everywhere. All the time. More and more, every day.'

The *Argo* creaked in the pause.

'Maybe I have brought back the memories?' he suggested. 'Or you're thinking of what happened on Mona?'

'I do not know,' she said. 'It bodes ill.' She grabbed his arm and squeezed. 'Be careful, my brother. All I see is fire. Destruction. Death.'

And with that, she went back to talking with the dog. Cadmus withdrew slowly, trying not to set too much store by her words – but, as usual, they clung like burrs to his skin.

The last leg of the journey was strangely serene. Sitting in the back of the cart, enjoying the broken shade of the cypress trees and watching boys training horses in the hot, yellow fields, it was almost possible to imagine that nothing had changed. Here he was, Cadmus the slave, accompanying his master back from his country estate; perhaps transcribing a letter to be sent upon their return; perhaps discussing who might win office this year, which province should be governed by whom.

But then Cadmus looked down at his blistered hands and feet. He could see the sinews beneath his pale skin, taut and strong from his days at sea. He had calluses on his fingers and palms from helping with the sail. And he looked at the boys and their horses and knew that he had seen things that they couldn't imagine in their wildest dreams.

He was changed, he knew. He even had a new name, if he wanted to reclaim it.

While he ruminated, they crested a hill and the magnificent heap of Rome came into view. It shimmered like a vision in the heat, its colours bleached by the sun. More carts and carriages and teams of slaves joined them on the road. Tombs, and the faces of their inhabitants, began to appear on either side.

'Here we are, Cadmus,' Tullus said. 'Home at last.'

Cadmus nodded and smiled, but for some reason this didn't feel in the least like a homecoming. After all he had been through, the place felt completely foreign. As the crowds grew, he felt like he was sticking out just as much as one of the *heroidai*. And then there was the added discomfort of Eriopis's ominous words.

He wished Tog were with him.

'Something wrong?' said Tullus.

He shrugged. 'I feel strange. Anxious.'

Tullus managed a little chuckle. 'Come now, my boy. We have travelled to the edge of the world, crossed wild, barbarian lands, and *now* you're getting anxious? Rome is the centre of civilization.'

'That,' said Cadmus, 'is exactly why I'm worried.'

XXXI

The Vicus Longus was seething with bodies, the washed and the unwashed, the sweat-drenched and the perfumed, every one of them in such a hurry they never gave Tullus or Cadmus a second glance. But then there was no reason why they should. Rome was full of young Greek slaves and old Italian men. Cadmus's only distinctive feature was his eye, and he kept it half-closed as though squinting against the sun.

They passed through the Subura, along the bottom end of the Forum and under the shadow of the Domus Transitoria. Cadmus's escape from the palace seemed to belong to a different age, and certainly to a different Cadmus. He wondered if the emperor was inside, and hid on the opposite side of Tullus as they passed one of its many huge entrance halls.

Walking up the Caelian felt very strange indeed. They had made this trip so many times before, every paving slab, every coloured marble facade, every trickling water fountain was familiar to Cadmus. And yet it felt like he shouldn't be there – like they were foreigners in their own city. The whole environment fitted him like a badly made tunic. The ground felt too hard under his feet, the noises of scampering slaves and hollering craftsmen too loud in his ears.

Arriving at Tullus's front door was stranger still. Nearly three months gone, and nothing had changed. It looked like it had on the day Cadmus had escaped the drunken Bufo with Tog.

Thinking of her made him suddenly unspeakably melancholy.

Tullus knocked on the door. There was no answer. He looked at Cadmus and raised an eyebrow. He knocked again.

Eventually the slot at eye level opened. It was no surprise when Bufo's bloodshot eyes appeared in the gap. It was a surprise, though, when Cadmus felt pleased to see him.

'Bufo, my old friend!' said Tullus. 'We have returned. I hope you've kept the place spick and span?'

Cadmus knew something was wrong when Bufo didn't reply – only his eyes gave anything away, and they spoke of something like fear.

The slot closed and the door opened. The grizzled old slave, face like a dried and salted olive, bowed as they entered.

'I'm glad to see you, Master,' he mumbled. He didn't even look at Cadmus.

They stepped over the threshold into the cool darkness of the atrium. Cadmus smiled at the familiar smells of burning lamp oil, incense from the household shrine, and somewhere underneath, faintly, pumice and papyrus. The wax faces of Tullus's ancestors glowered down at them from where they hung on the wall. Everything looked exactly as they'd left it. Apart from the slaves themselves. The Syrian, Clitus, looked thin and unwashed. Charis hovered somewhere behind a bust of Apollo, her tunic torn.

'What is it, old thing?' said Tullus. 'Aren't you going to complain about something? You're making me nervous, being so quiet!'

Bufo's dry lips parted, but he said nothing and hung his head.

'Of course he has no complaints,' said a voice that sounded like someone trying to tune a broken lyre. 'He's going up in the world!'

Cadmus saw the silhouette of a man with a thick

neck and oiled curls appear in the doorway to the garden.

'Yes, what an honour! You must all be beside yourselves with excitement! Telling all your little slave friends – *you'll never guess who* we *had to dinner.*'

It was the man's wild, jangling laugh that confirmed Cadmus's suspicions.

'Caesar, I, ah . . .' Tullus gibbered, and the emperor cut him off.

'Quiet, please.' The quietness and steadiness of Nero's words unsettled Cadmus deeply, more than if he had been spitting with rage. 'You took your time, both of you. Were you carrying him on your back, boy? Like Aeneas and his father?' He laughed again. 'You rather fancy yourself a hero, don't you?'

Cadmus looked at his feet. Nero stepped into the centre of the atrium, followed by his shadow, Epaphroditus. The huge forms of his guards – the false *heroidai* – appeared from the other rooms. How many there were, Cadmus couldn't be sure.

'Forgive me, Caesar—'

'When I first came here, I was intent on ransacking the place. Tearing it to pieces. And then I saw what a *beautiful* house you have. Such wonderful, old-fashioned Republican charm to it! So I thought I would simply move in and wait for you. Thankfully your old slave has been most accommodating of me and my guests. Day and night he has tended to us, hasn't he? Day and night!'

Tullus shifted from one foot to the other.

'We have only now returned from Britannia, Caesar. We were, ah, separated from the group.' Cadmus still didn't look up. His master was not a good liar. 'We found the grave of Medea, but there was no fleece. Perhaps you heard? A setback, certainly, but no need to, ah, give up hope . . .'

Nero smiled, and his features disappeared into his blotchy face.

'I have heard as much,' he said. 'But there was some good news to come from the expedition.'

'Good news, Caesar?'

Again, Cadmus shivered with a black premonition.

'We captured the girl. Perhaps you remember her, Tullus? The fiend who stole the fleece from me *in my very own home*?'

'It was not the real fleece, though, Caesar,' Tullus began to protest, but Nero continued.

'Of course you remember her. You put her up to the task.'

'I did no such thing—'

'Silence!' The emperor's voice became shrill and birdlike. 'You, and her, and the boy, all working together. I'm not an idiot. You have been working to undermine this project from the very start. But it is of no matter now. Like I said. We captured the girl, after she helped you escape from Britannia. And she told us *everything*.'

'Where is she?' said Cadmus, fear for Tog outweighing his fear of the emperor's wrath.

Nero clapped his hands. 'You really are quite extraordinary, boy. Defiant until the end.' He came forward and brushed his fingers over Cadmus's cheek with strange affection. 'Don't worry. I specifically asked for her to be brought to me, here at Rome. I have shown her just the kind of hospitality she deserves.' He withdrew his hand and put it over his mouth like a coy young girl. He giggled.

Something inside of Cadmus collapsed, and he staggered where he stood. He couldn't bring himself to think of what Nero might have done to her.

'She revealed some remarkable things, with a little persuading.' The emptiness inside Cadmus became a kind of roaring sickness. 'About your lineage, about the location of the real Golden Fleece. If I hadn't seen you and your sandal, I never would have believed it. But now it all makes sense. Jason's heir. A little Greek worm like you.'

Without thinking, Cadmus launched himself at the emperor, his small fists flying. He heard Tullus cry out, but nothing, not his master, not his reason, could prevent the cauldron of his rage from boiling over.

Nero's flesh was soft and spongy, and Cadmus hardly felt like his knuckles were making contact. The first few blows he struck seemed slow and weak, as though he were underwater – and then he felt the enormous, bronze-clad arms of one of Nero's guards wrap around his waist and pull him away from the tottering emperor.

The man squeezed, and Cadmus felt a rib crack. His vision darkened.

Nero watched him for a moment, and calmly wiped away the sweat that had erupted on his brow.

'As much as I enjoy seeing the life leaving your body, you're no good to me dead.' He nodded. 'Not yet anyway.'

The giant dropped Cadmus to the floor like a sack of olives. Nero stood over him and rolled him on to his back with a shove of his foot.

'Where is it?' he said, saliva cascading from his lips.

Even if Cadmus had wanted to tell him, it was agony to draw breath.

'Perhaps you won't say,' said Nero. 'But your master is made of weaker stuff.'

One of the guards unsheathed his sword and put it to Tullus's throat. The old man closed his eyes.

'You're very close, aren't you, for a master and a slave? Rather too close. Perverse, I think.'

'I am prepared, boy,' Tullus said. 'I already feel as

though I have lived more days than my fate allows. You needn't tell him on my account.'

Nero drew a thumb across his neck. Cadmus cried out.

'Stop!' He got to his feet. He had already lost Tog. He wasn't going to let them take Tullus as well. 'I'll tell you where it is. Don't harm him.'

His master protested, but Cadmus was already making his way across the atrium to the tiny *cubiculum* where he had slept every night since Tullus had brought him over from Athens. The *heroidai* followed him with their weapons drawn.

His bedroom was just as he'd left it: his stilus and writing tablets laid out on the little desk, next to them the oil lamp in the shape of a fish, and his one spare tunic folded neatly at the foot of the bed.

It was there, lying on top of the mattress. His old blanket, a wrinkled, soft, almost hairless piece of sheep's hide. Cadmus had slept underneath it every winter night, had tossed it aside when he was late waking, had trodden upon it when the floor tiles were too cold for his bare feet. He had spilt food upon it, had worn it over his head when it was raining heavily. Even now, when he held it in his hands, he found it hard to believe that this was the relic that had driven Jason to the ends of the earth. It seemed such a pitiful old thing.

The guards shifted silently under their armour as he returned to the atrium. Nero's face contorted with rage when he saw him.

'What is *this*?' he screamed, pointing at the blanket. 'Are you trying to fool me, or merely to hasten your death?'

'This is no trick,' said Tullus. 'This is the thing you seek, Caesar. Passed down from Medea, through the generations. Cadmus is the last of her children. Medus, his mother called him.'

Nero inspected the sheepskin for a moment, then seized it from Cadmus's hands and hurled it at the wall. It struck the shrine of the household gods and sent the little clay figures of the *penates* tumbling to the floor. They shattered where they fell.

'You seek to make a sport of me, do you? How *dare you*? Worms. *Less than worms.* Are you entertained? Does this amuse you?' His rage ended abruptly and his smile returned. 'Well. You have had your bit of fun. I cannot begrudge you that, now you are facing certain death. But now it is *my* turn to be entertained. Take them to the Campus Martius. Let's see how much of a hero's blood you really have in you.'

He turned to Epaphroditus.

'The fleece is hidden somewhere here. I'm sure of it. Keep questioning the old man and his slaves until it is found. By any means you see fit.'

XXXII

Evening was drawing on when Cadmus was led out of the house. As the door to Tullus's villa closed, he could hear the sounds of furniture and ornaments shattering. The sickness of fear had reached such an intensity that it had become a numbness. He couldn't feel his hands and feet. He couldn't even feel his broken rib. He walked with a hypnotized trudge.

Nero had whispered something to his guards and gone ahead with his head shrouded, so he wouldn't be recognized. It was a favourite trick of his – to move unnoticed among his people, to search out sedition and treachery, or to enjoy the baser pleasures of the city.

They left the Caelian Hill, made their way past the crowded Circus, under the Palatine and the Capitoline hills, where the river bordered the plains of the Campus Martius. It soon became clear, though, that they weren't heading to the Campus itself. Nero was taking him to the amphitheatre.

The great stone arena had been hemmed in by other building work in recent years, and rose in front of them unannounced. In the twilight it was a dark, imposing hulk of a building. The Games of Apollo had finished the previous week – gone were the pipe players and coloured flags and garlands of flowers. Now it was silent and empty. The arches on the lowest level were black as the mouth of hell.

Cadmus had lost sight of Nero. Alone, he was hauled through the gates of the amphitheatre, down a flight of steps and imprisoned in a pitch-dark cell.

He didn't know how long he was kept there. Certainly long enough to cry himself to sleep, over Tullus, over Tog, over his sister, alone on the boat among men who hated her.

He thought of his own impending doom, imagined the agonies that Nero was even now preparing for him, and knew that whatever he imagined probably wouldn't be half as bad as the real thing. He thought about how bizarre the last few months of his life had been. The stuff of myth. Only, for it to be a myth, someone needed to remember it and to pass it on. No one would remember Cadmus. No one would write stories about him. He would slip through the cracks of history.

He was woken from his uneasy half-sleep by a key rattling in the lock of his cell, and the strong, sweet smell of myrrh in his nostrils. The gate groaned on its hinges and Epaphroditus entered with a torch in one hand and an item of clothing in the other.

'The stage is set for your final labour,' he said. 'Nero has asked me to bring you this.'

He threw the material at his feet. Cadmus picked it up. It was his old blanket.

'He wants to give you a fighting chance,' Epaphroditus continued, unable to keep the smirk from his face. 'So he has agreed to give you your fleece back. If it is as powerful as you claim, you have nothing to worry about.'

Cadmus took it from the floor and folded it carefully. The feeling of the hide next to his skin calmed his nerves a little. But the longer he held it, the more absurd, the more hopeless his situation seemed. How could this be the Golden Fleece? It felt ready to disintegrate in his hands.

'You know,' said Epaphroditus, 'it is not too late for you. Just tell us where the genuine article is, and Nero might consider a pardon.'

'But this *is* the genuine article.' He paused. 'I think.'

'You and Tullus are as stubborn as each other,' the secretary sighed. 'Very well. If what you say is true, then it will save you, and you have nothing to fear. If it is not, then your trick will be revealed and you will be punished as you deserve. Rather neat, I think.'

'May I ask,' Cadmus said slowly, 'how the emperor intends to punish me?'

Epaphroditus laughed. 'Oh, no,' he said, 'I wouldn't want to spoil the surprise!'

He stood to one side and gestured down the row of cells.

'Follow me, please.'

Cadmus got to his feet and wrapped the fleece around his shoulders. Fear and fatigue had hollowed him out, as though he were a bronze replica of himself. He walked without feeling, without seeing, without hearing. The passageway led around the circumference of the amphitheatre, up some stone steps and stopped at a large double door, three or four times his height. Through the crack he could just see the sand of the arena, red in the firelight.

Epaphroditus disappeared and emerged carrying a short, military-style sword. He handed it over, hilt first.

'Here you are. I'm afraid they don't make them any smaller than this.'

Cadmus took the sword in one hand, surprised he was able to lift it.

'He wants me to fight?'

'That's right,' said the secretary. 'A chance for you to show your heroic credentials. When Nero gives the sign, the gates will open. Give them a good show, eh?' He patted Cadmus on the back and grinned. 'I'm sorry it had to end like this. I always rather liked you. But you didn't take my advice. You're a slave. All you had to do was play the game.'

Cadmus waited in the darkness, thinking nothing. There was only the sound of his pulse, the sharp pain in his ribs. Beyond the huge doors he could hear just one voice, echoing around the amphitheatre's empty seats.

A lonely trumpet blared. There was a shuffling of shadows at his feet and doors opened. Epaphroditus shoved Cadmus forward, and he wandered blindly into the arena. He entered to the sound of a single pair of hands applauding.

Behind him the doors slammed shut.

Cadmus had never been to the amphitheatre before – Tullus had always said that gladiators were a pastime of the uneducated. The space was an enormous oval, lit with torches and braziers on the end of poles. The games weren't usually held at night, so Nero, in his impatience, had obviously improvised while Cadmus had been locked in his cell. The only audience members were the emperor himself and his entourage – Polydamas on one side, slaves on the other. Epaphroditus eventually joined him.

When Cadmus hung back against the wall, the men who had opened the gates dragged him into the middle of the sand. Nero's giant guards stood in a ring around the perimeter.

'Here he is!' jeered Nero, laurels upon his head, goblet in one hand. 'Descendant of Jason! Descendant of the gods! What a heroic figure he cuts!'

Cadmus didn't move. Couldn't move.

'What is this?' Nero gestured around the amphitheatre as though in outrage. 'Too arrogant to even salute his emperor? A poor omen, wouldn't you say, Polydamas?'

Even from where he stood, with his blood pounding in his ears, Cadmus could hear the soothsayer's wheezing.

The emperor settled back in his chair. 'Well, we shall see where his defiance gets him. Let's show him his adversary.'

He drained another cup of wine, dried his fingers on the hair of the slave standing next to him, and gave the signal. The trumpet sounded once more, and the doors opposite him opened. From the darkness within came a young woman, as tall as the other guards, hair like moonlight tumbling down her back.

Cadmus dropped his sword in disbelief.

'Tog,' he said, the name barely making it out of his mouth.

She didn't reply. She looked tired. Or was that bruising beneath her eyes? She still held her sword tightly, he noticed. Her knuckles twitched on its hilt.

By now Nero was laughing so hard he had nearly fallen out of his chair.

'Now,' he said, voice echoing around the empty seats, 'the rules of these games are as follows. Obviously I would like to see each of you slice the other into tiny pieces. Perhaps you think you will not fight? If this is your choice, my *heroidai* will kill you anyway, so you will gain nothing. If you win the fight, however, I will spare you. Free you. Honour you, even. Perhaps, my girl, you would like a corner of Britannia to rule yourself? Perhaps, boy, you would like your master to live out his life in peace and comfort? Hmmm? I can make all these things so, you understand.'

Cadmus looked into the deep, blue pools of Tog's eyes and found her as placid and unreadable as ever. He realized, his stomach falling away from him, he had no idea what she was going to do. She had always been wilful, headstrong, self-reliant. She didn't need him. It probably seemed like a good deal to her.

For his own part, he knew that, whatever he did, Nero would kill him. He didn't trust a single drunken word he said.

'Tog,' he said. 'It's all right.'

She blinked very slowly, as though she were trying to master a pain inside her. Then she shook her head fractionally. Cadmus didn't know what that meant.

'Well?' screamed Nero. 'What are you waiting for? Pick up your sword, you *coward*!'

Cadmus heard the sound of bows being drawn. Around the arena, half a dozen guards aimed arrows at him and Tog.

He pulled his blanket up around his neck. There was only one way that they could both come away from this alive. He had to believe, with his whole heart, that he had the Golden Fleece upon his shoulders. After all of the strange things he had seen and heard, after all the hours spent in intellectual contortions, trying to rationalize, to prove, to disprove – all his questions could be answered right now, in this very moment. He either held the real fleece, or he didn't. It held all the powers that the stories said it held, or it didn't. He would die, or he wouldn't.

He found himself unexpectedly calm. A hint of a smile pulled at the side of his mouth.

'Just do it, Tog,' he said quietly.

'I don't want to.'

He bent down to pick up his sword, and when he came up he took a step closer. Nero began a slow clap.

'You don't understand,' Cadmus whispered. 'This is the fleece. The real one.'

Tog frowned. 'Are you sure?'

'Of course I'm sure.'

He tried to make it true just by saying it. But he didn't know. He couldn't know, until she had struck him. His whole body was shaking, he realized.

'*Come on!*' Nero shouted. 'I'm getting *bored!*'

'I don't want to,' Tog said again.

'You have to. Just try not to miss and cleave my head in two.'

A series of expressions passed over Tog's blank face, like clouds across an empty sky. Then she stepped backwards and made a couple of experimental strokes with her sword. Nero clapped again. The guards relaxed at their bow strings. Cadmus closed his eyes, tensed, and thought of nothing at all as Tog raised the weapon over her head.

He thought someone tapped him on the shoulder.

The amphitheatre went quiet. Cadmus turned and looked behind him. There was no one there. He turned again to look at Tog, feeling foolish. Her sword arm hung limply at her side, and in her hand was only the hilt, which smouldered slightly. The blade lay in glittering fragments upon the sand.

When he looked into Tog's face, he saw her skin had regained some of its colour. It was radiant, even.

It was reflected light. The blanket around his shoulders glowed golden. Silence spread around him, around the fleece, slow and warm as sunrise.

'It's true,' said Tog.

'I don't believe—'

Nero came stumbling down the tiers of seats with Polydamas behind him.

'He has it! He has the fleece! Take it from him, you cowards!'

But the guards didn't move. They stared at Cadmus in awe. One of them nocked and loosed an arrow at him. The iron head tinkled like shattering glass as it struck Cadmus's arm, and again Cadmus felt as though someone were touching him gently with their finger.

'You!' Nero snarled. 'You *useless creature*!' Cadmus thought the emperor was shouting at him, but he had turned to Polydamas. 'You *assured* me that he was lying! You told me the boy would die tonight!'

In his rage, he seized the soothsayer by his grubby robes and hurled him from the tiered seating down on to the sand. Polydamas's ancient bones fell in a heap, and there was a sound like twigs snapping beneath his robes. He didn't get up.

'And *you* . . .' Nero turned around to look for Epaphroditus, but the secretary had already fled. The emperor whirled around on the spot, until he almost tottered into the arena himself. He leant over the edge and snarled at his guards.

'I did not free you from gladiator school for your mercy! He is just a *boy*! Take what is mine, or you will be the ones illuminating the arena at the next games!'

They moved slowly, uncertainly.

Cadmus flung the Golden Fleece so it covered both his and Tog's shoulders, and together they ran across the arena, leaping over Polydamas's broken body. They made for the gate Tog had entered from, and disappeared into the darkness.

They ran back the way they had come, the glow of the fleece gradually fading. Cadmus's thoughts matched his feet, rushing and tripping over themselves. He wanted to say more to her, but he was completely out of breath and his broken rib hurt like a dagger in his side. Crossing the River Tiber he sprained his ankle, and Tog had to drag him to his feet like a dog on a leash. He hobbled on as fast as he could, but knew he couldn't go much further.

Rome's respectable population were in their beds by now, safe behind their slaves and gates and high walls. The streets had been given over to a different kind of citizen, who whispered and snickered and cracked their knuckles in the shadows. Cadmus felt pairs of narrow and greedy eyes watching them from corners and alleyways. He didn't feel much safer here than he had done in the amphitheatre, even with the fleece around his shoulders.

When they reached the shops alongside the Circus Maximus, he fell to his knees and grunted in pain. Tog pulled him upright again and they huddled in the doorway of a *taberna*.

Then she said suddenly: 'Someone's still following us. Don't turn around. They're at the end of the street. We need to keep going.'

'I can't,' said Cadmus, wincing. 'Please . . . can we rest a moment?'

Tog sighed. She helped him to his feet, led him into another, smaller alley and went around the back of the *taberna*. She threw her shoulder against the door once, twice, until it gave way. They fell over the threshold and scrambled out of sight, hiding themselves behind some stacked bags of flour.

Cadmus panted in the darkness.

'Are you all right?' Cadmus asked.

'Yes.'

'Nero said they . . . questioned you.'

'Yes.'

'Did they hurt you?'

She shrugged. 'Some,' she said.

'You seem . . .'

'What?'

'Well, better than I'd expect for someone who has been interrogated by Nero.'

She suddenly looked embarrassed. 'He didn't interrogate me.'

'He didn't? Then how did he know about me? How did he know we were going back to Tullus's villa?'

She scratched the side of her face. 'I talk in my sleep. I'd told them everything before I was even back in Rome.'

Cadmus couldn't help laughing. His rib sent a jolt of pain through his body.

'What?' said Tog. 'Aren't you angry?'

'Not in the slightest,' he said.

'Oh.'

She took the edge of the fleece in her thumb and forefinger. It had lost its glow by now. An old, thin sheep's hide, curling at the edges. There was nothing remarkable about it.

'It's not what I expected,' she said.

Cadmus nodded. 'It's not what Nero expected either.'

'Will you keep your promise, now I'm here?'

'What promise?'

'To give it to me?'

He thought of the *heroidai*, waiting for him at Antium. He had sworn to bring the fleece back to them. How could he get around that, and keep his promise to Tog?

Suddenly the light of a torch spread across the wall of the storeroom, distorting the hard edges of things and filling the space between them with living, malevolent shadows.

'Come out, little mice,' said a voice. 'Come out, come out.' A giggle.

Nero had come looking for them personally. The emperor himself, skulking around the backstreets like a common thief.

'There is nowhere to hide in this city. It is my city. It is my empire. There is nowhere, no nation on *earth* where you will be safe. I have as many eyes as Argus, and they see *everything*.'

He stood in the centre of the room, where the shop owner's table was piled with scrolls and tablets. He turned his sweating face slowly. Tog was preparing to launch herself at the emperor, but before she could Cadmus caught sight of that familiar brown blur darting out from their hiding place and crossing the room.

Nero saw the dormouse before he saw Cadmus or Tog. He squealed with terror as the little animal raced around his feet, and there was a clatter as he dropped his torch to the ground. Tog lunged forward – more to save the mouse than to attack the emperor, Cadmus suspected – and they collided. Nero grunted as the breath was knocked out of him and he fell into the table and the piles of accounts.

Then another sound, which reminded Cadmus of the *Argo*'s sail catching the wind, as the torch's flames lit the dry papyrus that had fallen to the floor.

Tog had already chased her mouse out of the door, but Cadmus was trapped. The fire greedily claimed the table and the chairs and the sacks of flour, and the tips of the flames were already reaching for the wooden shelves above them. Through the thick smoke Cadmus could see Tog outside. She was shouting something but at the same time one of the bags of flour exploded and her words were lost in a rain of burning debris.

Nero rolled around on the floor, semi-conscious. The mouse scurried away through the destruction and disappeared.

Cadmus had convinced himself that this was the end, when the Golden Fleece began to shine again – not with the red of the fire, but with a cool divine light of its own. He pulled it around himself tightly, and walked calmly through the flames, and over Nero's twitching body.

Tog grabbed him as soon as he emerged from the

burning storeroom.

'He's gone!'

'Who has?'

'My mouse! He's run away!'

She looked miserable. Cadmus didn't know how to console her.

'We need to go, Tog.'

They heard the emperor getting to his feet within, and set off down the network of alleys, Tog looking over her shoulder.

They came out at the foot of the Palatine, in front of the Circus Maximus. Here, a crowd had gathered to watch the smoke billowing out over the shops and the cheap blocks of flats, and when Cadmus looked back he could see that the fire had spread between two, possibly three buildings. The wind was strong, the shops were tightly packed, and the flames licked from roof to roof quicker than he could follow.

His sister's baleful words came back to him. *The flames. Everywhere.* How many times, he wondered, had her memories in fact been visions of the future?

Cadmus worried about the poor souls trapped in their tower blocks, but there was nothing they could do. They set off towards the Caelian Hill, to the villa, to Tullus – or whatever was left of him.

When they arrived, they found a bruised and frail

figure lying on a couch in the master's bedroom. The other slaves were attending to him. Cadmus approached his master slowly, wordlessly. The others turned around, and it was only then that he saw it wasn't Tullus who was laid out on the bed. It was Bufo. Tullus was helping the other slaves to clean his wounds and bring him water.

Tullus turned as Cadmus and Tog approached. The old man looked less surprised than terrified, as if he was seeing two shades returning from the Underworld. He experimentally laid a hand on Cadmus's shoulder, and then pulled him into an embrace.

'You . . .' he said, stepping back and looking him over in disbelief. 'And she . . .' He pointed at Tog. 'How . . . ?'

'I might ask you the same question, Master. Where are Nero's men?'

Tullus smiled briefly through cracked and swollen lips. Then his face fell and he turned to the figure of Bufo.

'Your fellow slaves decided to take matters into their own hands. Bufo here fought fiercest, but, ah, came off worst . . .'

Cadmus suddenly felt a huge surge of pity for the old toad. Loyal to the last.

'Will he survive?'

'I think so,' he said. 'I have sent for a doctor.'

Cadmus came forward and laid the Golden Fleece over Bufo. Immediately his leathery face seemed to soften.

'Master,' said Cadmus, 'we need to leave. Something terrible has happened.'

Tullus gave a wheezing laugh. 'I know something terrible has happened. Something terrible has happened on an almost daily basis for the last four months.'

'More than terrible. Catastrophic.'

He led his master out of the villa, and showed him the huge cloud of smoke, a dirty orange against the night sky, spreading like an umbrella pine over the city. The great fire was like a fierce, unnatural sunrise. The far end of the Circus Maximus had now caught, and the flames were making short work of its wooden frame. The roar of the conflagration was matched by the cries of the citizens as they watched their livelihoods being devoured.

'Oh, dear, Cadmus,' Tullus said. 'Your doing? Or hers?'

'Neither, technically. We can thank Nero for this.'

'Where is the Divine Caesar now?'

'I don't know. Somewhere out there. I think.'

Tullus stared at the burning city.

'If he is still here, then we cannot be, boy. Your sister is waiting for us. And the others.' He took a deep breath and coughed quietly. 'I think it is time for us to say farewell to Rome.'

The old man went back inside, crossed the ruined atrium and returned to his bedroom. Charis was chatting to Tog when they entered. The slave raised an eyebrow at Cadmus when she saw him, and grinned. Still playing matchmaker, in the midst of all of this.

'My friends,' Tullus began, in Latin, as though he were addressing his peers in the Senate. 'Due to forces beyond our control, Cadmus and I must take our leave of my family home; indeed, we must take our leave of the city we love so much; perhaps of the country too.' He surveyed their faces. 'But I will not be asking you to come with us. The path ahead may be a dangerous one, and I would not want you to endure any more misfortune than has already befallen you. But nor will I leave you here to be slaves to another man or woman.'

The group exchanged mute glances. Cadmus's heart swelled to hear his master speak like this. He looked at Tog, but she understood no Latin, and besides still seemed to be quietly grieving her lost mouse.

'I have stipulated in my will,' he continued, 'that you shall all be freed upon my death. Now, you may have realized, I am not dead. But in the circumstances, it is to my advantage to have the world believe I *am* a dead man, and I would ask you to believe it too. I am sorry there is no magistrate here, no ceremony to make the deed official. But I have something that will perhaps make my words feel a little more concrete.'

The slaves began talking excitedly. Tullus turned around to his strongbox, pushed into the corner of the room and, despite the evidence of being attacked with several blunt objects, unopened.

'I know you always thought me a terrible miser,' he said, producing a key from beneath his toga. 'But I never saw the need to spend my money on such trivial and fleeting things as ornaments and paintings and marble columns.' He opened the lid. The strong-box was full to the brim with thousands and thousands of gold coins. 'Perhaps,' he said, turning to the slaves, 'you might find a better way to spend it.'

XXXIII

For the first time since landing in Italy, the sky was overcast. Rome burnt, and the blanket of smoke had spread miles to the south, turning the beach at Antium to a deathly grey. The air was acrid, the breeze strong.

Cadmus waited with his sister on the quayside, blinking tiny flecks of ash from his eyes. Tog was standing by the *Argo*. The *heroidai* came and went, loading the ship with provisions. She watched them like a stern, imperious quartermaster, and then picked up a crate herself and followed them below decks. Cadmus rubbed Orthus behind the ears, more for his own reassurance than for the dog's.

Tullus returned from bribing the harbourmaster.

'All set,' he said. 'We're allowed to go as soon as we're ready. And I've paid him enough to forget our faces.'

'You can't be sure of that,' said Cadmus.

Tullus shrugged. 'We'll just have to trust he is as god-fearing as he claims,' he said, and set off for the *Argo*. 'Come on.'

Cadmus gritted his teeth. In the last few hours he had hoped, secretly, that Tog would decide to join them on their ship and sail into exile alongside him. But of course she would never have agreed to that. Almost as soon as they had left Rome, she had taken him to one side and told him she was going home. For good, this time. Her mouse's escape had been a sign, she'd said. She had saved him. They had helped each other on their adventures. But now it was time for him to return home.

Cadmus still hadn't worked out if she was talking about the mouse, or about him.

On the journey from Rome to Antium they had finalized their plan. No one else knew about it, of course. Unless his sister had found out through some means of her own.

Tullus made his slow way across the harbour, Cadmus close behind. Eriopis came last, guided by Orthus. When she had the dog with her, she hardly seemed blind at all – and she hated it when Cadmus tried to lead her like an invalid. Cadmus still found it difficult to think of her as family, but he had grown protective of her and her strangeness. After all he had seen, strangeness was something he had come to embrace. But others didn't know better. Sailors began to mutter and hiss and make signs at her as they passed, and Cadmus's blood boiled.

When they reached the *Argo*, Thoas was waiting for them but Tog had disappeared.

'The fleece is safely stowed,' he said formally. 'And we are provisioned for the journey back to Corinth. The wind has changed. It is time we left.'

Cadmus nodded briefly. 'Ready when you are.'

'You know,' said Thoas, 'you might still be welcome among the *heroidai*. You have proven that you have more of Jason's blood in you than the witch's.'

Cadmus shook his head and smiled. The fact that Thoas had to say 'witch' instead of 'Medea' was itself a reason why he could never go with them. And they certainly wouldn't take his sister in.

'That's kind of you,' he said. 'But we will make our own way once we get to Corinth.'

Thoas shrugged. 'As you wish.'

Tog suddenly emerged from below decks and stood between them, oblivious to their conversation. Her tunic looked a little more snug than usual. Cadmus hoped no one else noticed.

'I'm ready too,' she said, and coughed. There was an odd pause.

Thoas looked at her suspiciously for a moment, and then went to see to the ship and his crew. Tog leapt on to the quayside in a single bound.

'Where will you go?' she said.

'To Athens first,' Cadmus answered.

'Aren't you worried about Nero?'

'Nero has more pressing concerns right now.' He nodded to the pall of black smoke hanging on the horizon to the north.

'He will still come looking. Later.'

'Perhaps. But we're not going to Athens to settle.'

'You're not? But it is your home.'

'Not really. I'm starting to realize, Tog, that a home doesn't have to be a particular place.'

Tog frowned. 'Then where are you going? Eventually?'

'We're going to look for the others,' Cadmus said, with a flush of excitement he couldn't conceal.

'What others?'

'The other artefacts. The other heroes. Tullus may have left all his notes behind in Britannia, but we think we can piece it together from memory. And we have my sister to help us now. We're going to get them before Nero does.'

'And then what?'

'Keep them safe.'

'I see.'

Tog never gave much away at the best of times, but he could see she was trying to hide something. Perhaps Tullus could see it too.

'How will you get home?' said Cadmus quickly.

'Not by boat,' she said. 'Not again. I'll take the roads. I can buy a good horse with your master's money.'

She made a curious little bow in Tullus's direction, and the old man smiled back.

'Oh,' she said, suddenly straightening up. 'I have something for you.'

She reached beneath her tunic and brought out the wolf's head razor she had stolen from their house months ago. Through everything – the journey to and from Britannia, her enslavement in Greece, her capture by Nero – she'd somehow looked after it. Cadmus shook his head in wonder.

'Please be careful,' he said. 'Roads aren't much safer than a rough sea, especially once you're out of Italy.'

'She'll be safe,' said Eriopis. She was wearing the strangest expression, somewhere between dismay and delight. 'I think you both know that.'

Thoas began yelling, and Cadmus was glad for the distraction. The wind was up. The rowers were beginning to take their seats behind the oars. It was time to go.

Tullus laid a hand on Cadmus's shoulder.

'Come, Cadmus. We are not far from Rome, and Nero may well be sending his spies after us as we speak. We must be gone while we can.'

He climbed aboard with Eriopis, and after a few moments Cadmus could hear the old man fighting with the dog for a space on the prow of the boat.

Cadmus turned to Tog and finally did what he'd been meaning to do for months. He put his arms around her and squeezed. It was like embracing the trunk of particularly stout oak tree.

'What are you doing?' she said.

When it became clear that she didn't know what to do, he stepped back and saved her the embarrassment.

'Thank you,' he said. 'And I'm sorry.'

'Sorry? What for?'

'For everything. For getting you involved in all of this. For lying to you. For taking you to Athens.' He looked her in the eye. 'For that hug, just then.'

'There's nothing to be sorry for. What has happened has happened.'

He swallowed. Of all the things he had suffered, this was the most difficult to endure of all. He opened his mouth, but nothing came out.

Tog shook his hand.

'Go well, Cadmus,' she said. 'I will think of you.'

Before he could reply, her broad back was to him

and she was walking to the other end of the harbour as though she'd already forgotten he was there. He raised his hand in a feeble wave, which she didn't see.

As he climbed back on to the deck of the *Argo*, his eyes burnt uncomfortably, and his body felt two or three times heavier. He looked again and again over his shoulder, but Tog was lost in the forest of masts, looking for her own way home.

There was a chorus of shouting and a creak of timber. With a heave the sailors levered the boat away from the dock and began rowing the *Argo* out to sea. Cadmus went and stood on the prow of the ship, a little apart from Tullus and Eriopis. Sick to his stomach, tears drying on his cheeks, he certainly didn't feel like a hero. But then, even the heroes wept. They loved, and they lost. Indeed, it was their loving and the losing that made their stories worth the telling.

The sailors put up the *Argo*'s mast and pointed the ship south, keeping close to the coastline. It wasn't long before the stench of smoke began to clear, and the sky along with it. Cadmus looked to either side of him. Tullus had closed his eyes and was breathing the sea air deeply, the sun bringing a little colour back to his face. Orthus was stretched out on the deck, nose on his paws. Eriopis whispered to herself, an enigmatic half-smile playing around her lips.

A strange family, Cadmus thought. But they were his family.

Tullus saw him, nodded, and came over to speak.

'You know,' he said quietly, 'your British friend made a good point.'

Cadmus looked at his old master. His hair was so thin it looked as though it might blow off the sides of his head at any moment.

'What's that?'

'When – rather, *if* – we find the rest of these relics, what are we actually going to *do* with them? How do you propose we keep them safe?'

'Well . . . we can cross that bridge when we come to it, Master.'

'Not "Master". Tullus.'

'Oh. Yes. Sorry.' It still didn't feel right.

'We already *have* come to one of those bridges, though, my boy.' He lowered his voice so the *heroidai* would not hear him. 'Are you sure we should be just handing over the Golden Fleece to this lot? I know they're god-fearing and all that, but they don't seem entirely . . .'

'Sane?'

'Exactly. At any rate, I'm surprised that you're happy to just give it away. It is your inheritance, after all.'

Cadmus said nothing for a moment, listening to

the clap of the waves on the sides of the ship.

'You don't need to worry, Tullus,' he said. 'The Golden Fleece is in safe hands.'

The old man's head loomed into the corner of his vision.

'Whose hands?' he said.

Cadmus looked to the western horizon and found himself grinning.

'*Whose hands?*'

EPILOGUS

S hin-deep in seawater, rain-lashed and wind-scoured, the girl manoeuvred the remains of her rowing boat towards the cliffs. The vessel should have been under the control of four grown men, but the chance to steal it had come before she'd been able to recruit a crew, so she decided to be captain, helmsman and rowers all in one. Halfway through the crossing, she'd leapt forward to save the chest from rolling overboard, and in doing so had lost one of her two remaining oars. From then on, she'd had to paddle on both sides, and the exertion had nearly killed her.

As the boat slipped into the cliffs' deep green shadow, the waters became still and the wind ceased whistling around her ears. It was as though the land were drawing a blanket over her as she returned. The keel struck the sand. The girl leapt from her bench into the shallows and began hauling the boat up on to the beach.

She rested for a moment, tasting the salt on her lips, listening to the gulls. Her palms were bleeding and she hadn't even noticed. She looked at the battered chest, still lying in the corner of the boat, and couldn't help thinking of the strange, pale boy who'd been with her last time she'd made this landing. She hoped he was safe. He deserved to be. She was indebted to him for a great many things – not least for the contents of that box.

The sun was beginning to set by the time she felt she had the energy to go on. Great billowing columns of cloud mounted overhead, lit orange, pink, gold.

She went to the chest, undid the clasps and threw back the lid. The chest itself was soaked and salt-stained, but its contents were still dry. It looked so tatty, so unremarkable, folded like that. An old sheep-skin, hardly a scrap of wool left on it.

She unrolled the Golden Fleece and threw it over her shoulders. Then she found the cliff path and, singing quietly to herself, began to climb.

ACKNOWLEDGEMENTS

To my editor Kesia, *primus inter pares*, who found this a story of brick and left it a story of marble; to the sagacious Barry Cunningham for his faith and foresight; to Rachel Leyshon, Rachel Hickman, Jazz Bartlett, Laura Myers and all of the Chickens for their support, their guidance, and their extraordinary care for both author and idea; to the other Chicken House authors, for welcoming and helping me with open hearts; to Erica Williams, for another cover beyond my wildest dreams; to my eagle-eyed copyeditor Jenny Glencross; to Jane Willis, my agent, confidant and tireless champion; to all of the Highgate School Classics Department for being kind and funny and helpful when I needed you to be; to the High Priestesses of Classics, Heather Isaksen and Steph Melvin, who were far more generous with their time than they had to be and brought some much-needed scholarly rigour to the book; to all my students, and my young readers, for being a constant source of surprise and joy and inspiration; to Sophie Lynas, for the title suggestions, for the encouragement, and for everything else I didn't thank you enough for at the time; to Will Dollard, whose *humanitas* and *liberalitas* as both friend and critic knows no bounds: *in perpetuum, maximas gratias ago.*